HOUSE ON HARDING STREET

SUSAN PICK

THE HOUSE ON HARDING STREET

A NOVEL

atmosphere press

© 2024 Susan Pick

Published by Atmosphere Press

Cover design by Matthew Fielder

No part of this book may be reproduced without permission from the author except in brief quotations and in reviews. This is a work of fiction, and any resemblance to real places, persons, or events is entirely coincidental...except for when it's entirely on purpose.

Atmospherepress.com

For Charlie and Alex

With love and gratitude

PART ONE

1998

1

Ever since Julie's early morning call came with the news of Paul's death, I had been thinking about the enormous burden our father left us. A large, run-down house in a small, run-down town. Paul hadn't bothered with upkeep for years, swearing that the place was so solidly built that he would be spending money to fix what wasn't really broken. After all, didn't his father build this place with the best materials available? Hadn't he himself dealt with construction and building for his entire life? Who would know better than he would? Yet anyone with an eye could see there was a lot of work to be done here.

Not only was the house a crumbling castle, but it was also packed with Cutler family clutter. My parents moved in with my grandmother, who never completely moved out, even when she took a small apartment nearby shortly after Julie was born. Some of the closets and drawers were still full of her things. And Paul, so stubbornly and blindly proud of family history, refused to throw anything away. Now, my siblings and I would have to deal with all this debris.

Here at the Harding Street house after the funeral, the guests gathered in this familiar living room didn't seem to notice its shabbiness. Then again, Julie planned and prepared, cooked and cleaned, and generally put a sparkle and shine on things that had gone dull over the years. Because that's just what you do, right? When someone dies, you have the funeral, you host a reception, and you feed the mourners with your very best efforts, whether your grief is overwhelming or non-existent.

I looked around the room at people I knew when I was a little girl, my parents' friends, sitting on once elegant furniture that faded with Paul's fortunes, reminiscing about dinner parties that probably weren't as much fun as they remembered, trying to say positive things about Paul. How committed he was to the town. How funny he was.

In fact, if you asked anyone who knew my father what they remember about him, they would probably say that he was irreverently funny, that he had a quick wit, that he could always make you laugh. He built that reputation one zinger at a time, usually delivered behind the back of the person he was laughing at.

During the memorial service, the parish priest called us "Paul's brave children" as we all sat in the front pew of the same church where my parents got married, where our mother dutifully brought the three of us to Sunday School every week while Paul slept in, where I was scared into sitting absolutely still and silent during my grandmother's funeral. A church that, had my father died during Cutler Enterprises' prosperous years, might have been more crowded with employees, clients, even retirees who once respected him, filling up the pews. Now his family, his remaining friends, and a few former employees listened to a long-winded eulogy about a "compassionate civic leader" and a "trusted friend" and a "devoted, loving husband and father," delivered by someone who tried his best despite the fact that he clearly didn't know his subject very well. As Revered Blake declared that Paul and Cutler Enterprises had "literally built up this town by providing construction supplies for two generations," I was suddenly seized by the absurdity of it all, and I couldn't suppress my laughter anymore. Maybe the rest of the world had been deceived into thinking Paul was any of those things, but his wife and children knew better.

Now, with the service behind us and the hardest part of Paul's sudden death still to come, I watched as Julie's husband,

Henry, poured wine into the long-stemmed goblets from my mother's wedding crystal. Their son, Michael, struggled to stay on his best behavior, his mother patiently reminding him not to run through the dining room. My uncle Ron took over my father's usual seat, a winged-back armchair, with its cushion caved in and its flowery upholstery worn and yellowed from all the years Paul spent sitting there smoking and smirking.

I still thought of this as Paul's house, even though three generations of Cutlers lived most of our lives here. My grandparents raised their two children within these walls. Paul brought his bride, my mother Virginia, here to be the lady of the house, a role my grandmother took her time relinquishing. And then Paul's three offspring, two daughters and, finally, the son and heir, all grew up in rooms that had barely changed since Paul's own childhood. Now, the house was the only thing Paul still owned, and it and its contents were the sum total of our inheritance.

Detaching myself from the crowd, I watched Julie expertly carrying out the hostess duties. Even five months pregnant, my little sister was amazingly energetic. She mingled with the guests, kept the silver serving trays filled, and tended to Michael—all while showing the appropriate and expected mix of grief and stiff upper lip. She accepted hugs and sincere condolences, listening to everyone's favorite stories about Paul. Julie could make every guest feel at home, accept their compliments, flirt just a little, and cook up a storm. Watching Julie now, I felt a mixture of pride, envy, and regret, knowing as I had pretty much all my life that I was never going to be as gracious as our mother.

Julie's friendly, easy-going personality was identical to our mother's, but her looks definitely came from Paul. As pretty as he was handsome, she got his dark hair and eyes, his lean body, and his long legs. Most of all, she had Paul's bright, disarming smile. When one of those smiles came over her face, her eyes twinkled, and her dimples deepened in a way that made the lucky recipient feel like the only person in the world. The difference between Julie's smile and Paul's, however, was that Julie's always felt like an accomplishment, a reward for making her feel like smiling. Whenever my father smiled at me that way, I knew he was about to crush me.

On the other side of the living room, I could see Trip, drink in one hand, the other hand in the pocket of his trousers. Wearing the same classic gray wool suit and navy-blue tie I bought for him to wear to our mother's funeral, he looked more like a schmoozing businessman than a grieving son. Of the three of us, I thought Trip would be the most broken up about Paul's death since he continued to idolize our father, to rationalize his actions, to try to emulate him, right down to the sarcastic jokes. But now, he showed no signs of being at all upset. Gesturing with his glass and leaning intently forward, he almost looked like he was trying to sell something to one of Paul's friends.

Trip hadn't inherited our mother's gracious nature the way Julie had. He did have a certain charm that he could pour on when it benefitted him, but what he really got from our mother was the unusual grayish-green tint to his eyes. When Trip got tinted contact lenses that took the color all the way to green, Mom smiled and told him how handsome he looked. But I was pretty sure she was secretly hurt. And while our mother loved the natural wave in her hair that allowed her to maintain a style without a lot of setting lotions and curlers, Trip kept his fair hair cut short to control the curls. Today, I noticed as he took the last swig of his drink and excused himself to get a refill that he was beginning to show a little bit of paunch around the middle. He would probably share our mom's battle to control his weight, too. At least he wouldn't have to endure Paul's constant scrutiny and cruel quips about his figure.

Turning away from Trip, I caught a glimpse of myself in the ornate gold framed mirror that had been hanging above the sofa my whole life. In any other reflective surface in any other place, I saw a grown woman looking confident and successful, with her grandmother's bright blonde hair surrounding a pleasant enough if not particularly pretty face constructed of unremarkable features that didn't strongly favor either of her parents. Here, in the living room of my childhood home, I tended to see what was not there: I wasn't beautiful like my mother or athletic like my sister or charming like my brother. I didn't have even a fragment of my grandmother's glamour. The self-confidence that I had carefully constructed when I moved as far away from here as I could seemed to crumble away whenever I entered this house.

"So, how are you holding up?" Appearing next to me with her head cocked in concern, my aunt Elaine studied me carefully. Despite spending her childhood in her older brother's shadow, Paul's sister was a remarkable woman. Younger than my father by a little more than a decade, she always viewed him with a mixture of amusement and mistrust. She made a life for herself and became a successful businesswoman away from Cutler Enterprises. I figured out early on that's what I wanted to do, too. She was the one who showed me it was possible to survive a childhood dominated by a demanding father and gave me the courage to build my own life. When I decided to move to the other side of the country after college, she supported me more than anyone else.

This house had been Elaine's home, too, but she looked strangely out of place, so fashionably dressed, so stylish, so graceful amid the faded glory of all this shabby furniture. Her usually perfect make-up, however, showed the slightest bit of smearing. Dark smudges of mascara and a few trails through her rouge testified that she shed a few tears at her older brother's funeral.

"I guess I'm as close to all right as I can be," I admitted. "It's a difficult day."

"Well, difficult days are a Cutler family specialty, right?

Put on your brave face, as my mother would say," Aunt Elaine replied. "We've all gotten so good at that. Especially you, Madeline." She reached out to rub my arm, and I felt a little tremble in her fingers.

"That's the most important thing, isn't it? Keeping up appearances?" If Aunt Elaine detected the crackle of bitterness in my remark, she ignored it.

"Maybe it's okay to let your guard down once in a while now, even when it's difficult. What do you think?"

I shrugged. "I'll work on it." Without my father around, maybe it was a little safer to let my guard down. I just didn't feel ready yet.

Hours later, the mourners were gone, Henry had taken Michael home to bed, Aunt Elaine and Uncle Ron had gone back to the city, and so the old house was quiet again. Trip sat in the kitchen with a cocktail while I cleared plates and glasses off the dining room table for Julie to wash and put away. The three of us hadn't had many occasions to be alone together lately. So many unspoken issues hung in the air, but we stuck with small talk.

"Did you talk to Mr. Nichols's girlfriend?" Julie asked.

"Frank has a girlfriend?" I vaguely remembered Mom telling me that Frank and Jean Nichols had gotten a divorce, but it still surprised me to think of my parents' friends being in the dating world.

"Sure, why not? He's still a pretty good-looking guy for his age, and the divorce has been final for, I don't know, at least a few years." Julie shrugged.

"I talked to her," Trip said. "Nice house. Nobody home." He grinned at his own little joke and took another drink from his glass.

With a scowl at our little brother, Julie changed the subject and turned her attention to me. "Mrs. Bridges said Derek moved back home," she said.

Derek Bridges? I thought. Really, Julie? Bringing up my high school crush? We're going to go there? What I said out loud was, "I thought he was doing so well in Chicago."

"Maybe he was for a while," Julie reported, holding up a lipstick-stained wine glass for inspection before scrubbing it, "but his mom just said things didn't work out. Good thing he's single and didn't have to move a whole family back here." Julie paused to cast a sidelong glance at me.

"But why would he come back here?" I wondered, ignoring her heavy-handed hint. "I mean, Graverton over Chicago? Who makes that choice?"

"Well, Henry and I chose Graverton over lots of other places," Julie said sharply. "So, it's not all that unusual." Julie and Henry had decided to live here for reasons I would never understand. Good math teachers like Henry were in high demand, and Julie had a business degree. They could have gone anywhere. But in Graverton, Julie could find only part-time accounting work, and they mostly got by on Henry's teaching salary. They did seem happy, though, so I let it drop. Also, turning the conversation to the town effectively dismissed Derek Bridges from the room, and it gave me the opening I needed to talk about my priority: what we were going to do about the house.

"Okay, if you're so happy in Graverton and you're planning to stay, are you going to want this house?"

Julie looked stunned by the question. "Where did *that* come from?" she asked, frowning.

"Come on, don't act like it's coming out of the blue," I protested. "It's a reasonable question." I ticked the reasons off on my fingers. "You do still live here, and you guys are going to need more space pretty soon. And it would mean keeping it in the family. The way I see it, either you and Henry move in, or we have to sell the place."

"Whoa, whoa, slow down," Julie said, hoisting herself

carefully onto a stool at the kitchen table. "I don't know if those are the only two options. I mean, sure, we might love to move in here, but we can't afford this place right now. It needs so much work, and upkeep would be way more than we could handle. And then there's the increase in property taxes and all the extra utilities. I'm not sure it adds up for us."

She vaguely gestured around the kitchen as if it proved her point. This room had last been remodeled the summer before I started third grade, after my grandmother died and while my mother was pregnant with Trip. Mom was really proud of the then-trendy red-and-black countertops and the wrought-iron-looking cabinet hardware. But over the years, the counters faded to a fast-food chain shade of orange, and kitchen grime built up in the ornate patterns on the drawer pulls. Mom put in the effort to keep them clean, but I doubt Paul even noticed the dirt while he lived here alone. Only two burners on the stove still worked, and the oven temperature was erratic at best. The only updated appliance was a sleek stainless-steel refrigerator that I helped pay for when the old one finally broke down beyond repair. Whoever decided to live in this house would have lots of expensive renovations, replacements, and overhauls to do.

"And don't forget that Trip has a say in this as well," Julie added, nodding pointedly across the table at our brother, who was being uncharacteristically quiet.

"Okay, fair enough," I agreed. "What do you think, Tripper?"

Trip grunted into his drink, avoiding eye contact with me. "I have a plan. You guys know that. But I need to start making some real money first."

In the six years since Trip graduated from college, I had heard him talk about his plan every time we got together. I learned not to voice my opinion about how crazy it was to think he could resurrect Cutler Enterprises after all this time. He could always provide a reason why he couldn't get started on it just yet, even as he insisted it was a brilliant plan. First, he needed more experience, then better contacts in his network. Now, it was more money. With each of the four jobs he'd had, he started out working for a "really great guy" offering him "tons of opportunity." But within a year, each really great guy turned out to be a "son of a bitch." As I watched him drain his drink, I wondered if he would ever figure out that the only problem with these guys was that they weren't impressed by his last name.

"Maybe selling the house would get you some of the money you need?" I ventured.

"It would be a start, sure. But not nearly enough."

"Wait, you guys, I'm not sure I want to sell," Julie sighed. "I mean, selling it is going to be as much work as keeping it, with all the junk we're going to have to clear out."

"Well, why don't I just call a realtor in the morning, start feeling things out in terms of the market around here, see what our next steps should be." The big sister taking charge.

"Maddie, why are you in such a rush?" Julie asked, becoming quite exasperated with me.

"I have a job and responsibilities. I can't stay here forever. I have to get back to my life."

Trip set down his glass with a thud and glared at me defiantly. But without even looking at him, Julie held up her palm to silence him. "Maddie," she said with a slight warning in her voice. "We just buried our father a few hours ago. Trip and I aren't quite ready to have this conversation. We're sorry to intrude on 'your life,' but I really think we should at least wait until Dad's lawyer actually reads us the will."

I sighed, realizing I had pushed too far. "All right, all right. I just thought we should at least start the conversation about it, but clearly, we're not going to settle this tonight. Let's see what the will says and take it from there." I settled down on the last unoccupied counter stool, next to Julie. "So tell me how you're doing. Is this baby moving around as much as Michael did?"

We talked late into the night. About our parents' friends. About people from high school still living in town. About the funeral service. About anything but the future beyond tomorrow.

Eventually, however, Julie needed to go home and get some rest, and Trip's drinks caught up with him. While I stayed at the house, Trip preferred to stay with Julie and Henry. Adding a guest to their place made for close quarters, but at least everything there worked. I briefly considered checking into a hotel, but I remembered something Paul had always been paranoid about. "Thieves always check the death notices in the paper, and they know when houses are empty," he'd said more than once. All I needed was for someone to break in here because I refused to stay.

Alone in the house at last, I carefully locked the doors and turned off the porch lights. Then I made my way up the stairs. How many times had I climbed these steps in my life? As a child, taking them two at a time in my eagerness to find Mom and show her the A on my test. As a sleepy teenager, coming home late after a Saturday night of babysitting. As an adult, with my mother's frail frame leaning on my arm for support. It was strange to think that my last trip up these stairs might be just a few days away.

Once I reached the second floor, I stood still for a moment. I could turn right into the room I shared with Julie growing up. Or I could go the other way, down the hall to Paul's bedroom. Even though I had, for most of my life, so carefully avoided the spaces he occupied, I realized that I didn't have to do that anymore. Maybe I could reduce the power this house had over me by facing my dread head on.

A week ago, Julie came into this room expecting to find Paul asleep. She was in the habit of checking on him every few days, making sure he had groceries and his laundry was done.

More often than not, she woke him up, even if she arrived in the middle of the afternoon. I told her she was foolish because the more she gave, the more Paul would take. Pretty soon, I warned, she would be over there every day, doing more and more of his errands, and Paul wouldn't care how much time that took away from Henry and Michael, not to mention her job. Her response was always that I didn't need to worry, that she could handle Paul. I don't know if she ever thought about how she would handle finding him on the floor, clearly trying to reach the phone. The coroner said the heart attack was sudden and massive. Paul never had a chance.

Somehow, Julie had found the time to clean everything up. The bed was made, the carpet washed of any evidence that Paul died there, the tracks of the vacuum cleaner visible in the worn seafoam green nap. I could still detect the faint odor of bleach mixed with the lingering scent of Paul's aftershave and the decades of cigarette smoke soaked into the curtains.

Paul had made this room uniquely his own. Looking at the controls for the electric blanket peeking out from under the bedspread, I could see that it was turned up to the highest setting, something the manufacturer surely recommended against. On the nightstand, there was a shoebox full of medications. As I poked through the many bottles, I saw pills to treat high blood pressure. Diuretics. Multi-vitamins. Some pretty strong pain killers. Not a childproof cap on a single one of them. Great idea with a toddler visiting here regularly, I thought. Opposite the bed was the only dresser Paul had probably ever owned. The antique heirloom came up to my chin, its wood stained dark, the brass drawer pulls burnished to deep golden brown from decades of handling, a light coat of dust already settling on the diamond pattern carved into the sides. Across the top, Paul had placed some framed photos: Trip's college graduation portrait, Julie and Henry in their wedding finery, me as a toddler in my grandmother's lap, and a cheesy studio shot of Michael just before his first birthday.

Not a single picture of my mother anywhere.

With a sigh, I opened the top drawer of the dresser. It was packed full of papers bundled with disintegrating rubber bands, several cases made of cracked oxblood leather containing unused manicure sets, outdated prescription glasses, Christmas cards from people I had never met, decks of cards, even a box of lottery tickets dating back almost a decade. Every drawer and shelf and closet in the house was like this or worse. Sorting through these memories would be a long and messy business. But I was tired now and ready to put this day behind me.

As I started to close the drawer, something tucked in the corner caught my eye. I saw a yellowed envelope with my name on it, written in Paul's distinctive handwriting. Underneath my name, he had written the year 1972. In spite of myself, my heart began to pound as I searched my memory for any event from that year, when I was about nine years old, that Paul might have kept a memento from.

With trembling fingers, I picked up the envelope, my mind rushing through all the possibilities that could be waiting to ambush me in there. I was in fourth grade in 1972, awkward and shy, watching my classmates splinter into the cliques that would be cemented in junior high and absolutely unbreakable by sophomore year—the pretty girls gravitating to other pretty girls and the boys figuring out who was good at sports and teaming up accordingly. Some of the other kids could afford to scoff at those popular groups, preferring to sneak off to smoke or light fireworks or commit petty crimes. The rest of us watched enviously from the sidelines, always hoping to be included and always disappointed.

Reaching in and feeling the texture of grosgrain ribbon, I suddenly knew exactly what the envelope contained. The memory was ignited by my fingertips and burned its way through my arms and back into my mind. The cheap, shiny plastic disk dangling from the ribbon read "Spelling Bee Champ," and it should have made me proud. Maybe for a few short hours back in 1972, it had. But not today.

Blinking to control the tears stinging my eyes, I put the envelope back where I found it and closed the drawer gently. I stood in front of the dresser for a moment, just to make sure I wasn't really going to start crying over something that happened so long ago. I wrapped my arms around my own waist, holding my nine-year-old self and telling her it didn't matter that her father took away her medal. She had still won, still beaten everyone else in fourth grade.

"Damn you, Paul," I said aloud. "Damn you. You always find a way to get to me."

2

I woke up from a deep, dreamless sleep, wondering what time it was. Coming back to Eastern Standard Time from the West Coast, I hadn't quite adjusted, but I was pretty sure the light coming through the window was what finally woke me up. Taking inventory of the aches and pains in my neck and back, I remembered where I was: in my childhood bedroom, on the twin bed whose mattress still caved in right under my hip. The blue flowery sheets and matching comforter that Mom and I picked out decades ago were soft and smooth from countless trips through the washing machine, and I shifted into a familiar, comfortable position that avoided the sagging spot in the mattress. Finding my watch, I saw that I had plenty of time for a run before anybody would wonder where I was.

While I warmed up and stretched on the front porch, I considered what route I should take. I thought of the track at the high school, but then I remembered that on a weekday in the fall, it was likely to be in use by the students for whom it was intended. So I just took off up the street at an easy pace, figuring I would make it up as I went.

Given my emotional state, I looked forward to an hour of head-clearing endorphin rush. I started running when I moved to Seattle. As a brand-new resident without a lot of disposable income, I needed a low-cost activity. Through a local running club, I made some new friends and learned my way around. I also learned how working up a sweat was good for my mental health, my focus, and my general attitude about life. Not to mention losing the chubbiness that had always drawn a cutting remark from Paul. Today, I was eager to turn off my brain for a while, to feel more like Madeline from Seattle and not Maddie from Graverton.

At first, the bright blue morning sky, the sweet fragrances of early fall blooms, and the crisp, cool air helped me relax. But the sights I passed began to distract me. In my mind, the street where I used to live was typical of small-town America, with neat little houses and perfect stretches of green grass, with an occasional lawn ornament or an overturned bike in the driveway. I was running by the same houses I passed on my way to school so many years ago, yet they now seemed almost as faded and worn as the furniture in Paul's living room. Gutters were sagging, paint was flaking, shutters were missing, porch steps were crooked, and lawns seemed to have gone a long time without a good mowing. I knew our town suffered an economic downturn with a pretty significant loss of jobs, but being confronted with such visible evidence of it was jarring. Even on my last visit, just five years before, I hadn't noticed this much decay. I wondered if Paul had ever walked around and taken a good look at his neighborhood. And what he had told himself if he had.

The young man at the funeral home who handled Paul's funeral arrangements made an offhand comment about how the only local businesses making money any more were the hospital, the drug store, and the funeral homes. Being so young, he may not have realized the impact his words would have on members of the Cutler family. Or maybe he did. In any case, his observation was spot on: The town was growing old and not keeping enough of its children around to take care of it.

As I got farther away from Paul's house, a new running challenge presented itself. The sidewalks became more and more uneven and cracked, crumbling to piles of pebbles in some places. To avoid tripping or twisting my ankle, I slowed down and began to dance around these obstacles. I hoped I was being graceful, but then I realized I didn't need to be embarrassed. There were few cars on the street and absolutely no other pedestrians, much less runners.

By the time I made my way back to the house, the morning chill had given way to a warm, blue midday. I was sweating and hungry and dying for some coffee. Back in Seattle, my favorite barista would have my usual large French roast with one packet of sugar ready to hand me seconds after I walked in the door. I missed the familiarity and comfort of my faraway neighborhood and apartment, not to mention the dark, rich aroma of coffee and the sweet fragrance of muffins baking, the things that made my morning commute easier to bear. Here, I had to rely on what was in Paul's kitchen. As I paced the length of the driveway to cool down, I tried to remember what I had seen the night before. Not really anything I wanted for brunch. However, I remembered seeing an ancient coffee maker on the kitchen counter. I hoped Paul had some bagels or something somewhere.

While the coffee brewed, I changed out of my sweaty running clothes. On the way back down to the kitchen, I paused in the hallway. There was one room I had not yet ventured into—my mother's bedroom. Julie and I left a lot of tears in that room when our mother died, and I wasn't sure I could go in there, even now, without crying. My mother's things, her clothes and jewelry and knickknacks and stationery, were all gone. But the memories were still trapped.

Standing in the doorway now, I breathed in deeply, hoping to find some remnant of my mother's favorite fragrance. It always lingered in the air in here, on her clothes, even on her pillow. But Julie had taken the last almost-empty bottle of Chanel No. 5 home with her years ago, and there was no trace of it left in this room. Now, it just smelled dusty.

The furniture in here was smaller and more feminine than the bed and dresser in Paul's room. The headboard curved like a sunrise, facing a window that let in glorious morning light through delicate creamy curtains. Mom's desk sat in the corner, its top empty of her pens, her silver letter opener, and her framed photos of her three children. It had all been boxed up and carried off to Julie's house or mailed to mine. Paul probably hadn't been in here since Mom died.

The last time I was in here, after my mother's funeral, Julie and I perched on the bed while we emptied her jewelry box and laid claim to our favorite pieces. We were quiet until Julie suddenly asked me, "Did you ever think it was weird that Mom and Dad didn't sleep in the same room?"

I shrugged off the question. "She said he snored really loud," I said. "That's not so weird."

"I guess not," Julie said, "but when my friends would come over to visit, they always commented on it. Seems like our parents were the only ones who didn't share a bedroom."

"Well, let's see. When did she actually move in here?" I tried to remember. "It was GrandMom's room when I was little. She got her own apartment after you were born. Then it was empty for a long time. But we still called it GrandMom's room."

"That sounds right," Julie agreed. "I remember playing in here sometimes."

Smiling at the memory, I said, "Yeah, these big closets were full of so much great stuff for dress-up." Then I thought of something else. "I tried to talk Mom into making this the baby's room when she was pregnant with Trip. I really didn't want you to move into my room!"

"Boy, if that isn't an understatement!" Julie laughed. "You were so mad when Mom made you clean out your drawers to make room for me."

"Yeah, well, you were kind of a pest back then." She took a playful swing at me, but I was still good at dodging her. "Mom told me Paul wanted to keep this room the way GrandMom had it, so moving the baby in here was out of the question. So, you and I had to figure out a way to co-exist. Eventually." I went back to searching my memory. "I don't think she made a big deal about moving in here. I just remember coming home from school one day and all her stuff was in that closet. I asked her about it, and she just said, 'Your dad snores. I'll sleep better in there.' Somehow, I knew better than to ask about keeping it the way GrandMom had it. And that was the end of it."

Julie had an odd look on her face for a moment before she said, "Maybe we should've tried to find out more. I mean, I remember being scared that they'd had a big fight or something and they were going to split up. So, I watched them both really carefully for a long time, trying to figure out if somebody was going to leave."

"Nah, I think you're reading way too much into it. Besides, you know she would never have left him." I got up from the bed and opened the closet door. "So I think we're going to end up giving away most of her clothes. It's all pretty vintage."

We spent the rest of that day marveling at the dresses and pantsuits and blazers our mother had never gotten around to getting rid of, even though she hadn't worn them in years. We laughed at the out-of-date styles, tried to remember the occasions when she wore each one, even tried on a few, and it was even funnier somehow to see ourselves in these outfits. We sighed over her nurturing ways and tough love and then cried some more when we opened a desk drawer and discovered that she had kept all the letters we had ever written to her from summer camp and college.

Looking around her room now, after five years, my mind flooded with the overwhelming sense that I failed my mother miserably. Taking the job in Seattle even though I had another offer in a city much closer. Rarely calling home and even more rarely visiting. I had cut my ties to the town so cleanly and completely.

My parents had never come to my new city, hadn't helped me move into a bigger place when I got promoted, had never met any of the men I dated, had never understood how much I loved the way Seattle was so fresh, so green, so vibrant. I had reveled in my independence, my new identity, right up until the day I got the worst news of my life.

By the time she got the mammogram, the cancer was too far advanced for surgery to remove it all. I managed to get away from work for the final two weeks of her life, but the last thing she asked of me, I couldn't give her.

The four of us were at the hospital late one evening when the nurses herded us out for violating visiting hours. With her voice weak, Mom called me to come back. "There's something I want you to bring tomorrow," she said. "The Ferragamo shoebox in my closet." She closed her eyes and settled her nearly bald head back on the pillow, the effort to speak taking all her strength. "I need that. But don't mention it to Dad."

I knew immediately what she meant. A pair of stylish shoes that were a bit too expensive that she splurged on when I was a little girl, that she took so much delight in wearing. "Sure, Mom," I assured her. "I'll bring them, and I'll see you in the morning." I kissed her forehead and left the room.

But I couldn't find the box that night. I knew exactly what it looked like, with its distinctive cursive F at the beginning of the name. It had been in the same spot in her closet for years. However, when I went to get it, it wasn't there. I looked everywhere, on every shelf, behind other boxes, under her bed, in her dresser drawers. I looked in other shoe boxes, thinking maybe she had misplaced the shoes or forgotten that the box had fallen apart. I even checked the bathroom closet. I asked Julie if she had seen them, but she didn't have the same memories of those shoes that I did, and she seemed to have no idea what I was talking about. I had to go back to the hospital the next day and tell my mother the shoes were gone.

She frowned and shook her head. "Honey, the box is in my closet, on the shelf, where it's always been," she insisted. "Look again when you go home, please. It's important."

She died that night. I never found the shoes.

3

Paul hated lawyers. He considered them to be a necessary evil, a profession whose only reason for existence was that it existed in the first place. "If it weren't for lawyers, nobody would need a lawyer," he used to say. When I was in college, I dated a first-year law student for a while, and that made my father roll his eyes every time I mentioned him. "Oh, he's a liar? Thank God, I thought for a minute you said he was a lawyer." Now, as all the remaining members of my family sat in a hushed, darkened, wood-paneled room in the downtown offices of Ripley, Mitchell, and Fowler (Paul had referred to them as "Dewey, Cheatham, and Howe"), I couldn't help wondering if the guy who was about to read us Paul's last will and testament knew how his client really felt about him.

The partner seated behind the desk was not Ripley, Mitchell, or Fowler. There was a time when the Cutler family's business was a big deal, and even a mundane task would have warranted a senior partner's attention. However, the current senior partners had delegated this will reading to one Anthony Marossi, Esquire.

I didn't know Anthony, but I knew of him. He'd been a star running back for the Graverton High School Bulldogs when I was a freshman. He captured a football scholarship, but a fractured wrist cut his sophomore season short. Julie told me that everyone in her class talked in hushed tones about how sad it was that Anthony had to come back that way.

Sitting at his large desk now, Anthony had the world-weary look of someone who constantly wondered why his life had worked out the way it did and not the way he planned.

His dark hair, so thick and curly in his star player days, had thinned and retreated to the back of his head, leaving behind a few dark gray wisps across his forehead. He still had a physique the size of a football player's but with flabby bulges instead of bulging muscles straining against his white button-down shirt and tasteful but boring striped necktie. He also had the same twinkling brown eyes and easy smile I remembered my boy-crazy classmates gushing about.

"My condolences for your loss," Anthony began, his eyes resting in turn on me, Aunt Elaine, Trip, Julie, and Henry. "Mr. Ripley and Mr. Fowler both spoke very fondly of Mr. Cutler."

"Thank you so much," replied Aunt Elaine. "My father and my brother always said your firm did good work for them."

"I appreciate that, Mrs. Springer," Anthony said. "It was our pleasure." Pausing to purse his lips, he continued, "Let's move on to the business at hand, shall we?" He opened the thin file folder sitting on his desk, removing the top sheet of paper and fixing his gaze on it rather than looking at any of us. He took a deep breath before he spoke again, as if he was embarrassed to be telling us what we already knew. "Mr. Cutler liquidated most of his assets before his death. The stocks were sold off, the bonds cashed in. He took cash payments from his life insurance policies, or he let them lapse. And, of course, the business assets ..." His voice trailed off as he finally risked an upward glance to make eye contact with me. Next to me, I sensed Aunt Elaine's body stiffening reflexively, even as she looked down so that none of us would be able to read her expression.

I nodded, hoping Anthony wouldn't feel the need to go into detail. Thankfully, he just continued.

"Okay. So. I'll just go ahead and read this then: I, Paul Robert Cutler Junior, being of sound mind and body, declare that this is my last will and testament, as witnessed on this day, the fifth of August, nineteen hundred and ninety-six.

"To my sister, Elaine Cutler Springer, I leave the diamond

engagement ring that belonged to our mother."

I risked a sidelong glance at Aunt Elaine, somehow managing to bite back the derisive grunt that threatened to escape from deep down in my chest. She was still looking at her hands, clasped tightly in her lap. Because he had kept that ring to punish us both, it was a sore spot, and Paul giving it to her this way was undoubtedly meant as one more poke at the wounds.

"To my children, Madeline Virginia Cutler, Julie Marie Cutler Nowak, and Paul Robert Cutler the Third, I leave all my remaining assets, including the house at 167 Harding Street and its contents, to be divided equally among them." Pretty much as I expected. I sighed softly, thinking this will reading had been quicker and less painful than I feared, even if what came next would not be.

But then Anthony kept reading.

"As a condition for this inheritance, one of my children must take up residence in the house that has been in our family for three generations so that it may be passed on to their children. My heirs will continue to jointly own the house until such time as the resident can buy out the other two. My attorneys have been instructed to turn over the deed to the house only when one of my children moves in or when my heirs have provided sufficient proof that none of them is able to assume residence. Only then can my children sell the property and divide the proceeds."

We all sat in stunned silence. Leave it to Paul to come up with something this controlling. Trying to force us to keep the house! Manipulating us all, even after his death. Finally, I spoke up. "And just exactly what, Mr. Marossi, is sufficient proof that we cannot assume residence?" I asked, not even trying to control the bitter edge in my voice.

"Mr. Cutler's instructions on that were a bit vague," Anthony admitted. "The partners in the firm are supposed to determine that, what sufficient proof would be, but he didn't really give us much in the way of guidelines. I believe his real desire was to keep the house in your family, as you can probably tell. He wanted you and your brother to at least consider moving back here. If you don't want to, or you can't, you could demonstrate that you're unable to find jobs here that are comparable to the work you're doing now. And as for Mr. and Mrs. Nowak, I think Mr. Cutler understood that you would be the natural choice to assume ownership since you're already here. If you would prefer not to, he suggested that you show us financial statements that indicate whether you can afford to keep up the house." Even the usually easy-going Henry let out a disbelieving sigh at that.

"Seriously?" I snorted. "He thought I could find a job here, doing the same software development work I do in Seattle, for the same money? I'm guessing it won't be hard to demonstrate just how impossible that is."

"I can't really explain Mr. Cutler's motives here," Anthony said defensively. "He dictated all of this to me, I recorded it, and our notary witnessed it. But if I had to guess, just based on our conversations, it seems that he just really wanted you all to try and keep the house. He wanted it to stay in your family. He liked the idea of his grandchildren growing up there."

"You clearly didn't know our father very well, Mr. Marossi." My smoldering anger was threatening to burst into flame, but I couldn't stop myself. "I doubt very much that he had any motive other than to exert his authority one last time. He probably laughed himself to sleep every night for the past two years, thinking about the last great joke he played on me. On us."

"Maddie." I heard the warning in Julie's voice.

"I hope you're not getting ready to defend him," I said. "Because this is indefensible."

"I think the important thing now is to figure out where we go from here," Julie replied. "Trashing our father isn't going to accomplish anything right now."

"I'll stay," Trip said so suddenly, so sharply, and with so much assurance that we were all startled, even Anthony. Seeing our surprise, he said, "What? I've been telling you that my job isn't working out, and Dad always talked about me taking over the business someday. It's always been the plan."

"You also told us last night you didn't have the money you needed for that," I reminded him. "And there's no business to take over. Have you somehow forgotten that? What are you going to live on if you move back here?"

"Look, it's what Dad wanted! He wouldn't have put it in his goddamn will if he didn't want me to at least try!" Despite his rising voice, his cursing, and his reddening face, I could still see Trip as a little boy, always so sure of himself, always knowing exactly what he wanted and somehow getting it every time.

Before I could respond, Aunt Elaine stepped in. "This is not a discussion we need to have here." She meant that we should be keeping all this in the family. Not airing dirty laundry. Not fueling gossip. Not letting the cracks show. This was not how the Cutlers did things. "Mr. Marossi, is there anything else? Do we need to sign anything?"

"Um, no, that pretty much covers our business here, Mrs. Springer. Oh wait, I do have the ring he mentioned." Anthony opened his desk drawer and withdrew a small velvet box the pale gray color of concrete. He stood to hand it across the desk to Elaine, who took it gently but didn't open it. "Mr. Cutler entrusted this to our safekeeping last year. And as I read to you, we'll keep the deed to the house here for now until those, um, conditions have been met." Again, Anthony looked terribly uncomfortable. "So. Unless you have any other questions for me?" Judging by his expression, he genuinely hoped we did not.

"We'll be in touch if we do," Aunt Elaine said, rising from her chair and causing Anthony to do the same. Looking at the rest of us, she ordered, "Let's not take up any more of Mr.

Marossi's valuable time. I think you all have some important decisions to make together."

Knowing Aunt Elaine was right, I stood up, too.

"Thank you, Mr. Marossi," I said. When I extended my hand, it disappeared into his beefy fist. "You've been a tremendous help."

4

Leaving the lawyer's office, we found ourselves outside, blinking in the bright early afternoon sunlight. No one seemed quite sure what to do next. Then Aunt Elaine announced that she wanted to treat us all to lunch. "We should talk things over, think about the decisions you have to make," she reasoned. "We might as well be in a pleasant environment with some good food."

My head was still spinning with anger and disbelief after hearing about Paul's final attempt to control us. That caveat in the will was his way of saying, "You do what I tell you," one last time. And yes, it referred to all three of us, but I was the one whose life would be most upended. I didn't want to talk about the house, or the will, or Paul, or anything. What I really wanted to do was to flee, to get back on a plane and get back to my life. I built that life without any help from Paul, and I wasn't about to let him tear it down. But, as the oldest sibling, I felt a heavy obligation to help straighten out the mess Paul left us. So, I agreed to go to lunch. The sooner we worked this all out, the sooner I could leave Graverton and never look back.

If there was one thing the Cutlers were good at, because we were all constantly reminded of it, it was minding our manners. Trip pulled out Aunt Elaine's chair for her. We all placed our napkins on our laps, politely said please and thank you to our waiter, sipped our ice water, and waited patiently till everyone was served before we started eating. Aunt Elaine chatted with Henry about the classes he was teaching this year. She wanted to know how Michael was doing, how preschool was going, and what toys he liked. She asked Trip if he had a girlfriend, then expressed mild, affectionate surprise when he said no. We were all very careful to stare straight ahead, to stay in the here and now, to avoid any mention of Paul or Harding Street or Cutler Enterprises or what the hell we were going to do in the coming days and weeks.

Finally, when coffee was served, Aunt Elaine carefully laced her fingers together over her cup and began the discussion we were all dreading. "Well," she sighed, "that was quite a will your father left. Not really surprising, I suppose, knowing Paul, but that really doesn't make it any easier on all of you, does it?"

"You're right; it's not surprising at all," I said softly. "Of course Paul would seize one last opportunity to bend us to his will."

"Your dad could be very controlling. No one knows that better than I do. But maybe we could give him the benefit of the doubt here. Maybe Harding Street really was just that important to him and he wanted to keep it in the family." Aunt Elaine looked at me with pleading eyes, hoping to convince me that Paul's motives weren't vindictive after all.

I shook my head sadly. "No, you were right the first time, Aunt Elaine. He wanted to make things hard for us. For me."

"Why do you think this is just about you?" Trip's voice exploded from the other end of the table. "There are three of us, you know. I can live in the house. You can go on back to Seattle and forget about it."

"That's not how it works, Trip. Even if I leave tomorrow, somebody is going to have to pay the property taxes and the utilities, not to mention all the repairs it needs. Since we all legally own it now, we're all responsible for it. We can't just let the bills go unpaid. And if you quit your job, how are you going to pay them? Were you thinking you could just live in the house for free?" I was so upset that my voice was getting much too loud. I glanced around the restaurant to make sure the other patrons weren't paying attention to us. Nothing worse than a public scene.

"I'll figure something out. I always do." Trip's eyes were narrowing against his growing anger. "I don't understand why the house you grew up in, where all your memories are, isn't important to you, but it is to me. I don't want to lose it."

"You haven't lost it," I pointed out. "It's been dumped on you. On all of us. This is Paul's way of trying to force me to move back here when he knew that was the last thing I wanted!"

"Stop it, both of you!" Julie interjected, leaning forward to slap her hands on the table. "I would say we're pretty clear on where you both stand. Does anybody care what I think?"

"You said last night you didn't want the house," I reminded her.

"No, I said I didn't think we could afford the house," Julie corrected me. "I might just love to move in there. But it needs a lot of work."

"I have to agree there," Henry put in. "It would be fantastic to get that much more space. We would just be really hard-pressed to keep it up."

"So you guys want it, Trip wants it, and I can't get far enough away from it," I summed up. "None of which changes the fact that the place needs a hell of a lot of work before we can do anything at all."

"What's wrong with a little hard work, Maddie?" Trip's voice continued to gain volume with his increasing exasperation and his pre-lunch Bloody Mary. "Sometimes you have to work hard for what you want. When you have it too easy, you don't learn important life lessons. That's what Dad always told me. You don't learn how to fail. How to figure out what you really want and what you're willing to do to get it. When it is all just handed to you, you won't know what to do when you're faced with losing it."

"Really, Trip?" I couldn't believe what I was hearing. "That's what you think his will was about? Making us work for something? Because how the hell would Paul know anything about that? He's the one who had it all handed to him. The one who never knew anything about failing because everyone made things so easy for him."

"Yeah, that's exactly what I think," Trip replied, trying to stare me down. "And I'm ready to work to keep the house."

Locking eyes with my little brother, I suddenly felt my heart flood with sympathy. Somehow, even after all this time, after all that had happened, after all that Paul had done, he was still Trip's hero.

"Okay, Trip, if that's what you want, you should give it a try. I just don't think it's going to be worth the trouble," I sighed. "I think we're eventually going to have to sell it, take what we can get, and cut our losses."

"That house has been the Cutler family home for a long time," Aunt Elaine said. "That has to be worth something, doesn't it?"

"So you don't think we should sell it either?" I was surprised that Aunt Elaine would be sentimental about that place. Then another more hopeful thought occurred to me. "Maybe you and Ron could buy it from us and fix it back up. That way, it stays in the family."

"No, no, no, that's not what I had in mind at all," she replied quickly, raising her hands defensively and shaking her head. "Our lives are in the city now. We're not in a position to move. Even if we wanted to. Which we don't." Aunt Elaine looked around the table. "I just want you three to consider every option, that's all," she said. Looking straight at me, she added, "It is possible that your father just wanted to leave you a legacy. Something to remember him by?"

I snorted. "You mean like GrandMom's diamond ring? The one you have been waiting all these years for him to give you?"

Aunt Elaine pressed her lips together into a thin line, as if she was straining to keep a regrettable response from escaping into everyone else's hearing. It was something I had seen her do many times before responding to insults and snubs from her brother. She was a lot better at that than I ever was. After a moment, she said stiffly, "That ring has nothing to do with this discussion, Madeline. I want to believe Paul had his reasons for holding on to it, just like he had his reasons for leaving it to me in his will. But that's none of your business."

Aunt Elaine was the last person I wanted to have angry with me, so I immediately regretted bringing up the ring. As an apology, I covered her hand with mine and gave it a squeeze.

"Listen, Maddie, this situation disrupts all our lives, not just yours," Julie was saying. "No matter what we decide, there is a lot of work to be done, and it's going to take a lot of time. And probably money."

Which you don't have, I thought. What I said out loud was, "So what do you propose we do?" I was eager to get to a decision and, more importantly, a timetable. I thought of my comfortable apartment, my favorite morning coffee, my office with its view of Elliott Bay.

Julie sighed. "We have to clean out the house, I guess. That has to happen no matter what. If we're going to sell or if one of us is going to move in, a lot of junk has to go. Do you think you can stay long enough to get that done?"

"I can give you a couple of weeks, I guess," I replied. I really didn't want to use my vacation time here in Graverton, but there was that pesky feeling of obligation again. I could probably figure out a way to work remotely for a while. As much as I hated to admit it, they were right; this was as much my problem as anyone's.

"What about you, Trip?" Julie turned to our brother, who had leaned back in his chair with arms crossed over his chest. "Can you stay a while?"

Trip shrugged. "I don't have much vacation time accrued, and I won't get more till my one-year anniversary. I can stay a couple of days, at least. You know, bereavement and all that.

And I'm in sales, after all. I'm supposed to be out of the office most of the time anyway."

"And I'm close by," Aunt Elaine offered. "I can drive up to help when you need me. There may be a few things left from my parents that I want."

"What about the part about proving we can't keep the house?" I ventured. "What about that?"

"There was no real deadline on that in the will, so we can cross that bridge when we come to it," Julie said. I noticed that Henry had put his arm across the back of her chair and was leaning toward her. Always supportive. "Maybe selling off some of the stuff in the house will make enough to start with the renovations and repairs."

"Sounds like it's settled, then," Aunt Elaine said, clasping her hands together again. "See? A nice pleasant lunch was exactly what we all needed."

5

Another morning, another run through a neighborhood I knew but hardly recognized. I never saw anyone else on the street, although I wondered if people were watching me from their windows, thinking maybe they recognized me, maybe not. I remembered where the worst of the sidewalk cracks were and tried to avoid them. I figured out how to operate Paul's coffee maker, but it was so old that the coffee had a faintly metallic, even rusty taste. Hard to tell how long the coffee had been in the cupboard, and the filter basket on the machine had not had a thorough cleaning in quite some time. But a new coffee maker was just one more thing we would have to figure out what to do with, so I was grinning and bearing it. For now.

Groceries were another matter. I couldn't survive on the sparse provisions Paul had kept in the kitchen. Cans of corn and peas. Jars of tomato sauce. Blue boxes of macaroni and cheese. A loaf of bread that had gone stale weeks ago. Clearly, Paul had been shopping by two rules: what he liked and what was easy. I had sent most of the funeral casseroles home with Julie, telling her she had more mouths to feed at her house. So, the first order of the day was a trip to the market.

Countless times, I walked the aisles of this grocery store with my mom. Ownership had changed, but the basic layout was the same. As with nearly every supermarket anywhere, the produce, the meat, and the dairy cases lined the perimeter, and the stuff I had learned to stay away from was in the middle aisles. My cart was full of fresh fruits, vegetables, low-fat milk, eggs, and some chicken breasts when I ventured into the interior aisles to find oil and vinegar for salad dressing. While I was comparing the prices of unfamiliar brands of balsamic vinegar, I became vaguely aware that someone else had come into the aisle. I didn't notice him until he spoke.

"Maddie?"

Only family members called me Maddie now because I had made an effort to introduce myself, always, as Madeline while I was in college and continued to do so in Seattle. So, I didn't respond right away.

"Hey, Cutler." The voice was more insistent, more certain now. "That *is* you."

Before I even looked up, a shiver of recognition rattled its way through my body. I knew that voice. Derek Bridges grinned at me from the other end of my shopping cart, just as achingly handsome as he had been in high school. The same soft brown eyes, the same sandy hair, the same strong shoulders, the same spray of tawny freckles across his nose. The only thing different was the slight crinkling of laugh lines around his eyes, but if anything, it gave his face more character and interest. His black button-down shirt was open over his blindingly white T-shirt, tucked straight into faded Levi's. I struggled to control a tremor in my voice when I answered. "Hey, Bridges. Yeah, it's me." The teenaged me with the wild crush on this guy was long gone, so why had all her shyness and social anxiety come rushing back?

"Wow," he said. "Haven't seen you since high school. How you doing?"

"I'm okay, thanks," I replied, while a voice in my head screamed at me to say something, anything, more clever than that. Without looking at it, I nonchalantly tossed one of the vinegar bottles into my cart. "How about you?"

"Doing great, thanks." He moved his glance up and down, taking me in from head to toe. "Been back in town for a few months, and I keep seeing people from the old days. They all look their age, but you? You look amazing."

"I took up running a few years back," I said with a shrug, trying to give the impression that I got that kind of compliment all the time and it was no big deal. "I dropped a few pounds in the process."

Derek's smile faded suddenly, and his face clouded over with concern. "Oh. Wait. Your dad died, didn't he? My mom said something about going to Mr. Cutler's funeral. So sorry. That's why you're back in town, huh?"

"Yeah," I said. "I'm here for just a few more days to help get all his affairs in order, then I'll head back home."

"So where's home now?" The concerned face was already gone, and he was smiling that irresistible smile again.

"Seattle, actually."

"Whoa, Seattle. Got as far as Chicago myself, but now I'm back." It was his turn to shrug, shifting the small basket he was carrying to the other hand.

Nodding, I remembered what Julie said. "My sister mentioned that," I said. "I was kind of surprised, frankly. What does this little town have to offer after you've seen the bright lights in the city?"

"Long story, but basically, me and the nine-to-five suit-and-tie life were not getting along too well. Needed to do something different."

"Like what?" I wanted to know.

"Okay, don't laugh," he said, leaning toward me as if he were going to whisper a secret. "Went to night school. For culinary arts. Got to be a pretty good chef, so I'm thinking, open my own restaurant. Right here." He gestured vaguely around the store as if it represented Graverton in a nutshell.

"Really?" I blurted out, unable to keep my disdain for this place from rearing its head again. "Here? Why would you want to open a restaurant here?"

To my surprise, he didn't seem to take offense. Instead, he laughed. "Because there isn't one here. Not the kind I'd want to run, anyway."

"Well, what's your idea?" I was really curious about what he was planning and why he thought it would work.

"Lemme show you." With one hand resting lightly between my shoulder blades, Derek began to guide me around the store, pointing out the ingredients he would use to create healthy, gourmet meals. Telling me how he'd learned to cook by adding strong flavors instead of calories and fat. Nobody in Graverton was offering the kind of fare he would serve up, he assured me.

As attractive as I found his vision, I remained unconvinced. "It's a lovely idea," I conceded. "I just think it's going to be a really hard sell around here."

"No faith in me, huh?" he chuckled.

"It's not a question of faith in you," I reassured him. "I just don't have faith in Graverton."

"Damn, you really don't have a very high opinion of your own hometown, do you?" We were back in the produce section, where he'd convinced me to exchange the romaine lettuce I'd chosen earlier for some arugula to "spice up" my salads. "Why is that?"

I felt my face growing red, as much from a vague sense of anger as from embarrassment. "I was never very happy here," I said, averting my gaze.

"Well, you know, Cutler, some people are happy here. Always have been. It's kind of a nice place if you give it a chance."

"I gave it eighteen years," I shot back. "That was enough." I didn't mean to sound so harsh, but it suddenly occurred to me that flirting with Derek Bridges was utterly pointless, no matter how handsome he was or how flattering his attention felt. Even if his flirting was serious, even if I could show him that I was no longer the awkward girl he ignored in the tenth grade, it was still a dead end romantically. He was here, and I was never going to be.

Derek held up a hand defensively. "Hey, not trying to

sell you on the place," he said. "If I remember right, you've been itching to get outta here since high school. Always with your eye on the horizon. More worried about good grades and going to college than having fun in the moment. You and me, we didn't hang out that much, but the few times we did, you were kinda preoccupied. Always got the impression you felt like you should be studying, even on a Saturday night."

"Well, school was important," I snapped, just as defensive as he was. "I knew what good grades would do for me." And what less-than-perfect grades would do to me, but I kept that thought to myself.

"Yeah, that was kinda your MO, wasn't it? How you'd get so mad if you got a B-plus or something. You cried more than anybody I ever knew." He nodded at the memory. "And the grades that made you cry, I would've killed for." In his face, I saw that familiar pity beginning to return, along with amusement, both at my expense. Suddenly, I didn't want to take this walk down memory lane, to be hit in the face with these painful reminders, to relive the kind of heartbreaking episodes Derek clearly remembered all these years later.

"Well, speaking of getting outta here, I've got to go." I grabbed my cart, hoping a tight grip would hide the tremble of anger and irritation in my hands. I pushed past him. "Nice seeing you," I called over my shoulder.

At the checkout, a very pretty young lady gave me a big, friendly smile. "Hi, how are you this morning?"

"Fine, thanks," I grunted, barely looking up as I unloaded my groceries.

"Did you find everything all right?" she asked, trying to make eye contact, even as she scanned each item and pushed it toward the pimply young man getting ready to bag it all up for me.

"Yes. Yes, thank you." I paid with cash and hurried out through the automatic doors. Even now, trying desperately to hide that I was falling apart again.

6

As I unloaded the groceries back at the house, I was furious with myself for getting so upset. What did I care what this guy thought of me? Maybe at one time, I had wanted Derek Bridges to pay attention to me, but that was a long time ago. The opinion of someone who was naïve enough to think he could actually start a successful new business here was so unimportant. Why did it matter that my grade obsession was what he remembered? I knew why I cried when I didn't get an A, even if no one else ever understood. How could I explain what Paul would do, how his reactions would affect me for weeks, sometimes months? How could I tell anyone how hard it was to be the oldest child of a man who would never think anything I did was good enough? What it was like to be belittled when you fell even the slightest bit short of perfect? To make matters worse, my father always managed to cloud his meanness with humor to make it seem to anyone else like it was just a joke, that he just wanted to make me laugh, and I looked like a poor sport when I reacted badly.

Through my frustration and anger, one thing was cracklingly clear: I needed to get this house cleaned out and get out of here, once and for all. The sooner I got started, the sooner I could return to my own home, my own life, my new and happier memories, and my friends who knew nothing about any of this.

And I was going to start in Paul's room.

My rage fueling my burning resolve, I grabbed the garbage bags I had just bought and climbed the stairs. I stood in the middle of Paul's room again, hands on my hips, disheartened before I even began because there were so many places I could attack. I needed an easy victory. The dresser drawers already ambushed me once, and this was no time to risk that happening again. In a quick glance at the desk, I saw piles of papers, some of them held together with old, yellowing rubber bands that looked like they would crumble when I touched them, some stuck in a large brass paper clip desk ornament featuring the logo of one of Cutler Enterprises' suppliers. And there were some random heaps in such disarray that organization would likely take hours.

The closet, then. I figured Paul's clothes wouldn't trigger me as much as some of the other stuff in his room. Suits, shirts, and ties were pretty unthreatening. Paul hadn't gone to work for years, so it had been a while since he had any need for that kind of thing. Then again, he hardly ever threw anything away. Lately, he just seemed to want to be comfortable. Julie told me he recently discovered sweatpants. I thought I could just get the clothes out, determine if there was anything Trip or Henry might be able to use, and get the rest packed up for Goodwill.

The closet door creaked ominously when I opened it, as if it was protesting the search-and-destroy mission I was on. As I expected, casual shirts, shorts, and khakis hung closest to the door. There were still several suits in various shades of brown, gray, and navy blue. The shirts were mostly white, or had been once. Of the ties dangling from a rack next to the shirts, most were striped or solid or decorated with a subtle pattern, some frayed and threadbare and worn in the middle from being tied so many times. The business clothes were all very classic, the kind of cut that never goes out of style. I would give Paul that; he had good taste.

I grabbed as many suits as I could carry and slung them over my arm to carry them to the bed, where I looked at each one as I dropped it. They were about the right size for Henry, but teaching high school math probably didn't require a jacket and tie very often. Trip was the one who wore a suit to work every day, but I doubted that these would fit over his recently expanded beer belly. They were all in pretty good shape, though. Goodwill would be happy to get them.

I turned back to the closet to get another load, but before I took anything else out, I noticed the shelves in the back. I had probably always known they were there, though I never had much reason to go into this closet beyond possibly some long-forgotten hide-and-seek games. Buried behind so many suits, the shelves had been well hidden when I opened the closet door. Now, they were mostly bare, save for a couple of pairs of Paul's dress shoes in shiny black leather and a few folded pairs of sweatpants. And one shoebox.

A Ferragamo shoe box.

My whole body went cold. When my mother was asking for those shoes, I never checked with Paul to see if he knew where the box was—Mom specifically asked me not to mention it to him—and it hadn't occurred to me to look for it in his closet. Why would Mom have left it in here? Had she forgotten about moving it? It seemed so important to her at the time to see those shoes once more, I couldn't believe she didn't know where they were.

Then, with a jolt, I realized that Paul had to have put the shoebox there himself. Maybe he wanted to hide it from her, in his controlling way, knowing how much those shoes meant to her once. It was exactly the kind of thing he would do, just to be mean. The idea that he might have done such a childish thing, to pull such a cruel prank, one that denied my mother her dying wish and kept me from granting that wish, renewed my anger. Even though I was the only one who knew she was asking for them, that didn't make me any less furious. In fact, it broke my heart all over again to realize that Paul's little joke had caused me to feel so incredibly guilty after Mom died, so distraught that I couldn't bring her the shoes she wanted to see one more time, so anguished that I had to deny her one last happy memory. Once again, the tears burned the back of my eyes and distorted my vision, my body shaking so much I had to lean against the door frame.

 I don't know how long I stood there staring at the shoebox, all the guilt and anger and regret crashing through my mind. I was just about to reach for the box when I heard the front door open downstairs and Julie calling my name. She and Trip were here to begin the first of many days in the long and arduous process of going through the house. I hurried across the hall to the bathroom, where I splashed some cold water on my face before I replied, "I'm upstairs!"

Not wanting to share the shoebox revelation with Julie and Trip, I kept them downstairs to work on the dining room, which was going to take hours, maybe the rest of the day. All of Mom's wedding silverware and twelve place settings of china had gone to Julie's house five years ago, but the drawers of the massive mahogany sideboard were still brimming with serving pieces, table linens, centerpieces, and candles. We determined that each of us could take what we wanted as we found it, and the rest would go to an antiques dealer en masse. Not having emotional reactions to this stuff like we did, the dealer could determine what had value and worth, what we could donate, and what we should just toss. Even with all three of us involved in the effort, it was exhausting work.

 While we talked, I knelt in front of the sideboard, where I looked through the dozen or so sets of placemats and matching napkins stored in the bottom drawer. There were some that our family had used regularly over the years, and those bore the stains of many dinners in this room. I wondered how many times Paul had yelled at me for spilling something or making a mess that was represented by a faint brown outline on these often-used linens. *"What, is the moon in klutz for you,*

Mad Dog? Be more careful."

Julie laughed when I pulled out some candles in the form of little blond witches and jack o' lanterns and black cats. "Oh, I used to love those!" she exclaimed, holding one of the witches carefully in her palm. "Our Halloween decorations were always so cute, not scary. I remember going to my friends' houses, and they'd have these awful, bloody skeletons and vampires and Frankensteins all over. Any time I went to a sleepover in October, I'd have nightmares till Thanksgiving!"

"Remember how you and I would try to pick out the prettiest costumes? We wanted to be Cinderella or Sleeping Beauty. Oh, but then there was the year we were Barbie and Skipper!" The memories were flooding back to me. "That was your idea, right?"

"I think so," Julie nodded. "It might have been Mom's. I loved that blond wig with the straight bangs. I thought it made me look just like you."

I listed a few other costumes I remembered, all of them princesses or TV characters. "It never even occurred to us to be anything scary." I turned to Trip. "But then you came along. And all of a sudden, Mom was buying fake blood and fangs and knives and these rubber masks with bulging eyes and scars. The uglier, the better."

Trip grinned at the memory. "Yeah, Mom always got me some cute costume when I was little. A stupid Muppet from Sesame Street or a superhero or something like that. As soon as I was old enough to pick out my own costume, man, I went totally in the opposite direction!"

"Some of your costumes were so elaborate, you couldn't even see where you were going. Like that Grim Reaper thing you made. Between the mask and the hood, I had to hold your hand so you didn't fall or bump into somebody." Since I stopped trick-or-treating when Julie decided she'd rather go with her friends than with me, it fell to me to chaperone Trip, at least until he was old enough to go with his friends. I was pretty sure his little gang was behind a lot of the Halloween pranks I would hear about the next day, but he always got away with it."

"Jesus, I forgot about that," Trip snorted. "I didn't want you coming up to the houses with me, but I couldn't climb the porch steps without you. It was so embarrassing. Couldn't wait to go out on my own."

"Oh, hey, Maddie," Julie said, "I ran into someone from your class at the drugstore. Do you remember Cindy Ragno? Wait, what was her maiden name? Harper, I think? She heard you were in town for Dad's funeral, and she wanted me to say hi."

"Cindy Harper rings a bell," I said, "but I didn't know her all that well." In my memory, I saw Cindy as a cheerleader with a big bouncy perm and perfect makeup every day. She had been part of the popular posse that generally paid no attention to me unless they were making fun of my nerdiness.

"Her husband, Johnny, was in your class, too," Julie went on. She was sitting on one of the dining room chairs since getting her pregnant belly on and off the floor was becoming an arduous task. "I'm pretty sure they got married just a year or so after you graduated. Their oldest daughter was in Henry's class last year."

"That seems really young to get married," I remarked.

"Didn't they start going together in, like, your freshman year? They were sort of that 'golden couple' every high school seems to have. Always together. Every party, every school dance. It was the relationship everybody aspired to. At least the girls in my class did."

"It seems like you were paying more attention to my class than I was. I mean, I kind of remember that they were a couple, but since I didn't go to those parties and dances and stuff, I just wasn't that much in the loop." Anyone listening to me might think that I had chosen to avoid those social gatherings when the truth was I hadn't gone because I hadn't been invited.

Julie chuckled and shook her head. "Well, Maddie, you might be surprised at how many people paid pretty close attention to what was going on socially at their own high school, even outside their own class. It was generally a pretty big deal, what everybody talked about, who was dating who. Maybe it was just so much teenage drama to you, but it was the most important thing in the world to a lot of kids. You were probably the only one who didn't care at all."

"It wasn't that I didn't *care*," I protested. "I wasn't friends with that crowd, so I didn't hear the rumors or the gossip or any of that. Anyway, I cared about other things more, like getting good grades so I could get into a good college and get out of here. I mean, how many times did Paul say to me, 'Grades are everything'? And sometimes even straight A's weren't good enough for him."

"Dad told me that, too," Julie insisted. "I knew I had to get good grades. But I managed to have friends at the same time. You always seemed to be studying."

"It's kind of hard to say which came first," I said. "I had no social life, so I focused on grades, or I was so focused on grades that I had no social life. Either way, the result was the same: no social life. The popular kids didn't pay any attention to me, so I just tried to ignore them."

"Well, that's because they thought you were stuck-up," Julie said. "You acted like you were above it all, like you just couldn't be bothered with silly things like parties or school dances. And a lot of people thought you were a snob because Dad owned one of the biggest businesses in town. Like you were too good for everyone else."

I rocked back on my heels to stare at Julie in her chair as she unleashed this news on me. I couldn't believe what my own sister was saying. "What? People told you I was stuck-up? Who said that? You never told me that! In all this time, you never thought to mention it?"

In spite of my shock, Julie just shrugged. "I just figured

you were, like, doing it on purpose. That you were constructing that image or something so people would just leave you alone. As far as who said it? Some of my friends had older sisters or brothers in your class. They told me what they heard. And there were upperclassmen with me on the cross-country team and tennis. So, I overheard stuff. Not just about you," she added quickly, seeing the surprise and anger rolling across my face. "About everybody at school. I paid attention. I knew what was going on, what seniors and juniors to stay away from. Which ones were more likely to be nice to me. It just, like, made my life easier."

I was so shocked that I couldn't think of a response. Not only had I been completely clueless about the social goings-on at Graverton High School, but also my own sister had been clueless about how much I really did care, how much I wanted to be part of it, how much it hurt that I was never accepted in those groups.

Overwhelmed, I rolled onto my back and stared up at the ceiling. "How could they think I was stuck-up? I was so awkward. Zero social skills. What would I have to be conceited about?"

I heard Julie sigh, so I propped myself up on my elbows to look at her. "What?" I asked.

As she pursed her lips, she stared down at me hard. "Do you really want to know?" she finally replied.

"Well, now I do," I said. What did she know that I didn't?

Avoiding eye contact with me, Julie seemed to be choosing her words very carefully. "See, what would happen, my friends' older sisters would tell me they were surprised that I was, like, nice. Friendly. They said the Cutler girls were supposed to be, you know, rich bitches or something. They had the impression that our family owned half the town, we lived in this great big house, nobody else's dad would have a job without us, blah, blah, blah. You never talked to anybody, and they assumed that was why. You thought you were better than everybody else because we were rich."

"But that wasn't it at all!" I cried, sitting up again to lean closer to Julie. "Ever since elementary school, those kids didn't like me because I was smarter than they were. They called me dweeb. And nerd. And geek. And spaz. And crybaby. They made fun of me all the time. By junior high, even my friends in the neighborhood were avoiding me. Remember Allison? From down the street? She wouldn't even walk to school with me anymore after about sixth grade. It was like I was social cancer or something." I felt as if a dam had burst inside me, allowing all the memories, the hurt, and the rationalizations I had always suppressed to flood violently into the here and now.

"What, like you were the only smart person in your class?" Julie scoffed, dismissing me with a wave of her hand. "So, you were kind of stuck-up in a way. Assuming you were better than everyone, not because you had money but because you had brains. If you were so smart, how come you never figured out that's why people avoided you?"

I didn't even know how to respond. All this time, my own sister held the answer to the question that had kept me up at night all through high school, that made me cry myself to sleep, that cemented my resolve to leave Graverton in my dust. Why didn't I fit in here?

Standing up to stretch and pace around the dining room, Trip took my stunned silence as an opportunity to cut in with his own issues.

"You guys with your perfect grades," he snorted. "You managed to make my life hell." He was looming over us, shaking his head. Here we go again. While Julie had never before talked much about her social life or her knowledge of mine, Trip had complained many times over the years that his sisters had blazed a trail that was impossible for him to follow. "Every teacher I ever had in school had already had one of you in their class. Sometimes, both of you. All I heard about was how smart you guys were. The first day of every single fucking class." Planting his hands on his hips, he switched to a mocking falsetto voice. "'Oh, another Cutler. I hope you work as hard as your sisters.' Shit, I was behind before I even got started."

"Well, for some reason, Dad never held you to the same high standard as he did us," Julie reminded him. "When you got B's and C's, he made excuses for you. If I had ever gotten even one single B, I never would have heard the end of it. With you, he would say the teacher wasn't working hard enough to keep your attention, or you just needed to be challenged more, or you were bored, or something. It was never your fault. At least not in his eyes. You have no idea how much pressure Dad put on us."

"What are you talking about?" Trip was incredulous. "All my life, all I heard was how I was supposed to take over Cutler Enterprises someday, how Dad expected me to follow in his footsteps. Everybody was depending on me. It was so incredibly important to keep the business going, keep it successful. You guys thought you had it so bad. But I had my share of pressure, believe me." He crossed his arms over his chest, defying us to prove Paul was harder on his daughters than he was on his son.

"That's why your grades didn't matter as much," Julie pointed out. "Dad figured he'd give you on-the-job training at the company as soon as you finished college. All you had to do was get that far."

"Did you ever tell Paul you didn't want to take over?" I asked. "He probably wouldn't have liked that, but I bet he would've gotten over it. You are Paul the Third. In his eyes, you could do no wrong. In fact, he would have found a way to make it a good thing. To be proud of you for it."

"But I did want to take over!" Trip exclaimed. "I was proud to be a Cutler. People in this town respected Dad! The company was important to the whole town! I wanted to keep that going for our family. I still do."

Respected. Was. Past tense. And not just because Paul was dead. His reputation died a long time before he did. I wanted to point that out to Trip, but there was no reason to open those wounds. Everyone in Graverton knew the full story about Cutler Enterprises, and every member of the Cutler family, every former employee, had strong feelings about what Paul had done. It couldn't be undone now, no matter how much Trip wanted to try.

"You know, that's something I've always wondered about, but I never had, you know, the guts to ask Dad about it. Like, how he never really had a choice, did he?" Julie was saying. "I remember Mom talking about it sometimes, how GrandMom drilled it into Dad's head that the business was his legacy, how hard GrandDad worked to make sure he left his son with a solid future. I mean, how do you tell your parents you want to be a writer or a banker or a teacher or a fireman or whatever when you've lived with that kind of expectation hanging over you all your life? How do you say, 'I'm not interested in construction materials or running a business'? I don't think he could. I'm pretty sure Dad grew up thinking, you know, that's just how it's done. That it wasn't just his parents, but everybody expected it of him. And that's probably why he expected it of you."

It was true that whatever GrandMom wanted of Paul, he knew he had to deliver. And no one was more concerned with appearances and "the way it's done" than Paul had been. Still, I couldn't reconcile that with the reality of how Cutler Enterprises fell apart. "If you're right about that, then what he did makes even less sense."

"I keep telling you, Maddie, he did it for me," Trip insisted. "He was presenting me with a challenge. He didn't want me to have things too easy. I needed to prove to him that I was worthy."

I shook my head sadly. Poor Trip was so delusional. "You

were the *son*," I said. "The chosen one, just because you were a boy. He never, ever considered you unworthy. Me, on the other hand ..." I let my voice trail off. Was I ready to go into this topic with these two?

"Well, you know, I think you have that wrong, too," Julie said. "Dad wanted to be able to brag about you. That's why he pushed you so hard. He wanted to go to the office or to the Elks Club or wherever he was hanging out with his friends and tell them *his* daughter was at the top of her class. *His* daughter won the spelling bee. *His* daughter got into the best college. He did that with me and sports. When I won a junior tennis tournament or got a medal in the sprints. I didn't like the pressure any more than you did, but you were the one who seemed to just crumble under it. That made him even harder on you because you weren't giving him what he wanted. And you know how he was when he didn't get what he wanted."

I was starting to feel picked on and petulant. "What he wanted? What he wanted was to make me cry, embarrass me, make my life miserable."

"You're absolutely right. He did it because he could get a rise out of you. It was his way of winning, and you handed it to him on a silver platter every single time." Julie said all this in a matter-of-fact way, as if she had no concept of how damaging Paul's behavior had been.

"Yeah, I guess the ultimate prize was driving me as far away as possible. If what he wanted was to make sure I never ever wanted to be here, here in this house, here in Graverton, here in the same zip code with him, then he won all right. He won big." I could feel myself collapsing under the weight of all the anger and bitterness and regret that these memories were bringing down on me. By now, I was pacing around the dining room, too.

"Look," I tried to explain. "Maybe there was a time, when I was very young, that I thought I could work for the business. Maybe I even thought I could take over as boss, like he did. But at some point, I realized that wasn't going to work. Whether that was because I started to see that Paul was mapping it out for Trip or because my relationship with him was so broken, or for both reasons at once, I don't know. I don't remember. But the thing is, even when I didn't want to, I wanted him to want me to. I wanted him to think I was good enough. That was all he ever had to do. Tell me I was good enough. And he just never did."

The bile was rising in my throat the same way it had every time I sat at this dining room table. Even before we said grace at supper, I braced myself to fend off an argument with Paul. He would ask about school, about tests, about my grades, every night. He kept insisting the subjects I studied were so easy, "a baby could get an A." Then there were the ever-present comparisons to Julie. "It's not like you have sports to distract you," Paul would say. "Your sister gets straight A's, and she wins at tennis."

When I was home from college, it seemed as though Paul spent the months I was away trying to think of ways to get under my skin. I would start eating, and he would sit watching me, his own food untouched, that smirk twitching around the corners of his mouth. Mom would try to make pleasant conversation, asking me questions about my life or sharing some gossip about people in town that I might know. Eventually, however, Paul would interject his own commentary. Something about my manners or my clothes or how much makeup I was wearing. He expressed no interest in my life, especially after I moved away, instead just picking me apart when I ventured back into his domain. I tried to hold my own, but I always lost my cool, only to watch his grin spread into that full evil smile. As soon as that happened I always knew I had lost. Again.

In the heavy silence that followed my outburst, both Julie and Trip avoided my gaze. It seemed as though they both had more to say on the subject but were deciding against it for now. Julie began taking the crystal wine goblets out of the china cupboard and carefully wrapping each one in newspaper before gently placing them in a box for the antique dealer to examine. She held one up to the light.

"You know, I noticed this the other day after Dad's funeral," she mused, "there are only eleven of these glasses. But there's twelve of everything else—place settings and silverware and even the water glasses. I wonder what happened to the other one of these."

7

"Hey, Cutler. Hope you don't mind me calling. Got the number from my mom."

Standing in the kitchen, holding the exact same phone that never rang for me when I was a teenager, I listened in amazement to Derek's greeting, struggling to find the right response. But then, it didn't seem like I needed to respond because he just kept going.

"Listen, sorry if I made you mad yesterday. I was really enjoying our conversation, so I thought I'd see if you wanted to get a drink sometime. Maybe even dinner. Seems like you'd be a lot more fun to hang out with now than you used to be."

Hell, yeah, I'm fun to hang out with, I thought defensively. As an adult living far away from my hometown, I got used to being asked out on dates. It was no longer unusual, unexpected, or extraordinary for a man to enjoy my company. Like many professional women, I could make interesting conversation, share intelligent opinions, and display my sense of humor. That didn't mean I wasn't flattered by Derek's call. And there was definitely something bewildering but intriguing about a boy I once had a crush on, someone who remembered an awkward, unpolished version of me, calling me at my parents' house because he was interested in the reinvented me, so I felt completely flustered. My knees weak, heart pounding, and palms sweating, I stared at the phone as if the most clever remark to make in reply would magically appear there. When it didn't, I just said, "Yeah. Sure. That sounds like fun."

Derek took me to the same place Aunt Elaine had taken us all to lunch after the will reading. At dinner time, the lights were dimmed and there were flickering candles in crystal holders on every table. The hostess showed us to a cozy booth where the seats were plush and comfortable. Two or three other cloth-covered tables were occupied by older couples who looked as if they had been seated promptly at six o'clock.

Apparently, it was the only restaurant for miles that lived up to Derek's new standards now that he was an aspiring chef himself. "Spent the last few weeks visiting them all," he explained. "Research for my business plan. Since this place is pretty popular, I have to figure out what they do right and copy it, but be different enough to compete."

It seemed our date was going to be part of his research, too. As soon as we opened the heavy leather-bound menus, he began to fire questions at me. "What do you look at first? The appetizers? Or do you go straight to the list of entrees and then decide if you want something in addition to your main dish?" Then he wanted to know when I would look at the dessert menu: while I was considering the rest of my meal, or would I wait and decide based on how full I was after dinner? After I ordered and the waiter walked away, Derek asked about my choices. Why that salad? What would get me to order a steak in a place like this? Did I think about what wine I would want before or after I chose my entree?

Taking a sip of the California chardonnay I ordered to go with my grilled sea bass, I finally managed to squeeze in a question for Derek. "Is every dinner like this with you? I'm not used to having to think so much about all my meal choices. Or to justify them, for that matter. I should've suggested a bike ride or something instead."

"You're right. Sorry." Derek smiled that heart-melting smile and lifted his own wine glass full of cabernet. "Can't promise not to ask how you like your dinner, but if I do, it'll be as much because I want to make sure you're having fun as it will be for my research. Okay?"

"Okay," I agreed, clinking my wine glass gently against his. "But I don't think you need to worry. This is already the most fun I've had since I've been back in town."

"Yeah, well, you're here for a funeral, so I don't think that's a very high bar."

"That's true," I admitted, "but I didn't mean just this trip. For a long time, my visits have been pretty, well, I guess purpose-driven is probably the best way to say it. Christmas. Julie's wedding. My mom's funeral and now my father's. I come back to get something done, I do it, and I leave again. This time, there's more to do and I have to hang around a little longer. So it's nice to have some unexpected fun in the middle of it."

"Happy to provide it." As the smile returned to Derek's face, he gave me a little bow of his head and shoulders. "It's nice for me, too. Been so caught up in all there is to do to get this idea of mine off the ground that I haven't really taken any time to chill out. But I'm so excited about my restaurant, I don't even notice. You know?"

"I do know. I love the work I do, and it's really easy to let it take over. If I don't pay attention and stop myself, I end up spending too much time in my office. And then one night last summer, I'm at my desk, I look out to see the sun setting over the water, and I realize I had actually forgotten that Elliott Bay was even there. It had been so long since I looked up from my computer, I mean really looked up and looked around. It was a real 'I need a life' moment."

He asked me about my job, my company, why I loved my work, how I had discovered it was my passion. He was interested in Seattle. Did I follow the Seahawks? What neighborhood did I live in? And, of course, did I have a favorite restaurant there?

I asked him about his life since high school. Where had he gone to college? How had he ended up in Chicago? What had he done there? Why did he decide to go to culinary school? I watched him carefully as he talked. It didn't seem to me that he had changed very much at all since we were teenagers. Not only was he still just as handsome, but he was also confident without being arrogant, funny without being childish, interesting without being boorish. All the traits that I had admired from afar, that used to turn me into a tongue-tied twerp in his presence. Now, it was easy to listen to his enthusiasm, but I remained skeptical about one point: why did he want to open his restaurant here in Graverton, of all places?

"Seems like the market is ripe here," Derek explained with a shrug. "There aren't a lot of fine dining options, and I think people want them. And I can live here pretty cheaply. Bought a house here, in fact. After I sold our condo in Chicago, I could almost pay for it free and clear."

"Did you say 'our' condo?" I remembered Julie saying Derek was single, but I thought I had better be sure.

"Yeah, got it in the divorce. She got the car, and I bought her out of our place. She'd already moved in with the guy she left me for, so she didn't need a place to live."

"I'm sorry, I didn't know you were divorced," I said. Trying to gauge whether he'd be willing to talk about it, I ventured, "What happened?"

"Like I was telling you, got pretty burned out because my job was so stressful. There was always so much pressure. Keep moving up. Keep making more money. Keep buying stuff. Just didn't want to do it anymore. But she did. She loved it. Thrived on it. Put off having kids until she was where she wanted to be in her career. But she never got there. Couldn't understand why I wanted a change. Said she married me because I was such a go-getter. That was the life she always wanted to lead, and she didn't see any problems with where we were. And while I was trying to figure things out, she met somebody else. Somebody even more driven than she was. I guess they're happy."

"More importantly, are you?" I asked. "Happy, I mean?"

"Getting there," he said with a smile, "which is to say, I'm enjoying the journey." He lifted his wine glass in a mock toast and took a long drink. "Gotta tell you, Cutler, whatever you're doing in Seattle is working for you. You're not at all like I remember."

Thinking about what Julie had just told me, I took a deep breath and decided to just go ahead and ask. "How do you remember me? I mean, you said you remember me crying all the time and being grade-obsessed. But what else? Anything good?"

"Well, I sure remember you kicking my ass in the spelling bee at McKinley," Derek laughed. Then he set his wine glass down and twirled it by the stem for a moment before he went on. "But for real? Somewhere along the line, I guess we all got the impression that you were kinda, well, off limits."

"What do you mean, off limits?" I asked, surprised.

Squirming a little, Derek replied, "Well, you know, everybody had a parent or an uncle or a brother or somebody who worked for your dad. Nobody could take a chance on pissing off Mr. Cutler, like, somebody could lose a job, you know? Even if we weren't gonna take you out on a date, we couldn't invite you to the parties because your dad might find out what we were up to, might think we were corrupting the boss's daughter. Nobody really wanted to rock the boat, I guess."

I sighed and leaned back in my seat. "I suppose that shouldn't surprise me," I said. "Just one more thing my father ruined for me."

"Okay, probably shouldn't say this." Derek reached across the table to cover my hand with his. "But the way I remember it, it never seemed like it bothered you all that much. You know, being so focused on your grades and all. Everybody figured you just didn't have time for fun stuff anyway."

"So everybody was wrong about me, and I was wrong about everybody. I thought you all didn't like me, and you all thought I didn't like you. Was I really that clueless?"

"Seems like maybe we all were. Well, I say, let's just put that behind us and start from where we are now." He lifted his wine glass again. "What do you say?"

Raising my own glass and tapping his lightly, I smiled. "I like that idea."

By the time we polished off our shared dessert, the restaurant had emptied out. Derek leaned across the table and shared, in a conspiratorial whisper, "Restaurant people hate it when you do this, but I'm having such a great time, I wanna hang out a while." To the staff's chagrin, we lingered over coffee (really good coffee, like I hadn't had since I left Seattle), sharing more stories about our lives as single career people. When the check arrived, I offered to split it, but Derek waved me off. "At least let me help with the tip," I said. "We should probably leave a pretty big one."

"Okay, now that's the kind of thing restaurant people like to hear. Almost makes up for forcing them to work late."

When he dropped me off at the Harding Street house, Derek planted a brief, soft kiss on my cheek. "See ya, Cutler," he said. "Next time, I'll cook for you."

Next time.

8

It took a couple of days, but the three of us finally had the dining room packed up. I hadn't claimed very many items, balancing my desire to keep certain memories of Mom alive against the hassle of shipping fragile stuff all the way back to my Seattle apartment. I also took into consideration the limits of the space I had in a one-bedroom unit. So far, I had only chosen to keep a red glass candy dish because I always liked the way Mom kept Hershey kisses in it, even though the clank of the lid always gave me away when I tried to sneak one; a cake cutter with a beautifully elaborate blue enamel handle because I used to look forward to holding it to cut my birthday cakes almost as much as I did to eating the actual cake; and a sterling silver candle snuffer, just because no one else I knew had one of those and it would become a conversation piece, I was sure.

Trip took even less than I did. He kept talking about how much all this stuff was worth and how we had to make sure that the antiques dealer didn't cheat us, that we got the best possible price for everything he sold. He kept reminding us that he needed the money.

There was still the question of whether one of us, or I should say one of them, was going to live here. We had been delicately sidestepping that topic for the last couple of days, but we seemed to sense its presence all the time.

By the end of the day, we were all worn out, Julie most of all. Not only did the pregnancy drain her strength, but she was always awake early to care for Michael and help Henry get off to work. So, I did my best to pull together a dinner here from what I had brought home from the grocery store. With few culinary skills and even fewer kitchen tools, I couldn't offer a particularly elaborate meal, but Julie was just happy that she didn't have to cook for once.

While we were packing, Julie and Trip teasingly grilled me about my dinner with Derek. They had lots of questions, but I assured them there was nothing to tell. By the time we sat down at the kitchen table, we were all exhausted from the day's efforts and conversation, so we ate in silence. And that was just one room. So much more territory to cover.

Julie finally broke into the quiet. "How much longer do you guys think you can stay?"

"I have a few more PTO days, I guess, between bereavement and vacation," Trip said. "Might as well use them up before I quit this job."

"You've definitely decided to quit, then?" I asked. "Does that mean you were serious about moving back into this house?"

"Yeah, I was," he sighed, setting down his glass. "It might take me a while to figure things out, that's all."

"And you, Maddie? Can you stay a while longer? Much as I know you don't want to." Julie spoke to me but made no direct eye contact. Instead, she jabbed at the salad with her fork.

"I'm sorry, Julie, but it's hard for me to be here," I replied. "I checked in with my boss, and he says it would be fine if I worked remotely for a little while. I just need to be able to call in for some staff meetings and respond to messages and stuff. But I can't keep that up indefinitely. Let's say one more week, okay?"

"Today was kind of eye-opening," she admitted. "All three of us all day, and we got through, what, half the buffet and the china cupboard? Henry will have to help me, I guess. After you guys are gone, I mean. I'm really not supposed to be lifting anything heavy as it is. Another few weeks, and I won't be able to even if I try." She patted her swollen belly lovingly.

"So, is that the deadline for making a decision about the house? When I leave?" I wanted to know. I wasn't going to say we had to decide tonight, but I wanted to know when we would.

"Again, I remind you: This is not just about you, Maddie," Julie said, this time looking straight at me with hardening eyes. "This is a big deal for all of us."

"I didn't say it was about me or that it wasn't a big deal for anybody else. Stop twisting my words that way when I'm just trying to be practical and there just doesn't seem to be any point in putting things off. I can't see the housing market getting better around here any time soon. Selling the house now versus waiting isn't going to make any difference."

"That's *if* we sell the house," Julie said. "You keep talking as though that's a foregone conclusion, but Trip and I don't think it is."

Exasperated, I said, "Come on, be realistic, you guys. You can't think either of you could maintain this house. It needs so many repairs. Trust me, I've been sleeping here, and I can tell you the furnace leaves a lot to be desired. I'm freezing all night long, and it's not even winter yet. There's almost no water pressure in the shower, and forget about how long it takes the water to get hot. And when do you think was the last time Paul replaced any of the wiring? Or the water heater? We're probably lucky the place hasn't burned down. No, I think we just ask the attorneys what proof we need to give them that we can't live here so we can be rid of it and let it become someone else's problem."

"It was our home! It's not 'a problem'! Maybe you can be cold and unfeeling about it, but I can't!" Julie's anger was growing, her accusation bursting forth with the force of uncharacteristically violent emotions. "I've been right here this whole time, watching the house fall apart around Mom and Dad, and there was nothing I could do about it. You're right; Henry and I don't have the money to fix up this house. If we did, we would've helped Mom and Dad years ago! You're the one with the big bank account, but where were you all this time? As far away as you could get, pretending that all this had nothing to do with you. You tried to wash your hands of us, but you can't! Not yet."

"Oh no you don't!" My own frustration exploded with just as much force as Julie's. "You don't get to blame me for Paul's troubles! He made his own bed. GrandDad tried to make sure he had every advantage. Nobody was ever born with a bigger silver spoon in their mouth than Paul Cutler Junior. He was so entitled he never even bothered to learn about his own family business! How could someone who owned a building materials company let his own home get like this?"

I was standing up, gesturing around the room at all the evidence of Paul's neglect. "And his financial skills were even worse. He never paid a mortgage in his life. He had a guaranteed job when he finished college, and GrandDad paid his college tuition. Where would you be if you weren't paying Henry's college loans and a mortgage? Paul just flat-out blew it. He fucked up his own life, and he took Mom down with him! She might still be alive if he hadn't—"

"What happened to Mom had nothing to do with Dad!" Now, Trip was yelling at me, too. "She had breast cancer, for Christ's sake! How could that be Dad's fault?"

"They had no more money, Trip. After what Dad did! He lost his medical coverage, and Mom couldn't justify even routine trips to the doctor because it was too expensive. If she had gotten a mammogram sooner ..." I couldn't even finish the sentence. Throughout my life, my father had given me many reasons to be furious with him, but this was the one thing I knew I would never forgive him for. His selfishness cost my mother her life; I was certain of it.

"And still, you stayed away." Julie's voice had an even harder edge of accusation in it now. "Knowing what was happening here. Knowing you could help. You stayed in Seattle.

Oh, sure, you sent some money for a new fridge, and maybe that made you feel like you were some great savior. But you didn't show up until the end. Until it was too late to save Mom. You can say Dad was selfish, but you have to acknowledge that you are exactly like him."

That accusation hurt more than if she had slapped my face. No. I refused to even consider that possibility. I was nothing like Paul. I stayed away because I knew there would be a blow-up between us whenever I came back, and I wanted to spare my mother that anguish. She hated seeing me fight with Paul because she loved us both. But I was in no mood to explain that to Julie.

"How can you say that?" I cried. "I am not like Paul. I'm not!"

"You like to think so," Julie countered, "but you're just as self-centered as he was. Maybe more. And it's probably even worse with you because you don't acknowledge it. You took off. You left us all in your dust. Now you're trying to blame it all on Graverton. Like we all drove you away instead of you always thinking you were just too good for the rest of us.

"And the few times you managed to grace us with your presence—like my wedding—it was as if you were doing us all such a great big favor. Like we wanted you here, so you came. Not like you wanted to be here for us."

She was swinging a verbal sledgehammer now, carried by its momentum, determined to pound me into gravel. Pacing around the kitchen as if motion would help her blow off all this built-up steam, she barreled on. "It completely destroyed Mom to never see you, to hardly ever even hear from you. She kept up a brave face, but I was here; I could see how much she was hurting. You didn't even pay any attention to her. It was always all about you. And how you wanted to get away from here, from Dad. And you're trying to do it again! To just dump all this on me and Trip! Like you and your life are so much more important than the rest of us."

Still not satisfied that she had driven her point home, Julie kept going. "You have the life Mom and Dad gave you, you know. Dad because the business made enough money for us to live like we did. But it was Mom, too. Without her, you wouldn't have the life you have now. To her, the home she built here for us, for herself, it was her greatest accomplishment. She was so proud of all of us, of all this. Of making sure we had the best possible start in life. And you shit all over it. It wasn't good enough for you. You broke her heart into a million pieces. Worse than Dad ever did."

As her eyes were blazing at me and her words hung heavily in the air, I wanted to swing back. To defend myself and prove that I was nothing, nothing at all, like my father. But the words stopped in my throat, forced back down by the sudden, terrifying, painful realization that maybe she was right. I had been selfish. I hadn't paid enough attention to Mom. In fact, I hardly knew what was going on in her life the last few years before she died. Had I ever really known her? Really seen her?

"You're being so unfair," I heard myself say, my own choking voice betraying me.

"Am I?" Julie countered. "How would you know? I was the one here, the one who saw it all happen. How was that fair?"

"Mom wanted me to be happy." My arguments were weak, even to my own ears, but I needed time to process Julie's accusations.

"Of course she did! That's why she never said anything to you, never asked you to come back here and help her, never complained about Dad. My God, Madeline, you really don't see beyond your own little bubble of needs. It's all about you. Just like Dad."

"If I'm like Dad, so are you," I said, hearing Paul's low, barely controlled, angry rumble coming out of my own mouth. "Figure out where you can hit me so it will hurt the most. Then swing for that spot as many times as you can. Maximize the damage, then sit back and revel in it. With a big smile on your face."

"I'm not enjoying this, believe me." Julie wasn't even looking at me anymore. "And if Dad enjoyed it, it was because you rose to the bait every single time. And did you ever stop to think how that affected me? I came home with good grades, with a trophy I won, anything I did, and then Dad would hold it out to you. If you had even once congratulated me, been happy for me, instead of getting pissed off at him, maybe he would have stopped. He was trying to pit us against each other, and you helped him succeed. He loved that. He thought he was pushing you to achieve more. Pretty soon, you and Dad would be fighting, and you were running away crying, and everybody forgot about me. And I just kept wondering, what do I have to do? How do I get him to notice me? So, yeah, by all means, tell me how I am the one who's like Dad."

In the thick silence that settled over us like a dust cloud when she finished her rant, Julie seemed to know she had crossed a line, but it didn't look like she intended to apologize or back down. "Come on, Trip," she said finally. "We should probably go. And maybe we shouldn't all be here in the house at the same time anymore."

"Jesus, Madeline," Trip muttered to me as they walked out the door.

Angry and hurt by Julie's words, I cleaned up the kitchen after our makeshift dinner. Trip is still really good at getting out of helping, I thought. Maybe I should just leave tomorrow. Get back on a plane, no phone call, no note, no nothing. If Julie thinks I'm so much like Paul, then I should act like him and think of only myself and what I want. And by not disagreeing with Julie, Trip was telling me he was on her side. The two of them could just figure everything out. Why did I need to be involved at all? I didn't care how much money we got for the house. Julie was right about that part; I did have my own money now. By the time we sold the house and divided the proceeds among the three of us, the amount would be inconsequential. So, let them handle it.

All alone with my anger, I started to get irritated by absolutely everything, from the sirens outside destroying my peace and quiet to the cheap dish soap Paul had kept under the sink. How had he gotten anything clean with this stuff? Everything was just wrong. It seemed like my past, my ties to Graverton, all of it, was in pieces at my feet and the only thing to do now was to get out of this house. So, that's it, then, I decided. I'm leaving first thing in the morning.

As I got ready for bed, one regret began to nag at me. I wouldn't get the "next time" Derek alluded to after our dinner date. But who was I kidding? Even if he really did want to see me again, it wasn't like it was going to turn into any long-term thing anyway. If I didn't leave tomorrow, I'd leave next week or the week after that. He was determined to stay here. So it was silly to feel any regret at all. Still, when I heard the phone ringing, I hurried to Paul's bedroom, remembering that I had seen a phone by his bed, excited to think maybe this was Derek calling. After all, it wasn't likely to be Julie calling to apologize.

It was Henry. He was crying.

PART TWO

1969 – 1972

9

I loved to go shopping with my mom, just the two of us. Walking through the department stores at the mall, we held hands, and she pointed out dresses and shoes and scarves that would look nice on me when I grew up. "That's a very good color for you," Mom would say, holding something pretty up close to my face. Or she would tell me that I was going to be tall and slender some day and that style was just made for my kind of figure. For me, it was less about fashion and more about having my mother's undivided attention. No Daddy to make stupid jokes about the clothes, no little sister whining that she was tired.

On one particular trip in early spring, we concentrated on new warm-weather clothes for me because of my most recent growth spurt. My skirts were too short now, and my father wouldn't stop rolling his eyes and chanting, "I see London, I see France," whenever we were in the same room. So I had a few new, better-fitting outfits in a bag, and I was thinking about how much fun it was going to be to wear them to school. We were on our way to look for the shoes that, as Mom explained, would "complete this new wardrobe." But strolling through the ladies' shoe department, my mother spotted a pair of pumps that made her stop in her tracks. She picked one up with awe in her eyes and said softly, "These are beautiful." I remember the shiny patent leather, a shade of dark blue that was not quite navy, not quite royal. They had white leather trim and a higher heel than she was used to. I could tell by the look in her eyes that these shoes were calling her name. The price tag made her set them back down, but she didn't walk away. "I want to try them on," she said aloud, but I wasn't sure she was really talking to anybody but herself. "I probably won't buy them, but just for fun." She grinned and wrinkled her nose playfully. "What do you think?"

A few minutes later, she was walking around the shoe department with a lift in her step that I'd never seen before. I was too young then to know that shoes had the power to make walking feel like dancing, to turn your feet into works of art, to change the simplest outfit into a fashion statement. Watching my mom that day, the way she smiled, the way she daintily lifted her heel to flex her foot in front of the little mirror on the floor, was my first clue.

She debated for a while about whether or not to buy the shoes. They were kind of expensive, but money wasn't an issue for us because our family business was doing pretty well. My grandmother saw to that. Mom and I both knew my father never hesitated to buy himself anything that made him that happy, so I told her she should get them. "They make you even more beautiful, Mommy," I said. She smiled and cupped her hand against my cheek. Ultimately, she drew her department store charge card out of her wallet and said decisively, "I'll take them."

And for the next few months, she wore those shoes with delight and pride to parties, out to dinner, to church, anywhere she could. She worried about them if there was even a remote chance she would get caught in the rain. She closely inspected the white trim for the smallest scuff marks and quickly cleaned away any she found. She always returned them to their box, carefully wrapping each one in tissue paper.

My father was the one who ruined those shoes. Looking at the charge card bill, he casually questioned her about the total. "Most of that was for Maddie," she told him, "but I bought myself a nice pair of shoes, too." Dad arched an eyebrow at me and commented that I must be developing expensive taste. He didn't say anything about Mom's shoes at first, just mentioned the purchase every time she wore them: "Those are the shoes you bought shopping with Madeline."

Eventually, though, he noticed that she got lots of compliments on the shoes, and he started teasing her about them in front of other people. Out for a family dinner one night, we ran into a couple of their friends. Instead of exchanging the usual greetings, my father pointed at Mom's shoes. "Check out my wife's Ferra-GAH-moze," he drawled. "Ask her how much I paid for them."

Mom tried to laugh it off. "Paul! You're embarrassing me!" I watched her cheeks burn even darker than her rouge. Not only did she not talk about money, ever, but she also hated having unwanted attention drawn to her. She turned to their friends, shaking her head. "Isn't he awful?"

But that was only the first time it happened. Every time Dad commented, Mom blushed. "Oh, I know they were a silly indulgence. I just really liked them," she would tell him. They came home from a cocktail party one Saturday night, and it looked to me like my mom was fighting back tears. She went straight to her closet and put her shoes away.

After a while, I noticed that they didn't come out of the box as often anymore. One evening, Julie and I were sitting on the bed, watching Mom get ready to go out. When she turned her back to me so I could zip up her dress, I said, "Your blue and white shoes would be pretty with that, Mommy."

"You're right, sweetie," Mom replied, "they would." Taking a long look into my eyes, she smiled with pride and lightly touched my cheek. "You are developing such a good sense of fashion! But I think they're more of a summery shoe, don't you? And they're kind of out of style by now. Everybody is wearing lower heels now that it's autumn."

I don't remember seeing her wear those shoes again, but many times over the next several years, I did notice that the distinctively branded box remained in her closet. Those shoes may have been her last big splurge because the next year, everything changed.

10

"Maddie? Your mom just called. She wants you to come home right away."

My friend Allison's mother stuck her head into the TV room where Allison and I were watching Saturday morning cartoons. That was the best part of a sleepover: staying in your pajamas half of the next day and zoning out in front of the television to watch your favorite shows. It was barely ten thirty now. Way too early to go home.

"Aw, Mom, does she really have to? It's so early!" Allison whined, looking away from the TV only because there was a commercial on.

"I'm afraid so, honey," Allison's mother said sternly. "There's a ..." she paused awkwardly. "Family situation at Maddie's house. She needs to be there."

I didn't know what "family situation" could be so important, but I knew it didn't sound good. Reluctantly, I hauled myself off the couch cushions that we had spread all over the floor so we could get closer to the television set. Allison didn't get up. She turned her attention back to the show while I went to her room to get dressed and collect my stuff. Her mom watched me with a sad look on her face, an expression I didn't realize was sympathy. "Give your mother my best," she said, gently touching the back of my head. "Bye, Maddie," Allison called as I walked past on my way out.

Allison lived on the same block, so I didn't have to cross a street to get to her house. That meant I could walk there and back alone. I trudged home slowly, swinging my overnight bag and muttering complaints to myself. My sleepover was ruined.

Allison was probably never going to ask me over again. I had been hoping to stay there till at least lunch. Maybe we could have even spent the afternoon together. But no. I had a "family situation," so I had to go home early. It was so unfair! With every step, my petulance grew until I was downright angry when I got home.

"Mom?" I yelled, coming into the kitchen. "I'm home!"

I thought it was kind of strange when she didn't answer. She should be expecting me, after all, since she was the one who made me come home so early. I went looking for her, preparing to let her know how unfair this whole situation was. I found her in the living room, sitting in the armchair opposite the one where my father always sat. He wasn't there. Mom was staring into space like she hadn't even heard me come in. There was a crumpled tissue clutched in one hand, and her tear-stained face rested on the other. I had never seen her look so utterly defeated. All my irritation evaporated. Something was terribly wrong.

"Mom? Allison's mom said we had a family situation." I went to stand in front of her, putting my hands gently on her knees. "What does that mean? Did something happen?"

From her red and swollen eyes, I could tell my mother had been crying for a while. Whatever it was, it was bad, probably worse than I was imagining. "Mommy?" I said, nearly in tears myself just seeing her look so sad.

After a long moment, she sat up straight and looked at me. "It's GrandMom, sweetie," she sighed, her voice cracking. "She had a stroke last night. And she ... she died, honey. I'm sorry." Her arms were wide open by the time she got to "sorry," and I was flinging myself into them. I tumbled into Mom's lap and let my tears flow against her chest. No matter how bad I imagined a family situation was, it wasn't this! GrandMom was dead? That was just not possible. She had dinner with us just a couple of nights ago. And she was fine! There had to be some mistake.

Wrapping me up in a warm hug and rocking me back and forth like I was still a baby, my mother kept repeating, "Shh, shh, it's okay, it's going to be all right. GrandMom is in a better place now."

"But I want her here in this place," I sniffed.

"I know you do, honey," my mother said, trying to soothe me by stroking my back. "We all do. It's okay to be sad about it. Just remember that you're sad for yourself because you're going to miss her. And for Daddy and for Aunt Elaine because they lost their mother. But you're not sad for GrandMom. She's at peace."

"I think she's sad that she's not with us," I insisted. "She loved us. She would rather be here, I know it."

"Well, she did love you very much. You're right about that. And she's here, as long as you remember her. Right?"

"I want my GrandMom, not my memories." I stubbornly resisted the comfort she offered, as if my mother could do something to change the situation if I just refused to believe in it.

"I know. But you still have your dad and me and your sister and Aunt Elaine. Lots of people in your life who love you just as much as GrandMom did. We'll all remember her together. Always."

I stayed snuggled in my mother's lap for a while, trying to think all this through. "Where is she, anyway?" I finally thought to ask.

"Her body is at the funeral home now. That's where Daddy is."

"She didn't die there, did she?" I wasn't quite sure how all this worked, how somebody got sick, maybe went to a hospital, maybe not, but somehow got to a funeral home once they were dead. GrandMom was the first person I knew who had died.

"No, no," my mother explained. "GrandMom was playing bridge with her friends yesterday afternoon like she always does on Fridays. But she left Mrs. McKenzie's house early because she didn't feel well. Said she had a bad headache. Mrs. McKenzie called her later to see how she was doing, and she got worried when GrandMom didn't answer her phone. So she called here, and Dad went to GrandMom's to check. He found her in bed, but she wouldn't wake up." Mom started crying again at the part where she said GrandMom didn't feel well. Years later, when I learned more about strokes, I wondered whether my grandmother and her bridge partners had ignored signs that might have saved her if they had recognized them in time. But as a little girl, all I knew was that I had lost my GrandMom and she had died all alone. That was bad enough.

Mom and I sat crying softly in that chair for a while until my father came home. As soon as he came into the living room, his eyes red and swollen, too, I climbed off Mom's lap and ran to him. He picked me up, something he had not done for a long time because I had begun to resist his shows of affection and I usually tried to get away from him when I thought he was going to grab me for a forced hug. But at this moment, I needed one as much as he did. While he held me tight, I tried to ignore the smell of cigarette smoke on his clothes. I really hated that smell, and I felt like I was suffocating, but I didn't squirm away like I usually did. When he put his face against my neck, I could feel that his skin was wet with tears. Suddenly, he was shaking with sobs, dampening my shirt, and making a small, pitiful wailing noise that it seemed like he couldn't control. I think this was the scariest moment I had experienced in my life. I had never seen my father cry before, so, closing my eyes tight, I kept my arms around his neck until his shoulders stopped shaking. Then he kissed my cheek and put me down without saying a word or looking at my face.

That night, I could hear Julie crying. She wanted to leave all the lights on because she was scared that GrandMom's ghost would come to visit us.

"There's no such thing as ghosts," I reassured her, trying to sound like the big sister. "Anyway, GrandMom loved us. Even if she could come back as a ghost, you don't think she would hurt us, do you? There's nothing to be scared of."

My father was uncharacteristically quiet in the days and weeks after GrandMom's death. He didn't crack jokes or tease us. He had little to say about the news we watched on television or about what was going on at the company. The only time he seemed to pay close attention to Julie and me was the day of the funeral, when he inspected our outfits very carefully. He frowned at my new navy blue dress.

"Doesn't she have anything black, Ginny?" he asked. "She should wear black. It's a funeral. What will people say if she's not wearing black?"

"I'm sorry, Paul, but they don't really sell many black dresses for seven-year-old girls," my mother replied. "Especially not at this time of year. I was lucky to find a sleeveless jumper for Julie. There will be black velvet dresses all over the place during the holidays, but not now. This is dark blue. It's close enough."

"What about that dress she wore last Christmas? It was black, wasn't it?"

"It's too small for her, one. And even if it did fit her, it is a heavy wool. With long sleeves. She'll roast in it."

"Have her put it on," my father insisted. "Let me see."

My mother wasn't used to arguing with my father, and I could tell she didn't want to start now, given how deep he was in his grief. Still, I could also tell she wanted to stand up for me. But finally, she sighed and told me to go and see if I could find that dress.

The dress was in the back of my closet, along with several other things I had outgrown and that were waiting for Julie to grow some more. I wiggled into it, but I couldn't zip it up. So I went out to prove to my father that the dress was too small.

"See? She can't even get the zipper up anymore, never mind how short it is," my mother declared when I returned to the living room.

"Come here, I bet I can get it zipped up," my father said. He spent several minutes tugging at the zipper and telling me to hold my breath. I was starting to sweat under the high collar and the long sleeves, and I could barely breathe, it was so tight around my waist. There was no way he would make me wear this, was there?

"Turn around, Madeline," my father said when he finally overpowered the zipper. He looked me up and down and nodded his head. "I want you to wear this. It's black. You should always wear black to a funeral." It was not a question or a suggestion.

"Paul, that's ridiculous," my mother put in. "It's July, for God's sake. She can't wear a long-sleeved wool dress in the middle of summer! I don't care if it is black. Do you want her to pass out? Look at her face. She's already drenched in sweat."

My father looked surprised. Whether it was because he had not, in fact, noticed that I looked like I was melting or because my mother was actually standing up to him for a change, I couldn't tell. Maybe he thought I should be willing to suffer for appearances or for GrandMom's sake. In any case, there was a long, uncomfortable silence. In my discomfort, I wiggled a little and gave the dress a tug. The movement was too much for the dress to bear, and I heard a loud ripping sound as the zipper became detached from its seam.

"Well, now do you believe it's too small?" Mom declared, barely keeping the I-told-you-so tone out of her voice. "She can't possibly wear it now."

My father didn't like to lose, and he definitely wanted to make his final point. "I wish you had tried harder to find her a black dress, Ginny. I told you I wanted them to wear black."

"Yes, I know, and I just explained to you why I went with navy blue instead," Mom said. To me, she added, "Go change back into your other dress. Hurry, now. We don't want to be late."

I backed out of the room, watching my parents stare each other down. It wasn't until I was back in my room that I realized I wouldn't be able to unzip the dress by myself.

11

The first day back to school after Christmas vacation was so hard. The days before we left were fun-filled because the teachers incorporated Santa and reindeer and wreaths and holly and snowflakes into all our lessons, artwork, and games. Classrooms were brightly decorated, and there were Christmas parties to look forward to. Gingerbread men and hot chocolate! At school! Even if it was dark outside when my alarm clock went off, it was easy to get out of bed in the morning when you knew the day ahead held that kind of wonder. And it was getting you that much closer to Christmas Day.

Then, the day after New Year's, it was suddenly all over. The mornings were bleak and dreary and cold, with no bright Christmas lights on the porches on the way to school. The colorful and glittery decorations were gone from the classrooms, and the teachers were ready to get back down to business. No more parties, no more fun. Valentine's Day was too far away to look forward to. It was so depressing.

That year, going back to school in January seemed even worse because my family had just had the most incredible Christmas ever. Our tree was huge, bigger than anyone else's, my father kept saying, and certainly bigger than any we had ever had before, so my father bought lots of new fancy ornaments to cover its branches. Many of them were delicate and breakable, and he was reluctant to let me be the one to hang them. "Remember the Christmas earthquake?" he asked. "When you crushed one of those little houses in GrandMom's ornament collection?" Even though I was only three years old when that happened, I did remember it clearly since my father brought it up every year. So, I watched in envy as he carefully arranged these new silver and gold glass shapes so that you could see them clearly when you looked at the tree. And if any of our guests failed to notice them, my father pointed them out.

Every night in December, it seemed my father brought home some new holiday season treat that we didn't usually get. Pizzelles from the Italian bakery. Fruitcakes. Fancy nut assortments. There were some Christmas treats especially for him, too, and those went straight into the liquor cabinet. When Aunt Elaine came for Christmas dinner, even she seemed surprised that my father had gone so far overboard with this holiday. She said her Christmas gift to herself was a strand of perfect pearls. They seemed absolutely luxurious to me, and I desperately wanted to try them on. I didn't dare ask, though, because my father was sure to make a joke about my clumsiness and recommend against it.

It didn't occur to me to wonder why my parents were being extra generous this year. I was just glad my father was in a good mood most of the time, and he seemed less interested in making fun of me. I also didn't notice how much of the excess seemed to be focused mostly on him. Sure, Julie and I got pretty much everything we asked Santa for, but that wasn't unusual. Our mom made such a fuss over each gift we opened—what a pretty doll, how cute you'll look in that sweater, we can read that book together—we didn't really notice that she wasn't opening many gifts of her own.

Once, I got a little sad, realizing that, for the first time, my GrandMom wouldn't be with us for Christmas. I kept it to myself, though. I didn't want to risk ruining my father's good mood.

When I got home from school that first day after vacation, I felt defeated. It had been a very long day, just as I had known it would be. Although the playground was lively before school, as all the kids compared their gifts and showed off the new clothes they were wearing, there was nothing fun happening in the classroom. Even my teacher seemed excessively grumpy. At least our tree was still up and would be until the weekend. It would take Mom, Julie, and me a long time to put away the ornaments and tinsel and stuff. My father's only job was to lug the bare tree out to the curb, where the garbage men would make it disappear. In my post-holiday sadness, all I wanted was to sit in the living room and look at the tree for a while. I was about to shout out to my mother to let her know I was home, but then I heard her voice and realized she was on the phone.

"It was all of Madeline's money," she was saying with a heavy sigh. "He's spent so much of it already. And all on himself. On such frivolous things! Every ridiculous purchase, he would say it was something he'd always wanted. He refused to put any money aside for the girls' education, for a rainy day, for any reason. Nothing for repairs or maintenance here at the house. Nothing. Most men would take better care of their families in such a situation. I know you would."

Madeline's money? I didn't have any money. Then I realized what she meant: GrandMom. My father inherited a lot of money when my grandmother died. I didn't know how much, and I would never have asked. But had he really spent all of GrandMom's money on Christmas? That seemed to be what my mother was saying. I knew this was a conversation I shouldn't be listening to, but it was fascinating to hear her criticize my father. She hardly ever did that, and certainly never with anybody not named Cutler.

"Well, if you call all new furniture for his office 'investing in the business,'" Mom was saying now. "I don't really think that it's going to help increase sales or anything."

After another pause, she laughed, but not in a happy way. "Me? Nothing more than my usual Christmas gifts. I got some new jewelry that he'll insist I wear every time we go out for the next couple of months. He'll point it out, tell everyone he got it for me, allude to how much it cost without actually saying. That's what he does every year."

I wondered who was on the other end of that call. It would be unusual for her to confide in her friends like this. She and my father were both very adamant about keeping private matters private. We didn't discuss our family's business outside of our family. And to hear my mother talking about money was particularly earth-shaking.

"Oh, I didn't have to tell Elaine. She could see for herself as soon as she walked in the house on Christmas Day. She took me aside after dinner and asked if I was okay. What could I say? I told her, of course, everything is fine. She's a Cutler. She knows what that means, but she also knows that neither one of us can do anything about it."

I couldn't see Mom from where I was standing in the kitchen, but I assumed she was sitting by the phone table in the front hall. When she stopped talking, I heard a glass clink as she set it down on the table.

"No, I'm sure she was much smarter with her share. She bought herself some pearls, but as far as I know, that was her only splurge. Other than that, though, she hasn't spent any of the money. At least not that she told me about."

After another pause, Mom started to wrap up the conversation. "Well, I really appreciate you listening to me complain. But I need to get going now. The girls will be home any minute, and I don't want them to catch me crying and drinking in the middle of the day. That would be hard to explain."

Hearing that, I decided I should quietly get myself back outside and pretend I had just gotten home. Before I did, I heard her say, "Yes, lunch would be nice. Next week, then. Goodbye."

By the time I called out, "I'm home!" as I came back in the kitchen door, Mom had wiped her face and put her glass in the sink. No one would ever know she had just been talking about money issues. Without saying a word, I gave her a big hug.

She laughed as she hugged me back. "Are you okay, sweetheart?" she asked, holding me away from her body so she could look at my face. "Did something happen at school today?"

"No, I'm just glad to be home," I replied, hugging her again. "It's hard to be back in school after Christmas. It was nice to be home with you every day."

A couple months later, Julie and I were helping Mom make dinner. My father came home from the office early, and he fixed himself a cocktail right in the middle of the kitchen. Mom smiled at him patiently as she waited till he moved before she could open the refrigerator or cabinet doors. Finally, he sat down with his drink and began watching her closely.

"Hey, Ginny, have you been trying to lose those holiday pounds you gain every year?" he asked suddenly. "Because if you have, I think they've found you again."

Surprised, Mom turned to look at him. Then she glanced over her shoulder as if she was trying to see her own behind. "Why? Do you think I look fat?"

"Well, you don't have as many chins as Chinatown yet," my father clarified, "but those slacks are way too tight." He turned toward me, raising his eyebrows and tilting his head toward my mom as if to say, "You can see it, too, right?"

"It's strange that you would say that because I haven't had any appetite at all lately. I would've thought I was actually losing some weight. But if you're noticing it, then I guess I'll make myself a salad for dinner."

As soon as my father turned away, I frowned at his back. That was a mean thing for him to say to her, and I knew it hurt her feelings even if she didn't say so. However, I also knew better than to say anything on her behalf because then he would focus his attention and criticism on me. And I was already painfully self-conscious about my own appearance. I tried to shrink away from his field of vision and concentrate on shelling the peas.

It was Julie who rose to Mom's defense. As she took silverware out of the drawer to set the table, she said, "I think you look beautiful, Mommy. You're not fat at all."

"Thanks, honey," Mom said, smiling as she watched Julie go back into the dining room. For just a moment, I saw my mother's glance fall on my father, but it was hard to read her expression. She wasn't sad or angry, exactly, but it looked as if she wanted to wish for something, something she knew she'd never get.

When Julie came back to the kitchen, my father stuck out an arm to stop her and wrap her into a tight squeeze. He kissed the top of her head and said, "You know I was only teasing your mom. She would want us to let her know before it got out of hand, right? That's what family is for." He stood up. "Did the paper come yet?" With that, he took his drink to the living room, where he waited, smoking a cigarette and reading the paper, until the three of us had dinner on the table. Mom watched us eat as she slowly nibbled on her salad. Even so, I heard her throwing up in the bathroom the next morning.

I don't remember how long it was after that conversation that our parents told Julie and me that we were getting a new baby brother or sister in the fall. We were absolutely thrilled at the prospect. Julie expressed an immediate preference for a baby girl, but I didn't care one way or another. Babies were so cute and so soft and so much fun to have around. I declared my willingness to help with absolutely everything. Diapers. Feeding. Playing. Rocking to sleep. All of it. I couldn't wait.

The reality was much more difficult. As Mom's belly grew, she was more tired, and Julie and I were given more chores to help her out. I whined pretty openly about giving up my own room. "Why can't the baby have GrandMom's old room?" I wanted to know. "I'm the oldest. I should get to keep my own room."

"I'm sorry, sweetie, but that just won't work," Mom told me. "We're keeping that room open for guests for now. And anyway, I don't think Daddy is quite ready to change things in his mother's old room. You can understand that, can't you?"

I had another idea, which I thought was brilliant. "Well, why don't we just move to a bigger house? Then we could all have our own rooms and a guest room besides."

Mom got a good laugh out of that one. "Move to a new house just so you don't have to share a room? I don't think so. Even if I wanted to and we could find a bigger house and move in before the baby comes, you know your dad will never leave Harding Street. He grew up here. He loves it. You'll have a hard time convincing him that it's not big enough."

So, sharing a room became unavoidable. I did try to delay Julie moving in as long as possible, refusing or "forgetting" to clean up or clear out space, but eventually, new baby furniture arrived, and the room needed to be painted a good nursery color. Julie wasn't any happier about it than I was, but she was better at keeping a stiff upper lip. As we carried her clothes down the hall to "our" room, she said softly, "Don't worry, Maddie. I'll try to stay out of your way."

One autumn morning, Julie and I woke up to find Aunt Elaine in the kitchen making our breakfast. Or rather, she was looking through the cupboards, trying to find something easy to give us. "Where's Mom?" I asked, suspicious.

"Good morning, girls!" Aunt Elaine greeted us. "Your mom and dad went to the hospital to get the new baby. They called me last night after you went to bed. I'm supposed to get you ready for school before I go to work. But I need your help. Where does your mom keep the cereal?"

Julie opened her mouth, and I knew she was about to say we were only allowed to have cereal for breakfast on Saturdays.

So, I quickly shot her a look that warned her not to. Aunt Elaine was fun, but she would still be reluctant to break the rules. Better that she just didn't know about them. "It's in there," I said, pointing. "I'll get the bowls."

By the time we got home from school, we had a new baby brother. I couldn't remember ever seeing our father so happy. Granted, I was pretty little when Julie came along, so I didn't really remember much other than having GrandMom to myself for a few days before my parents brought home this new doll that I wasn't allowed to play with. But with a baby boy, my father called everyone he knew to announce the birth. He even called his friend at the newspaper to get the birth announcement on the front page.

There was never any discussion about the baby's name. Of course he was Paul Robert Cutler the Third, and of course he was the rightful heir to Cutler Enterprises. We all agreed that the nickname Trip (you know, like "triple," because he's the third, as I always had to explain to other kids) was kind of cute for the little one, and it would keep everyone from getting confused with two Pauls in the house.

When Mom and the baby came home from the hospital, there was a lot of fanfare: blue balloons everywhere, a big "IT'S A BOY" sign in the front yard, and some champagne on ice in the dining room. As soon as the car pulled up in front of the house, my father jumped out and ran to the passenger side. He opened the door, took the baby out of Mom's arms, and carried him inside. As Mom struggled to get out of the car, Julie and I ran out to hug her. She seemed happy to see us, but she didn't hug us back very hard. "Can you girls help me get out?" she laughed. "I'm still a little weak." So we each held one arm, and she stood up very carefully.

Inside, my father was showing the baby to the few guests who had already arrived. "Ooh, Ginny, he has your blond hair," our next-door neighbor exclaimed.

"Yeah, but his strong chin is all Cutler," my father replied.

"And he's got big hands. He should be a good ball player one day. Isn't that right, Trip? You even have a good ballplayer name: Trip Cutler. Yeah, announcers will love saying that name."

If the baby agreed with that assessment, he had a funny way of showing it. Trip chose that moment to let out a newborn wail that was shocking and scary to Julie and me. How could something so little make a noise that big? And was he going to do that a lot? We looked at each other with wide eyes, wondering what our parents had gotten us into.

But the wailing didn't last long. Mom rushed to where our father stood and took the baby back into her arms, which immediately silenced the screaming. "Yes, I know," Mom started cooing. "All these new people, it's so scary. You were just wondering where your mommy went, weren't you?" Swaying slowly, she jostled him gently, and the baby seemed to calm down instantly.

"She'll turn him into a mama's boy if I'm not careful," my father joked to his friends.

"I don't think that will be a problem," Mom laughed. She reached up to touch my father's cheek. Which was a little surprising because she was rarely affectionate with him. "You'll mold him in your image, I'm quite sure."

"Well, he will be the one carrying on the Cutler name." With that, my father turned to the guests, rubbed his hands together enthusiastically, and asked who wanted some champagne.

For the next few hours, our neighbors, my parents' friends, and some of my father's business associates dropped by to gush over the baby and drop off gifts for him. Some thoughtfully brought casseroles so my mom wouldn't have to cook. She was becoming visibly tired from all this attention, not to mention the baby getting fussy, but my father didn't seem to notice. He kept encouraging people to hang around, have another drink, hold the baby, and come up and see the room we decorated for him. I wanted to tell my father that maybe we should let Mom rest for a while, but I didn't dare. At one point, I saw her standing alone, apart from any conversation going on around her. Her arms wrapped protectively around her own waist, her gaze seemed to be focused far away, not looking at anything or anyone in the room but at something only she could see. While I watched her, the front door opened to let in another guest, and the beginnings of a smile swept across her face, and her eyes lit up just for a second. But then Mom waved a friendly hello to my father's secretary, the hopeful look gone as quickly as it appeared, and then she returned her focus to that faraway place.

I kept wishing Aunt Elaine would come because she could stand up to my dad, tell him Mom and the baby needed rest. I wished I could do it, go over to my mom, gently guide her to her own room for a nap, and reassure her that I would take care of the baby. I didn't think she would listen to me, though. It would have to be Aunt Elaine.

But when Aunt Elaine finally did arrive, I quickly forgot about asking her to intervene. There was a tall, handsome man with her, someone I had never seen before. And she was smiling in a way I'd never seen before either. As they walked into our house, she took his arm and guided him to where my father was holding court in the living room.

"Paul! Congratulations," she said, planting a quick kiss on his cheek. "I want you to meet Ron. Ron Springer. Ron, this is my brother, Paul, the proud papa."

"Very nice to meet you," this new guy said, shaking my father's hand vigorously. "Elaine talks about you and your family all the time."

My father remained cautious. He allowed his arm to be pumped in this enthusiastic handshake, but he didn't smile back at this Ron guy. "Thank you for coming," was all he said.

Aunt Elaine jumped right back in. "So where's the mommy? And my beautiful new nephew? Oh, there you are! Let me see this precious little bundle of joy!" Mom had returned to the living room after changing the baby upstairs. She smiled broadly at Aunt Elaine and turned her body so that Elaine could get a better view of Trip, now snuggled comfortably (and quietly) in a fuzzy blue blanket.

Ron hadn't moved. He stood next to my father, watching Aunt Elaine. The look on his face was strange to me. The dimples in his smooth cheeks and the laugh lines around his eyes were very visible, and there was an odd sort of glow in his face that seemed to be coming from his eyes and his goofy grin. While Ron focused on my aunt, my father stared at Ron, with his eyes hardening. That look was not strange to me. My father seemed to be deciding that he didn't like this new guy, just based on his appearance. When my father finally spoke, Ron seemed surprised, as if he had forgotten that there was anyone else in the room.

"So, Springer. What do you do?" my father asked.

"Oh, I'm a CPA," he answered. "Right now, I'm in the finance department at the hospital. Keeping records straight and such."

"Well, maybe you could see your way clear to knocking a few bucks off the bill for my wife here. Getting that baby was a pretty expensive ordeal."

When Ron laughed in response, I knew I liked him very much. His laugh had an almost musical sound, and I could see myself trying to say funny things to him just so I could hear it again.

"Sorry," he said. "I don't really handle patient billing. I wish I could help you out."

"Yeah, me, too." My father seemed reluctant to let the joke go. But then Aunt Elaine called Ron over so she could introduce him to my mother and the baby and then to Julie and me.

He squatted down so he was looking us both in the eyes.

"Your aunt tells me you two are the important ones in the family," he told us in a whisper, as if the three of us were in on our very own secret. "If I'm going to keep dating her, she says I need you guys to like me." He winked. Then he stood up and slid an arm around Aunt Elaine's waist. She beamed at him, and her expression was very much like the one he was watching her with earlier.

It probably took me longer than it should have to realize that they were in love. And that is what two people in love looked like. I wondered if my father had looked at my mother that way once.

12

With a new baby brother in the family, who was, of course, much too young to do anything wrong, I seemed to be the target of my father's scrutiny and criticism more often than ever. I didn't help my mother enough. I wasn't studying hard enough. I wasn't beating my friends at tennis.

So, this day was so critically important, and I had to do everything perfectly. And I did. I could hardly believe it. I won.

I was the McKinley Elementary School Spelling Bee champion.

Standing on the stage, I couldn't stop shaking. Except that now I was excited, not nervous anymore. Not only would I be taking a medal home, but I also had a year's worth of bragging rights, something nobody else in my class could say. All the preparation, all the sleepless nights, all the hard work, it all paid off.

I could tell my father I won.

Maybe he would smile at me for real for once, not with the smirk that always came before the worst of his teasing. He'd have something to brag to his friends and employees about, and he loved doing that.

Even better, I had avoided the consequences of losing. My father would never let me live that down. I was barely nine years old, but I could already write my father's lines for him: "How could you miss *that*? It's so easy. A baby could spell that." Or he'd tell me that he was a champion speller and a straight-A student and the teachers' favorite when he went to McKinley. Why was I such an embarrassment to the Cutler family? For weeks, I lived in fear of that outcome.

I came into school that day a bundle of nerves. Sitting on the stage under the bright lights, having to keep my knees together and be ladylike in my skirt, unable to see the other kids in the audience but more than aware of their whispering and snickering, my heart was pounding so hard I was sure my blouse was actually moving with each beat. I clasped my hands tightly in my lap to keep them from visibly trembling. I watched my classmates take turns at the microphone, getting their word from Mrs. Stapleton, repeating it, then spelling it, sometimes correctly, sometimes not.

In the first round, the words were ridiculously easy. Still, a few kids were so nervous they could miss something like "earth," forgetting to include the A or putting an extra N in "banana." When it was finally my turn, I walked to the microphone slowly, just so I wouldn't trip. There was a light at the judges' table so I could see Mrs. Stapleton. She looked up and said, "Madeline, your word is 'dull.'"

"Dull," I said confidently. "D-U-L-L. Dull."

It was hard not to smile as I headed back to my seat. That was easy! But then I saw Derek Bridges watching me, and my smile faded. Derek was probably my biggest competition. Not only was he handsome and popular, but he was also really smart, meaning everyone wanted, even expected, him to win. And I had a huge crush on him. Being so close to him and having his attention focused on me sent my already hammering heart into overdrive.

Then, I heard one of the other kids mutter, "Of course she knows that word," followed by a chorus of giggles. But Derek frowned. As he turned toward the source of the remark, he hissed, "Shut up." He was defending me! I was so thrilled. Until he added, "Talking's against the rules."

With each new round, the words got harder and more kids left the stage. My second word was "slumber." Again, I got it right without hesitation. Again, I heard someone say that it was a perfect word for me because I'm so boring.

Finally, there were only four spellers left. Derek Bridges, Jenny Pettry, Sammy McFadden, and me. Sammy began the round.

"Sammy, your word is 'guitar.'"

With a deep breath, Sammy began, "Guitar. G-I-T, no! Wait. G-U-I-T-A-R. Guitar."

There was a very long, tense pause before we heard Mrs. Stapleton say, "I'm sorry. The rules don't allow you to start over. Please take your seat."

We all watched poor Sammy, shoulders slumped and eyes cast down, slowly leave the stage. I felt sorry for him, to get this far and then make such a careless mistake.

Jenny was next. "Your word is 'recommend,'" Mrs. Stapleton said.

She seemed pretty confident when she started. "Recommend. R-E-C-O-M-E-N-D. Recommend." Jenny stood there for a few seconds, still smiling, still confident, until Mrs. Stapleton sighed. "I'm sorry. That's incorrect. Please take your seat." Walking down the stage steps, Jenny seemed genuinely confused. What had she done wrong? There was some applause as she made her way to her seat, her friends trying to console her and convince her she had done really well.

Although I felt a little sorry for Jenny, too, I suddenly realized how close I was to winning this whole thing. And I realized how close I was to Derek. I risked a glance at him. As usual, he looked pretty sure of himself.

It would not be an easy victory. Back and forth we went. Voyage. Avenue. Forecast. Vacation. Laughter. Mountain. Graceful. Chimney. I could hear our classmates letting out sighs of relief or grunts of disbelief every time Mrs. Stapleton said, "That is correct."

Then she said, "Derek, your word is 'successful,'" and I felt my high hopes come crashing down to earth. Of course Derek would know that word. It described him perfectly, from grades to sports, to friendships, to his future, to pretty much everything he ever did. Of course he was going to be successful in this Spelling Bee. What in the world had made me think I could win?

Whether Derek didn't know how to spell successful or he just got nervous, I'll never know. But I will always remember the look on his face when Mrs. Stapleton told him, "I'm sorry. That's incorrect." A lot of whispers rumbled through the audience before she continued. "According to the rules, Madeline must spell the next word correctly to win. If she misses it, you both get another chance." For one fleeting moment, I considered missing on purpose, just to give Derek another chance and maybe make him like me a little.

But no. I could not lose.

"Madeline, your word is 'construction.'"

I almost laughed. Was there a word any Cutler knew better than "construction?" With a smile, I said, "Construction. C-O-N-S-T-R-U-C-T-I-O-N. Construction."

It was the longest, most torturous moment I had ever endured before Mrs. Stapleton said, "That is correct. Congratulations, Madeline. You've won this year's Spelling Bee."

With the polite applause ringing in my ears, I turned toward Derek, and I suddenly realized he was obligated to shake my hand. He'd look like a sore loser if he didn't. His face still shrouded in disappointment and disbelief, he grudgingly extended his hand. I took it, and even as he deliberately squeezed my hand a little too hard, I felt a trembling thrill run through my body just from touching him.

"It's tradition with the McKinley Spelling Bee that the winner can continue spelling if he or she wants to. You can go until you miss. What do you think, Madeline?" As Mrs. Stapleton smiled warmly at me from the judges' table, it seemed like she really wanted me to. And I was a little curious to see how many more words I could get right. So I shrugged as if it was no big deal and said, "Sure."

Normally, I hated having so much attention focused on

me, but this was kind of fun. After all, I had already won. There was no more risk, no more reason to be nervous. It was a chance to use all those hours of practice I put in with my mom.

Neighbor. Wheelchair. Discovery. Machine. Doubtful. Newscast. Pioneer. I was on a roll. Shoulder. Camera. Beautiful. I didn't know how many words Mrs. Stapleton had on her list, but I was determined to spell them all.

"The next word is 'evening.'"

Another easy one, I thought. "Evening. E-V-N-I-N-G." Too late, I realized my mistake, and my hand shot to my mouth in horror. I stood in the middle of the stage, humiliated, overwhelmed by an urge to cry, sure everyone was laughing at me. How could I have made such a stupid mistake?

"I'm sorry, that's incorrect," Mrs. Stapleton said. "But you've done a great job today, and you're still our Spelling Bee Champion." She came up on stage to shake my hand and award me the Spelling Bee Champ medal, a gold foil disk hanging on a midnight blue ribbon. A few people applauded half-heartedly, but mostly everyone started shifting in their seats, anxious to finally be dismissed.

It took me a minute or two to get past feeling defeated about missing such an easy word and to realize that it didn't matter, that I won. I had already won ten words ago. I was the McKinley Elementary School Spelling Bee Champion! Not Sammy. Not Jenny. Not even Derek. Me.

I ran all the way home and burst through the door, shouting for my mother. She was in the kitchen with Julie. "Oh, sweetie, I've been waiting all day to find out how you did," Mom said, hands clasped in front of her heart. She leaned toward me and lifted the medal away from my chest. "You won? You won!" Her smile grew even bigger, and she threw her arms out to pull me into a hug. "Oh, my smart girl! I'm so proud of you." With her hands still on my shoulders, she extended her arms to study me. "This calls for a celebration.

And I know just what to do."

Finished with her snack, Julie slid off her chair, seemingly unimpressed with her sister, the Spelling Bee Champion. She stopped in her tracks, though, when Mom pulled her shiny new mixer from the cabinet. "Are you going to make her a cake?" she asked, eyes suddenly wide.

"I think a spelling bee champion deserves a cake, don't you?" Mom said, setting the Mixmaster down and starting to retrieve the flour and sugar and cocoa and butter and eggs and all the other things that meant a delicious dessert was in the works.

"Can we help?" Julie asked, getting back on her chair and onto her knees to get a better view of the mixing bowl.

"Well, you can," Mom said, "but this is Maddie's reward, so we should do it for her, don't you think?"

While Mom and Julie measured and mixed, I talked excitedly about the spelling bee. How nervous I was. What words I got. What words tripped up my competition. How Derek finally messed up and I swooped in for the win.

"And even after I won, Mrs. Stapleton kept giving me words to spell, and I kept getting them right. But then I finally missed, and she gave me the medal."

"Well, what did you miss?"

I was talking so much and so excitedly that I hadn't noticed my father leaning on the kitchen door frame until he spoke. He shouldn't have been home from work yet. Why did he have to choose today, of all days, to leave his office early? He had his arms crossed over his chest, and he looked at me expectantly. His expression told me it had better be a pretty hard word.

Except that it wasn't, of course. I'd gotten careless, probably because I was tired or I was just excited about winning. But I knew my father expected more than that. He would say I should still be spelling even now. I frantically looked around the room, trying to find a word that was really hard to spell, something I could tell him that he wouldn't make fun of. But I came up empty.

"Madeline?" He was getting impatient. "What was the word that you missed?"

I looked down. "It was 'evening.' I just made a dumb mistake, that's all. I had already won by a mile."

"Evening? You're kidding!" He was laughing at me. "That's so easy. A baby knows that. Good thing they didn't give you that while the Bridges kid was still standing. He would've crushed you."

I tried to protest, to tell him how many hard words I had to spell to win. I thought he would be proud that I actually won by spelling "construction."

"Construction? That's almost like cheating, to give *you* that word." Then that sly grin, the one I knew so well and hated so much, began to make its way across his face. "You know, when I went to McKinley, the Spelling Bee rule was, if you missed a word, the other guy got a chance to spell it right. Isn't that how it works?"

"Well, no, not exactly," I started to explain, not yet understanding why he was asking. But before I finished, my father said, "Evening. E-V-E-N-I-N-G. Evening."

The next thing I knew, he was lifting the medal over my head. "I win," he said smugly, twirling the medal on its ribbon around his index finger. He looked at me for another very long moment, still grinning, before he said again, "I win." He made a big show of hanging my medal around his own neck. Shaking his head but still smirking, he turned and left the kitchen.

I felt my mom's hands on my shoulders. "Come on, let's finish making your cake," she said softly. She kissed the top of my head. "I know you're the real winner here."

I got to cut the cake after dinner. Mom had made my favorite: chocolate cake with fudge icing. And I got to use the fancy cake knife with the pretty blue handle. But being asked to spell "chocolate" and "plate" and "frosting" and "dessert" and all the other words my father fired at me took all the fun out of the celebration. When he noticed that I kept looking down at my lap, he snorted and shook his head. "Come on, Mad Dog, can't you take a joke?"

When my mother came to my room to say good night and tuck me in, she reminded me that she was really proud of me and she knew I had done a really good job at the spelling bee.

After she turned off the light, I whispered into the dark, "Why can't Dad ever say that?"

PART THREE

1998

13

I found Henry in the emergency room, bent over in a chair, head in his hands, and looking utterly defeated. When he saw me, he stood and hugged me hard.

Over the phone, he had told me, in a low, breathless voice broken by hiccups, the relevant details. Just a few blocks from Henry and Julie's house, some guy had run a red light and broadsided Julie's car. He walked away without a scratch, while Julie and Trip were both transported to the hospital in ambulances. The police had said there didn't seem to be alcohol involved. They probably meant the other driver, but I breathed a silent sigh of relief that Trip hadn't been the one behind the wheel. This whole situation was bad enough without him being in that kind of trouble.

"Are they all right?" I asked into Henry's shoulder.

He released me and wiped his eyes on his sleeve. "They're both alive, but it's bad. Really bad. Trip has a lot of broken bones. And Julie, she ..." He choked up again, so I reached for his arm.

"She what?"

It was a real effort for him to collect himself. "She's still unconscious. She hit her head pretty hard. And her legs, they're broken pretty badly, almost crushed, and ..." His voice trailed off as he choked back another sob. "They don't know when she'll wake up or even if she will, and they can't even say if she'll be okay when she does ..."

"And the baby?"

"The baby seems to be all right, thank God. That's a miracle, really. They're talking about something called 'placental abruption,' which means a part of the placenta came away from the wall of her womb. They say it's not uncommon, especially where there's trauma to the mother, but it's something they have to keep an eye on. But Julie's stable for now. They say she'll be here for a while." With a deep breath, he added, "A long while."

"And they don't know when she'll wake up?" I needed her to wake up soon so we could talk.

"No," Henry sighed. "They just keep saying it's too early, we have to wait. It's all just so much to process." His voice trailed off as his eyes welled up again.

"And Trip? Lots of broken bones? That's all?"

"He's banged up pretty bad," Henry explained. "One of his arms is broken in a couple of places, and he cracked a rib. Lots of cuts and bruises. He should heal up okay, though. At least that's what they told me. You may get more information as his next of kin."

"Oh, wow. I hadn't thought of that. I guess I am, now that Paul's gone."

I sank into the chair Henry had been occupying. I nearly lost the only two remaining members of my immediate family and our last words to each other were so awful.

"Can we see them?" I asked.

"The doctors are still in with Julie. But I think you can go in where Trip is," Henry said, nodding toward a room down the hall. "He's probably sleeping. Pumped full of painkillers."

I stood by Trip's hospital bed, my little brother looking small and helpless to me, the way he had as a baby. I remember watching him in his crib, thinking how fragile he seemed, how he could be broken so easily. No wonder our mother hovered over him, making a fuss whenever she thought he was even a little bit uncomfortable. As he grew, I had begun to think of my brother as indestructible. There was no obstacle he couldn't see his way around, no hurdle he couldn't confidently clear.

Now, here he was in this bed, his arm swaddled in white bandages, his face swollen and purple with bruising. The machines attached to him blinked and beeped to signal vital signs I didn't understand. I desperately wanted him to open his eyes and tell me he was fine.

"Madeline?" I heard a voice behind me.

"Dr. Faulkner!" I was incredibly relieved to see a familiar face. Dr. Faulkner had treated my parents for years, including performing my mother's mastectomy. He was also their friend, moving in the same social circles, going to the same parties. He knew us all really well. The look on his face—sympathy, compassion, understanding—told me he knew exactly what I was going through. First, my father, now this.

"I'm glad I was the one on call," he offered as he returned my hug. "Your brother's going to be all right. It's just going to take him a long time to heal."

"That's what Henry told me. But the news about Julie isn't so good."

"Well, we don't know for sure yet. With her pregnancy, it will be risky to do surgery, but without it, we can't tell the extent of the damage. We could deliver the baby now and then see what's going on with her head injury, but that's risky, too. For now, we've got her stable, and that's the important thing. We'll keep her in a coma so her body focuses on the baby. We give her some time to heal, and then we'll see what happens."

I understood exactly what he meant by that. Julie might never be the same. Hoping for better news to focus on, I asked, "But there's no danger to the baby right now?"

"The baby's vital signs are strong so far," Dr. Faulkner confirmed. "She should be fine."

"She?"

"Oops," he said with a faint smile. "I should be more careful. I assume the parents didn't want to know?"

"Well, they never really said one way or another, at least not to me," I admitted. "At this point, though, it's probably the least of their concerns."

Dr. Faulkner reached for Trip's chart hanging on the end of his hospital bed. "Yes, your brother is doing all right. He'll be sore for a long time, and he'll need help with everyday tasks while the bones knit, but eventually, he should be good as new." Looking at the chart, he frowned. "Hmm," he grunted.

"Something wrong?" I asked.

"Oh, they didn't list your brother's blood type on here. Do you happen to know what it is?"

"No," I said, but then I remembered something. "Oh, wait. I think O positive? Is that the universal donor? When he was in college, he donated blood for some fraternity service project, and then he complained that the blood bank wouldn't leave him alone. They kept wanting him to come back. I think he did donate a few more times." I smiled with some big sister pride. "He has a good heart; he just likes being able to gripe about stuff."

A strange look passed over Dr. Faulkner's face, almost too quickly for me to notice, a little widening of his eyes, a slight sucking in on his cheeks. But then he turned away, closed the chart, and returned it to its place. "Okay, I'll make that note then," he said briskly. "I need to speak to Henry now. You may want to hear this, too, about your sister."

Dr. Faulkner explained everything one more time. The bottom line was they just didn't know. We would have to wait.

Michael was staying with a neighbor, so Henry and I both remained at the hospital, me sitting by Trip's bed and Henry holding Julie's hand all night. Trip woke up once, turning his bruised face toward me. The beginnings of a sleepy smile moved across his swollen lips, and he nodded.

"You're here," he said so softly I almost didn't hear.

"Yes, I am," I replied, touching his hand. "I'm here."

14

When I finally returned to Paul's house after a long, mostly sleepless night at the hospital, I couldn't believe that just a few hours before, I was determined to leave, to return to my own life, this very morning. Well, that wasn't going to happen now. I still wanted to, believe me. I yearned to cut and run, to sever my ties to this place once and for all. And the fact that somebody, two somebodies, actually, needed me desperately just made me want out that much more.

But I couldn't abandon my family. Not now. Not like this. The guilt I was feeling about Julie leaving here so angry tore me apart.

There was so much to do. Call my office and try to figure out how I could be away even longer than I originally planned. Get something to eat. Shower and become presentable. And that was just in the next few hours. In the long term, it was going to fall on me to pack up the house now without any help from Julie and Trip. And I wouldn't be able to press them about a decision on selling any time soon. Standing in the front hall, feeling so overwhelmed I could hardly move, I didn't know what to do first.

Luckily, Aunt Elaine was already on her way. It took some doing to convince her she didn't need to drive to the hospital last night, but she insisted on coming this morning. I'd always depended on her guidance and advice, so I was relieved to know I could talk to her soon.

While I stood in the kitchen, trying to figure out what to do first, the phone rang. I was starting to hate that noise. But I was grateful to hear Derek's voice.

"Hey," he said softly. "Heard what happened. Through my mom. You okay?"

Hearing the kindness and concern in his voice made me start crying all over again. Derek knew about the accident and that Julie and Trip were both in the hospital, but I also tearfully confessed to him how we'd had such a blowout argument before they left, how that was making me feel so much worse.

"It's not your fault. You know that, right? Your argument with them didn't have anything to do with that asshole running a light. They're going to be fine. You have plenty more sibling squabbles in front of you, trust me."

I couldn't bring myself to tell him the rest, how I planned to take off this morning, just leave, not look back. The weight of that guilt hung in the air around me, like a dense gray Seattle fog. What I managed to say aloud was, "I suppose it means that I'll be here a lot longer than I thought."

There was a pause before he answered. "Guess that's what you call a silver lining, huh? At least for me. Kinda glad you're sticking around, in spite of the reason why. You're the most interesting dinner companion I've had since I got back to Graverton. Shit, since the divorce. Just don't tell my mom I said that."

Wiping the last of the tears away with my wrist, I said, "Thanks for making me smile in the middle of all this. And if I have to stick around a while, I'm glad you're here, too."

He promised to bring me some dinner later. "Something even better than grilled sea bass. See you then."

Over the coffee and bagels Aunt Elaine was thoughtful enough to bring me, I filled her in on the situation, the relatively good news about Trip, the uncertainty about Julie. She just let me talk, listening carefully and waiting patiently whenever I had to stop to dab at my tears.

"Look, honey, you don't have to make any plans or decide anything today," she said when I had finally poured out everything that had happened since last night. "Or even this week. Just take baby steps. Like my mother used to say. How do you eat an elephant? One bite at a time."

I laughed at that. "That's funny. I do remember GrandMom saying that. I never understood that expression. Why would you want to eat an elephant in the first place?"

Aunt Elaine chuckled. "Well, I never thought of it that way. Why would you, indeed?"

"Some of her other sayings made more sense," I remembered. "Like, 'Use it up. Wear it out. Make do, or do without.' I guess that goes a long way toward explaining why there's so much crap in this house. Nobody ever wanted to throw anything away."

"That's true. My parents were pretty frugal, even after my dad started making good money. I think they were always afraid it could be taken away somehow." She paused and shook her head. "But they were so generous with Paul and me. They never denied us the things we wanted. Especially your dad."

"That doesn't really surprise me," I said. "He was pretty used to getting what he wanted when he wanted it. If your parents were frugal, he was the exact opposite. He lived like the money was never going to run out."

Her response surprised me. "Maybe you shouldn't be so hard on your dad, Maddie," Aunt Elaine said. "At this point, you're not going to get any explanations or apologies, or whatever else it is you're hoping for. Your dad was who he was. Sure, he was spoiled. But the expectations for him were so high. He was Paul Cutler the Second. Supposed to be just like his father. In every possible way. It's hard to see how he could have turned out any differently.

"It took me a while to understand," she went on. "But when I think about our childhood and how my mother had Paul convinced the sun didn't shine till he got up in the morning, well, how could he help being the way he was? He really thought he was the only one who could do the job because he'd been told that his whole life. That's why he boxed me out. It wasn't that he didn't think I could do it. He was just so sure he could do it better. Because everyone had told him that every single day. My father laid out that path for him, and he never really had any choice in the matter."

"You know, Julie was just talking about that exact same thing, Paul never having a choice about his own life and career. But somehow, I just don't feel like sympathizing with him. You saw how he treated me. Nothing I did was ever good enough for him. And when I fell short of his expectations, he was so cruel. If he never had any choice, why did he try to take away mine? That bullshit with making me pay off my own college loans if I didn't move back here. And now he's trying to trap me in this house with this will nonsense. He still wants to take away my choices!"

Aunt Elaine took a deep breath before she spoke. "Did you ever stop to think that maybe he couldn't pay your college loans? That he was in financial trouble even then, and he was too embarrassed to admit it?"

"But I thought the company was doing so well in those days. He was always so cocky, so willing to throw his money around."

"Well, I didn't work there very long, but even I could see that a lot of his business practices weren't sustainable. I tried to tell him he needed to make some changes. He didn't want my help. He kept telling me that his people knew what they were doing, that everything was fine. He never even bothered to learn much about the business himself. He liked all the executive perks, making the decisions, taking customers out for lunch, having the big luxurious office. He didn't want to hear that he was making mistakes." Aunt Elaine shook her head sadly at the memory. "But I didn't realize how bad things actually were until it was too late."

"Don't blame yourself for the mess Paul made," I said

angrily. "Clearly, you would have made a much better chief executive. But GrandDad wouldn't put you in charge because you were a girl, and Paul did everything he could to make you quit. You might even have been able to save the company."

"Well, I guess we'll never know, will we?" Aunt Elaine arched an eyebrow at me. "Just like you'll never know how your dad really felt about you. Whether you realize it or not, your dad was proud of you. He bragged about you all the time. All three of you, really, but he was pretty impressed with your career. I think he really thought you would want to move back here someday and put all your computer know-how to work for Cutler Enterprises."

I was really not in the mood to be convinced that my father was a good guy after all. "Look, we're just going to have to agree to disagree for now," I said. "Paul is gone. I can't do anything to change our relationship at this point. You can try to change the way I remember him if you want to, but I warn you, that will be an uphill battle."

"Well, at least we'll have lots to talk about," Aunt Elaine grinned, taking another sip of coffee. Then her expression changed. "But your sister and brother are the more important reason I'm here now. What do we need to do for them? For Henry?"

Hours later, at the end of a very long day that began with Henry's phone call the night before, I opened the front door to Derek's knock. He held a large cardboard box with a towel over the top, and I smelled roasted tomatoes, basil, oregano, and melted cheese. "Lasagna," he explained, "the ultimate comfort food. Lucky for you, it's one of my specialties."

I pointed him toward the kitchen, where he put the box on the counter and removed the towel with a flourish, releasing even more of that mouth-watering aroma. Using the towel, he lifted a casserole dish out of the box. Then he held up one finger and headed back to the front door. "There's more," he called over his shoulder. A minute later, he reappeared with a bowl of green salad and a bottle of red wine. As I watched in exhausted silence, moving only to gesture at the cabinets where he could find dishes or the drawers full of utensils, he laid out a lovely, simple supper for us.

"I can't tell you how much I appreciate this," I said, lifting a very large forkful of steaming pasta to my mouth. "I don't make meals like this for myself even when I have all the time and energy in the world."

"Well, I did promise to cook for you," Derek said, "but I was thinking of something a lot more elaborate so I could show off for you a little. Get you on board with my restaurant idea."

"This is plenty elaborate, believe me. And I'm so hungry right now, I'd eat it even if it wasn't this delicious. You don't need to convince me you're a good cook."

While we ate, Derek talked about all the different places around Graverton that he had checked out as possible restaurant locations. I was happy to let him keep up the banter, not really wanting to discuss my day at all.

When we finished eating, Derek motioned for me to sit still while he carried our plates to the kitchen sink, where he rolled up his sleeves and started washing the dishes. I poured myself a little more wine and watched him. The navy blue crewneck he was wearing stretched tightly across his broad shoulders as his arms moved through the washing motions, and the T-shirt underneath the sweater peeked out above the jeans hugging his butt and thighs. It made a lovely picture. With all the wine I'd drunk and all the fatigue I was feeling, the edges of his image began to soften and blur, and it suddenly seemed like a vision, a view into a parallel universe where everything about my life turned out differently. What if I had never moved away? What if I had gone to work for

Cutler Enterprises? What if I had married a Graverton boy like Derek and settled down here, in my childhood home, the way Paul wanted? This is what it might have looked like. At that moment, it didn't seem so bad. Leaning my cheek against my palm, I kept my eyes glued to this man I'd known my whole life and yet hardly knew, cleaning up a special dinner he made just for me, sitting in a house I'd been desperate to escape just twenty-four hours earlier.

When all the dishes were clean, Derek turned towards me to get the towel and start drying them. But seeing me gazing at him so dreamily stopped him in his tracks.

"Geez, Cutler, you're fading fast, aren't you? How are you even still awake?" Shaking his head, he decided, "Gonna get out of your hair now. You need to get to bed."

"You could stay," I answered softly. Maybe I could find out a little more about this alternative future I was imagining and how nice it might actually have been.

Derek walked around the table and squatted next to my chair. Taking my hand, he said, "Yeah, I could. Under any other circumstances, I would. Oh, man, I really want to. But not like this."

"You don't have to worry about my father finding out," I ventured.

"Well, that is true," he said, laughing. He stood up enough to leave a quick peck on my forehead. Before he could step away, I tilted my head back so that I was looking right into his eyes. His incredible, warm brown eyes. Putting my hand on the back of his neck, I pulled his face to mine. No brief smooch, no gently brushing his lips against my skin. Not this time. Not now. I wanted, needed, demanded, and received a passionate kiss. I wanted to express all the emotion I was experiencing. Release all the tension in my body. Fill myself with hope and with the strength to get up tomorrow morning and do what needed to be done. It was a lot to ask of one man and one kiss. But it delivered.

Derek pulled back after a few moments. Brushing the hair off my face, he said, "You're making it tough; I'll give you that. Still not staying, though. Wouldn't feel right. But I have a hunch it might be right one of these days." Then he kissed me again. "See ya later, Cutler."

And he was gone.

15

"Can I see Mommy?"

Michael had remained stoic and serious when Henry explained how Mommy got hurt so badly that she needed to stay in the hospital. He had stayed silent even as a few tears rolled down his little round cheeks, but he had nodded his understanding and hugged his daddy with all the force he could muster.

Now alone with me, Michael asked more questions. Harder questions. And I was incredibly bad at answering them. "No, I'm afraid you're, um, you're going to have to wait a while." How could I explain this without frightening him? Was it okay to lie? Would I be contradicting something Henry already told him? Trying to think quickly, I said, "Mommy needs to rest, and if you were there, she would want to talk to you and play games with you and stuff. So we're just going to let Daddy be with her for now."

I knelt in front of him to tie his shoes so I avoided looking directly into his eyes. Even so, he seemed to know it was hard for me to explain all this.

"Is it because I'm too little? Because they don't let little kids in there? I would be quiet, and I wouldn't touch anything. I promise."

"No, it's nothing like that, honey. It's just like I said. She wants to see you, too. She just needs her rest."

"What if I just went in and gave her a kiss, and then I left? I wouldn't make her tired, really I wouldn't."

"That's a very sweet offer, buddy." How did this kid get such a big heart in just a few short years? "Maybe in a few days, okay?"

I'm not sure which was harder at this point—taking care of Michael or cleaning out Paul's house. Both seemed to remind me of parts of myself that I didn't want to think about. And then Michael said something that made me realize that substitute parenting was definitely the more difficult task. "What if Mommy dies before I can get there to kiss her?"

"Oh, Michael, your mommy isn't going to die!" I cried, falling back onto my heels to look up directly into his eyes.

"Everybody dies," he insisted. "My grandpa died. And I didn't get a chance to kiss him goodbye." His statements were very matter-of-fact, and he never took his big round eyes off my face.

"Well, that was, um, that was different," I began carefully. "Your mom got hurt pretty badly, that's true. But she's in the hospital where doctors and nurses can watch her every single minute. They'll know exactly how to take care of her if anything happens. If all those people had been watching your grandpa, he might not have died. The thing is, we didn't know that he needed to be watched. His heart didn't give him any warning ahead of time. Do you understand the difference?"

Michael nodded solemnly. "I guess. I still want to see my mommy."

"I know you do, buddy. Your daddy and I will make it happen as soon as we can, okay? Now, go find your jacket. It's time to go."

When I talked to Derek later, I confessed how absolutely overwhelmed I felt. Trying to be a dutiful daughter to the dead father I was still so angry at, the devoted sister to the people who desperately needed so much healing, the gentle and loving aunt to the little boy who was trying to process so much pain and who could sense that I was, too. "This is so not what I signed up for," I sighed.

"Nobody signs up for this shit, Cutler," Derek said. "It's the price you pay to be part of a family."

"As they say, you can't pick your family."

"Yeah, well, they didn't pick you either," he reminded me. Not exactly the comfort and compassion I was fishing for. "But you're all they've got right now, so there's nothing to do but do it." After a pause, he added, "Hey, you know what? You may be all they have, but at least you've got me. Looks like I'm gonna have to be the one to give you a good kick in the ass now and then."

"Thanks, I think." I appreciated having someone to vent to, even if Derek wouldn't let my pity party last very long. And it didn't hurt that I really enjoyed talking to him. Maybe it wouldn't be so awful to hang out in Graverton for a little while longer.

16

After Julie and Trip's accident, my days fell into a routine. Wake up early. Run. Get to Julie and Henry's house to take Michael to daycare. Then stop by the hospital to spend some time with the patients. Trip needed help with everything, including eating. Then I checked in with work in the afternoon, just as my office was opening up on the West Coast. Initially, that was a really cumbersome task, given that Paul hadn't updated his phones in a really long time, and I had to deal with an incredibly slow dial-up modem. But eventually, after a few trips to the office supply store (which was miles away from Graverton), I had things working at a faster pace. Late in the day, I picked up Michael, took him home for dinner, and got him ready for bed.

Then there were the nights. Released from all these family obligations for a few hours, I dragged myself back to the Harding Street house, where I barely closed the door behind me before I began the debate with myself: Did I want to see Derek or not? Half of my brain remembered how lovely it was to have a comfortable conversation with someone so interesting, how distracting it was to look into a handsome man's eyes, how life-affirming it felt to kiss him. But somewhere else deep in that same brain was the embarrassment of drunkenly propositioning him and getting turned down. Derek and I had talked several times since that night, but neither of us broached the subject of another date. He seemed to have fallen into the supportive friend role, and I wondered if I would ever live down my humiliation enough to see him again. So my nights all ended the same way: with me climbing into bed alone, hoping to get enough rest to face the next day.

When I could, I devoted a few hours to cleaning out the house. Through it all, I kept telling myself, you can go home soon. This will all be over soon. I missed my cozy apartment, my corner coffee shop, my office, my runs along the water. Even more, I missed the peace and quiet of living alone, the freedom to come and go as I liked, and the idea that my time was my own.

And just when I convinced myself that I could handle it all, I would find something in the house that triggered a memory I had tried to leave behind. Yearbooks with precious few signatures because I just didn't have that many friends. Photos of the five Cutlers on vacation at the seashore from that time when Paul wanted to teach me how to surf and I was too terrified to leave the beach. The tassel from the cap and gown I wore to my high school graduation, after which my father wouldn't stop talking about how I wasn't the salutatorian, much less the valedictorian, and it was probably because of that one time I got a C on a midterm. Julie's tennis trophies. A key chain that had once held the keys to Trip's sixteenth birthday present: a new car.

One morning, I tapped softly on the door to Julie's hospital room, even as I slowly opened it. I wasn't worried about waking Julie; nothing about her condition had changed, and she was still unconscious. No, knocking was more for Henry's benefit, announcing my presence so he could pull himself together if he needed to. I had caught him crying a couple of times. Now, he was just sitting in the chair by the bed, looking at the math tests spread out on the blanket covering his wife.

When he looked up and smiled at me, I thought, yet again, how handsome he was. His dark-blonde hair had receded from his forehead somewhat in the years I'd known him, but he still had those clear, icy blue eyes that weren't the least bit diminished by the horn-rimmed glasses he wore. He wasn't tall or particularly muscular, but he always seemed to wear his jeans and button-downs with a casual ease that many men with more enviable physiques never seemed to achieve. When they started dating, Julie told me that Henry's intelligence was the sexiest thing about him, but I had a hunch she had fallen for the whole package and the smarts were just icing on the cake.

"Hey, Madeline, I'm glad you're here," Henry said quietly, rising from his chair. "Let's go outside so we can talk." Gently putting his hand between my shoulders, he guided me back out of the room and down the hall to the lounge.

He sat down in one of the institutional gray vinyl cushioned chairs and leaned forward with his elbows on his knees. I imagined it was the pose he struck when he was trying to get a student to work a little harder in his class. "So, Tony Marossi was here," he began.

"Paul's attorney?"

"Yeah. He thinks we have a good case against the other driver, and we could get a pretty nice settlement."

"And, of course, he would handle it for you." I hadn't thought of Tony as an ambulance chaser, but maybe a case like this didn't come along very often around here.

"Look, I'm not crazy about the idea of suing somebody," Henry sighed. "The guy is actually related to one of my students. It could get awkward. It's just that the hospital bills are piling up. My insurance through the school district is pretty good, but the doctors are telling me Julie's going to need long-term care even after she leaves the hospital. They're probably going to want to keep her here till the baby can be delivered safely, and then I'm at home with a newborn and a preschooler. I'm going to need help."

I looked at him carefully for the first time in a while. The worry lines on his forehead were deeper than I remembered, and there were shadows under his eyes that even their bluest blue could not disguise. All this had been hard on him, and now the wear and tear was beginning to show.

"It's totally your call," I reminded him. "I don't have a say in this."

"I know," he said. "I just thought you should know what's going on. And I want to know what you think."

"I'm no expert, but this kind of case can drag on for a while, right? And in a small town like this, people will take sides. The fact that she's a Cutler probably won't help you any, either. People might still be mad, want to get even with Paul somehow. If you go to a jury ... Well, like you said, awkward." I didn't want to focus on the negative, but I felt like he should consider everything. "You would have to decide whether you're really in it for the long haul. On the other hand, you are going to need the money."

"There's a lot to think about," Henry acknowledged. "Although Tony seemed pretty sure the guy would be willing to settle out of court."

"That would be good. What about Tony's cut of the settlement? Is it one of those deals where he only gets paid if and when you win? Or are you going to have to pay him as you go?"

"We didn't get that far into specifics. He just wanted me to think about it." He paused and looked me straight in the eye for a moment. "There's your brother to consider, too."

Oh, wow. I hadn't thought of that. Trip was a major consideration in this case. Not just a witness but also another plaintiff. "Let me guess. Trip was the one who called Tony in the first place?"

"Oh, yeah," Henry confirmed with a nod and a short, harsh laugh. "I tried to tell Trip that I wanted to think it over, maybe even wait till Julie's awake and alert and discuss it with her before we make any decisions, but that didn't seem to cool him off one bit."

"Does Tony need both of you to sign on?" If there was

conflict brewing between Henry and Trip, I didn't want to get caught in the middle.

"He said that was best. Truthfully, I'm leaning that way, but I still want to get some more input. Even wait for Julie's if I can. Speaking of which," he put his hands on his thighs and stood up as he spoke. "I need to get back. They tell me she's not really aware of when I'm there and when I'm not. I just kind of like to be there anyway, you know?"

I headed down the hall to visit Trip. He was recovering slowly and getting anxious about being stuck in the hospital. As soon as I entered his room, he started chattering excitedly about Tony's visit. "He thinks it could be seven figures, Mad," he declared after giving me an overview of everything he heard the attorney say. Which didn't include anything about legal fees or what would happen if the suit wasn't successful. Tony had dangled dollar signs in front of my little brother's eyes, and he was hooked.

"Slow down a little, Tripper," I cautioned in my best big sister voice. "Make sure you think it through before you make any decisions."

"What's to think through? Of course the guy was at fault. Of course he should pay for our pain and suffering. He nearly killed a pregnant woman. We can't lose!"

Famous last words, I thought. Aloud, I said, "As much as I'm sure Tony wants you to think this is an easy win, you never know which way courts will decide any given case. Juries are fickle, unpredictable. And a jury in Graverton might not be all that sympathetic to a Cutler. You have to know that. I really don't think you should start counting the money just yet."

My warning fell on deaf ears. Waving his hand to bat away my concerns like an annoying gnat, he kept right on talking about what he would do with all that money. "It would be more than enough to live on while I do the work on the house! I could get myself set up in business, like a whole new and improved Cutler Enterprises. On a smaller scale, sure, but I could build it back up, just like GrandDad did. I wouldn't have to keep working at this dead-end job I have. I'm telling you, Maddie, this could be the best thing that's happened to me in a long time." Only my brother would think a catastrophic car accident could be the best thing to happen to him.

"Henry said he talked to you about it," I interjected cautiously, trying to remind Trip that this hadn't happened just to him and Julie might not agree it was such a great thing.

"Yeah, yeah, we talked," Trip said dismissively. "He said he wants to think it over, maybe even wait till after the baby is born, but really, what's to think about? They're going to need the money, too, probably even more than I do."

I listened to his blue-sky dreaming for a while longer. He had big plans for a whole lot of money he didn't have yet and might not even get, but there was no telling him that. By the time the hospital staff brought Trip's lunch, he'd convinced himself that he was going to become the filthy-rich savior of our little hometown. For the first time, I looked forward to helping him eat. At least it would shut him up.

17

"So, I guess you heard about Trip and Julie maybe filing a lawsuit against that other driver." I settled into a chair at the kitchen table with my coffee cup. On this crisp autumn Saturday morning, Aunt Elaine was sitting across from me, holding her mug in both hands, close to her face. She'd come to the house to help me clear out some more closets and drawers, but at the moment, we were procrastinating over coffee. I had finally figured out some tricks for coaxing a pretty decent brew out of Paul's ancient coffee maker, and Aunt Elaine treated me to some fresh croissants from her favorite French bakery.

"Yeah, your brother was quite excited about the prospect when I dropped by to visit him," Aunt Elaine said. "I get the feeling Henry is more hesitant."

"I'd say that's about the right read. Henry wants to consider everything, every possibility, before he signs on. He may even be using some mathematical formula to calculate the probability of a win. And he really wants to know what Julie would think. But he also seems to realize that they have a long road ahead of them." I sighed. "Trip, on the other hand, is already spending the money. Calling it a literal silver lining. They haven't even filed a suit yet, and he's talking like he's going to get enough money to support himself for the rest of his life."

Aunt Elaine shook her head sadly. "Trip is a Cutler man," she sighed. "He wants what he wants, and facts and reality aren't going to get in his way. Your dad was like that. So was mine, for that matter."

"Really? GrandDad was like Trip? I always thought he was such a hard worker, that he built up the business by never being satisfied, never enough, always more. Trip's always been allergic to hard work."

Even though she brought up the topic, Aunt Elaine suddenly seemed reluctant to talk about her father, the grandfather I never knew except by reputation. She hesitated a moment before she responded. "I think he started out that way. That's how people who knew him at the time described it, anyway, that he focused on his company always, that nothing else mattered to him. And that's why he worked so hard. But somehow, once he was successful, he started to feel like he was entitled to it, you know? And not just entitled to success, but to more. Always more. To respect and deference. To praise. To always getting credit. He expected everyone to be grateful to him somehow, that they should make allowances for him. And he became kind of a bully. He was always working to maintain his position or, even better, to continue to rise, and he treated a lot of people really badly along the way. But he never seemed to feel guilty about it. If he and my mother lost friends over business deals, so be it. Like he just thought he could buy new friends eventually."

The story of my grandfather was a local legend. Every Cutler knew all the details because Paul liked to tell it, and that meant we'd heard it often. Born here in Graverton. As a teenager, lost his own father. Took a small inheritance and squirreled it away. Never touched it. He had plans for it, GrandDad always said. Big plans. When he started his own construction materials business in a small warehouse downtown, it took a while for him to make any money. Once he did, he made a lot of it. At that point in the story, Paul liked to grin mischievously and say something mysterious. "Nobody is entirely sure it was all above board, but my dad definitely had his ways."

The company expanded, GrandDad hired lots of people,

and those men made lots of money. In the post-war years, people were starting families, building bigger homes, needing more retail stores, paving more roads, and Cutler Enterprises had all the materials they needed. Late in his own mother's life, GrandDad bought her the things she'd had to do without all those years, including a house. Unfortunately, she died after living in her big, beautiful Harding Street home for only a year.

But Paul Senior wasted no time in replacing the lady of the house. The woman I was named after, Madeline Keener, came to work at Cutler Enterprises as a bookkeeper. Early on, she set her cap for the boss, and being as smart as she was beautiful, she figured out ways to get his attention. The few other women who worked at Cutler Enterprises as secretaries gossiped furiously about Madeline, clucking their tongues and shaking their heads and saying, "Well, I never," over and over again. GrandMom never responded to them, but she filed it all away in her memory. Before long, she wasn't working for Paul Senior anymore; she was married to him. And those secretaries were summarily replaced.

Growing up, I knew GrandMom's beauty and smarts had set a standard I was expected to live up to. I was supposed to use them to snare a rich and successful husband, like she had. Being rich and successful on my own? That never seemed to occur to anybody. Except Aunt Elaine. And eventually, me.

"Everybody always talked about GrandDad in such glowing terms," I remarked. "It must have been hard to be the daughter of that guy, especially when you know differently."

"Well, GrandMom and your dad never had a bad thing to say about him, that's for sure." Aunt Elaine stared into her coffee mug, avoiding eye contact with me. "And I started out feeling that way. When I was a little girl, I adored him. He was big and strong. So handsome. And generous. But as I got older, I realized that Paul was his favorite. He was so proud of his son and heir. I was just supposed to be window dressing." I was surprised but sympathetic to see her eyes glaze over with tears. "I started to see more of his bullying side. He kept trying to marry me off like I was part of some business deal. If there was another company he wanted to do more business with and that guy had a son, he would dangle me as bait. 'Let's merge our families and our businesses,' he would say like it was the best idea he'd ever had. It never worked. These business owners weren't interested in 'merging,' knowing that with my father, it would actually be a takeover. And I didn't want to get married then. For some crazy reason, I still thought I had a chance to be an executive at my own father's company." She paused and closed her eyes. "Then he finally pushed me too far."

Setting her coffee mug down, she looked off into space. "I haven't thought about this in a long time. I tried hard to forget it."

"Why? What happened?"

After another long pause, she told me the story. "My father fixed me up on a blind date with the son of somebody he wanted to do business with. The guy was a crashing bore, but somehow, he thought he was God's gift to women. We went out for dinner, and he talked about himself the whole time, making a big deal about ordering for me. A steak and some expensive wine. Then I thought he was driving me home, but he winked and said he knew a shortcut. We ended up on that road that leads to the cemetery. In those days, it was dark, and there was never anybody on it."

I had heard stories like this before; almost every woman has. I reached across the table and took Aunt Elaine's hand. In a very small voice, I asked a question that I was afraid to know the answer to. "Did he ... hurt you?"

She shook her head. "Not that he didn't try. I managed to get my shoe off and hit him in the face with my high heel. That left a mark. So, he slapped me and called me a bitch and said I could tell my dad the deal was off.

"I came home and told my father what happened. He

didn't believe me. In fact, he was angry at me for ruining his plan. And that's when I finally told him to cut it out. That it wasn't going to work. I wasn't going to go into some arranged marriage. It was archaic and insulting, and I wanted to make my own way. I don't think he ever quite forgave me, but I do think giving me a job at the company was his way of making it up to me."

"I'm sorry that happened to you," I said softly. "It makes the way Paul treated you seem even worse."

"I don't know if he knew. I certainly never told him about it. But he was so much like our dad." She paused, shaking her head. "Well, except that his sense of entitlement didn't come from his own hard work, you know? He was Paul Cutler the Second and therefore deserving of all the same respect and admiration our father had. Like it was transitive or something. The only problem was he didn't bother to take the time to learn how to run things. He thought he could just show up, sit in the office, make a few calls, and have everybody come to him for decisions. The processes were already in place, right? They ran smoothly before; why would he need to interfere? The money should just keep rolling in. And it did for a while. Until it stopped."

I don't remember exactly when I figured out that my father was a less-than-competent businessman, but I know I was aware of it by the time I left home to go to college. "It bugged him a lot when I didn't ask for his advice on any of my decisions," I said. "My major, my first job, my finances once I was on my own. Paul had all kinds of ideas about what I should do with my life. And my money. I just ignored him because I knew he didn't have any real insight."

Aunt Elaine nodded. She was familiar with this facet of her brother's personality.

"I guess my father tried to teach him about business, but Paul was such a know-it-all that he ignored any advice he got, no matter how valuable it was. Truly, it was a tribute to your grandfather that Cutler Enterprises lasted as long as it did."

"You were here when ... well, when it all went down," I said. "Did he talk to you about it at all? Give you any sense of why?"

"You've got to be kidding," Aunt Elaine laughed. "Paul consult me on something related to the business? Never in a million years. I was as surprised as everyone else."

With a sigh, I reiterated what I knew she had heard again and again. From me and my mother many times over in the past few years. "I still don't understand. How could he do that? After everything GrandDad worked for. His whole legacy. And he really yanked the rug out from under Trip in a big way. I don't know if Paul would've explained himself to me, ever, but now I'll never get the chance to ask him."

"Okay, sweetie, I know this isn't going to be a popular opinion with you, but I'm going to put it out there anyway." She leaned across the table, resting her hand on my arm and looking me squarely in the eye. "I think it killed your dad to walk away from Cutler Enterprises. I really do. He knew it meant he'd failed. And that was the one thing he never thought he could do. My mother worked so hard to turn everything he did into the best thing ever. She built him up so high that she had to keep him from falling because that would be one epic crash if it happened. It took a while, but then it all finally came tumbling down."

I didn't want to give my father the benefit of the doubt, but what she said made sense. Even so, I insisted, "That doesn't explain the how and when, and why he decided to screw over so many of his employees. And my mother."

Aunt Elaine could see by my expression that I remained unconvinced, and she looked like she was about to say something else but thought better of it. She drank the last of her coffee, then stood up. "Well, why don't we get to work?"

We decided to begin with Paul's desk, a spot that seemed so intimidating the last time I came into his room. It was stuffed with papers and files and documents that may or may not be important, and I didn't want to be the only one to determine which was which. There was probably some family history hidden in there, too. Aunt Elaine would be just as interested in that as anyone else.

While we sorted papers, Aunt Elaine asked about my job, my social life, my vacation plans. It felt good to talk about the life I built in Seattle. But it also made me that much more anxious to get back to it. I fell into the comfortable banter, smiling a little to myself as I finally began to look forward again.

After wading through piles of old phone bills and canceled checks and insurance policy updates and credit card statements, all of which were outdated clutter that we could just toss, I got to the bottom of one of the desk drawers. As I closed it, I felt some resistance, as if something had fallen behind the drawer. I reached my arm all the way in, and, sure enough, I felt the corner of a page seemingly stuck in that dead space. With some effort, I brought it out into the light.

It was a Certificate of Appreciation made out to Paul. There was an old-fashioned spiral border and an embossed seal. It was hard to read because the typeface was some kind of fancy lettering, but eventually, I figured out that it had come from a hospital somewhere in Pennsylvania. Basically, it was thanking my father for "his unselfish acts of generosity that not only saved a life but gave a community hope."

On my knees in front of the desk, I stared at this certificate, trying to figure out what it meant, while Aunt Elaine kept chattering away. When she noticed that I had stopped responding, she looked over at me. "What is that you found?" she asked, moving toward me to peer over my shoulder.

"I don't know, actually," I admitted, holding it up so she could see. "I've never seen this before. It looks like Paul was a hero a long time ago." I pointed at the date; Paul would have been about 20 years old.

"Oh," Aunt Elaine exclaimed, taking the paper from my hand. "I think I know what this is. From when your dad was in college. There was a little girl who was in the hospital at the university while Paul was there. She needed blood transfusions, but she had some unusual blood type or something. They were trying hard to find a donor close by, so they put out a call to the students. I don't really remember all the details; I just remember that my parents were so proud of Paul for stepping up. He was a match for this little girl, and he went to the hospital just about every other week for a whole semester so he could donate blood to her. They said that was the only reason she survived. No wonder Paul kept this."

It took me a minute to wrap my head around the idea that my father had done something for someone else, a stranger, that didn't benefit him in any way. That wasn't his usual MO. At the same time, something else was nagging at the edges of my mind. Suddenly, I realized what it was.

"Wait," I said. "Paul had an unusual blood type?"

"Well, I think he's AB. It's not that unusual, I guess, but it's the least common type. You didn't know that?"

"It's never really come up before, but I think I need to find out," I said. "Because it might answer a very important question."

Aunt Elaine looked at me quizzically. "What are you talking about?"

"Probably nothing. I, um, I just want to know for my own health history."

The fact was, I didn't want to say until I knew for sure. But I might finally have come across an explanation for Paul's actions.

18

After spending the day with Aunt Elaine, I visited Trip at the hospital as usual. For the first time in a long time, I looked at my brother with fresh eyes. As pretty as our mother had been, he was just as handsome. How often I wished I had gotten her eyes. Today, Trip's hazel eyes, still surrounded by fading bruises, were flashing with giddy anticipation. Tony Marossi had received an initial settlement offer from the driver of the other car. And, of course, Trip wanted to jump on it. He wanted the money, and he didn't want to wait. Which was entirely contrary to Tony's advice and Henry's wishes. Funny how he looked like Mom, but if I closed my eyes when he talked, I could easily think I was listening to Paul. So much money. So much he could do with it. Marossi doesn't know what he's talking about.

There were two reasons not to accept the initial offer, the lawyer said. First, the fact that the other guy made the offer so quickly indicated that he knew Julie and Trip had a pretty good case against him and he was eager to avoid going to court. And Julie's situation was far from resolved. Still unconscious. Doctors still unsure of the extent of the damage. Still concerned about the baby. Keeping Julie under observation was the best thing for both of them. And knowing whether or not she was permanently disabled would make a big difference in the settlement. According to Tony, if Julie couldn't walk or there were any problems with the birth, or, worst of all, she suffered any permanent damage, the case would be so much stronger because Henry would need even more resources to care for her and the baby.

So, Trip told me how he got himself another lawyer.

"My guy says we can file separate suits," Trip explained to me almost before I even sat down next to his hospital bed.

"It seems to me if you could be patient, you would stand to gain even more," I reasoned as I handed over the Coke he begged me to bring him.

"Yeah, but court cases are always iffy," he said as if he had all kinds of firsthand knowledge of lawsuits. "You said so yourself. You just never know which way a judge or jury is gonna go. You run the risk of coming away empty. I say take the sure thing." It sounded to me like he was echoing his new attorney's words. I wondered how big a cut of the settlement this new guy would take and whether Trip had factored that into his plans for the money.

"What will you do with it?" I asked, even though I was afraid of the answer.

"Quit that fucking dead-end job, for starters," Trip grunted, closing one eye and peering into the Coke can. "Then I can invest in starting my new business."

I held in the heavy sigh I really wanted to heave at that moment. It was frighteningly easy to foresee the next several months of Trip's life once he got his hands on this money. I imagined him gleefully starting out by getting himself a more expensive car and maybe some new suits, rationalizing that he would need to look the part of a successful business owner. He might even move to a bigger apartment in a better neighborhood, all thoughts of moving into the Harding Street house gone. He would dip into the money every month to pay his living expenses while he slept in, made an occasional call to a potential investor, stayed out late with his buddies, talked a good game about his business ideas to people who couldn't possibly help him achieve his goals, and generally reveled in not working. He might call me at my office from time to time to tell me his latest brainstorm; he might even ask me to invest with him. But there would be nothing concrete. No business plan, no marketing, no prototypes, nothing practical that might require effort, and so no progress toward an actual money-making endeavor. I would ask for those things, as would any investor, and he would get mad at me for not having faith in him. Eventually, in a year, maybe less, depending on the level of his extravagance, the settlement money would run out, and Trip would be scrambling for cash again. He might sell the new car or get a roommate. He would have a thousand excuses for why his business, the rejuvenated Cutler Enterprises, never got off the ground. It wouldn't be his fault, of course. In fact, it would probably be mine for refusing to give him the loan I already knew he was going to ask for. And then he would charm his way into another job that he would tout as the greatest possible opportunity for himself, a way to make "real money," beginning the familiar cycle all over again.

And with this new job, Trip would declare, as he did every time, that this time would be different.

For the next hour, I listened to him gripe about his job, steering clear of giving him advice or observing that maybe he could handle certain situations a little better. Finally, it was time for me to leave so I could pick up Michael. I patted Trip's leg through the sheet, and I told him, "I'll see you tomorrow."

"I don't suppose you could sneak in a beer for me when you come back, could you?"

19

"So I have a question for you," I said when I finally got Dr. Faulkner on the phone. "What was my father's blood type?"
A very long, uncomfortable silence followed. I imagined him at his desk, rubbing his temples, trying to decide how to respond. "If you're worried about violating doctor-patient confidentiality, I think that expires when the patient dies, don't you?" I said, hoping to help him overcome his qualms about telling me what I needed to know.

"Legally, I suppose it's a gray area," Dr. Faulkner ventured. "But ethically, it's much more complicated. I'm pretty sure I know why you're asking, and that means a lot of other people will be affected by the answer."

"Actually, I think you may have just given me my answer," I said. "How about this? I'll just make some statements, not ask any questions. You can correct me if I'm wrong, but if I'm right, you don't have to say anything. Okay?"

After a long pause, he replied, "I'm listening."

"I know now that Paul had an uncommon blood type. Aunt Elaine thinks it's AB. Biology was never one of my strengths, but I remember enough from the genetics unit to know that blood type is hereditary. And certain types can't produce other types. Am I right so far?"

"Yes, that's correct. It's basic genetics."

"Okay, so if my father had AB blood, he couldn't have produced a child with O positive blood. Which is what Trip told me he has." I left that to hang in the air, not only to see if Dr. Faulkner would correct me, but also to give myself time to fully acknowledge what I had just said out loud. When Dr.

Faulkner remained silent, I began to feel my heart beating faster, my hands trembling. He was right; a lot of other people would be affected. And the implications were so far-reaching and staggering to contemplate that I could hardly speak.

"Who knew?" I finally asked. "Did Paul?"

"I have no idea, honey," Dr. Faulkner said softly. "I only just figured it out myself when you told me your brother's blood type at the hospital. And I couldn't say anything about it even if I did."

"Thank you, Dr. Faulkner. I really appreciate it. And I'm going to keep this between us for now. Honestly, I have no idea what I'm going to do with this information."

"If you want my advice, don't do anything. You'll only hurt the people you tell. There's no reason to do that now."

As I hung up the phone, I took some deep breaths. I couldn't be sure that Paul somehow figured out Trip wasn't his son. If he knew, it would explain so much. Why he had done what he did with Cutler Enterprises. Why he had been so cold to Mom at the end of her life. He had been betrayed, and he had to punish her for it as harshly as he possibly could. Crushing everything that gave her joy, even if it meant he toppled right along with her. Snatching away what was most important to her, especially her hopes and dreams for her son. Paul would blow everything up rather than create a legacy for someone else's kid. Trip was just collateral damage. It all made sudden, sickening sense.

I found surprisingly little comfort in finally understanding why my father had done what he did. Somehow, I was even more angry that revenge was his motive. He had hurt so many people in the process, not just Trip and my mother, but lots of people in town, people who had worked for him, for GrandDad and for the business for decades. I knew he could be mean, I knew he didn't like to lose, and I knew he had a capacity for cruelty. But this was shocking.

I also had to decide what to do with the burden of this

information. Trip probably deserved to know, but would he want to? Once I told him, there would be no un-telling him. And Julie. She was not unaffected by all this. What would she think of our mother? Our father? If she ever found out on her own about Paul's blood type, it might be only a matter of time before she connected the dots to Trip's O positive blood, just like I had. Dr. Faulkner might be right—I should just leave it alone. But what if he was wrong?

My head was spinning. I wouldn't be able to make any decisions until I had considered every option, every possibility, every outcome. I needed to talk to someone.

When I finished telling my story, Derek leaned back in his seat and shook his head. A few hours ago, he seemed happy to hear my voice on the phone, even after I told him how badly I needed to talk to someone, to get an opinion from someone unaffected by my shocking discovery. I asked him to meet me outside Graverton, somewhere no one would be interested in listening in on our conversation. I think he was intrigued, and when I told him he was really the only one I could talk to, he agreed to come. Now, his expression reflected the magnitude of everything I had just unloaded on him—the meaning of different blood types, my theory about the business, and how I needed to decide who needed to know.

"Wow, Cutler. That is some soap-opera-level shit," he said, rubbing his forehead, eyes wide. "What do you want me to tell you? That your brother and sister deserve to know? That you should just leave it alone? Don't have a good answer for you. Can't really even tell you what I would do, because I don't have a clue. No matter which way you go, it's risky."

"That's the thing. Every time I think about keeping quiet about it all, I think about what will happen if Trip and Julie find out some other way. What will they think if they somehow figure out that I knew and didn't tell them? They might never speak to me again, and they're the only family I have left. Then again, telling them could just as easily wreck everything. They might be mad at me for ruining their memories, for throwing Trip's whole identity into chaos, for slandering our mom. There's no upside either way."

"Seems like you're kind of playing God no matter what you do," Derek acknowledged. "Think I would probably keep it to myself if I were you. Just doesn't seem to be any benefit to telling them."

"What really puzzles me is how Paul figured it out," I said. "All those years, he was so proud of his son, of Paul the Third. Maybe he connected the dots when he found out Trip's blood type, but I don't know if that whole donating blood thing is something Trip would've talked to him about. Something else must have happened, or someone let something slip. But it does explain his actions."

"That is the missing piece in this puzzle," Derek said. "You may never know what happened between your parents." He looked at me and gently reached his hand across the table. "This is so not what you need right now, is it?" I turned my hand upward so that his fingertips were lightly stroking my palm. Maybe he thought that was a comforting gesture, that he was helping me relax. But the actual effect was the exact opposite. I stretched out my own fingers to touch the inside of his wrist.

"Well, the situation puts a whole new layer of complexity on my feelings about my father, and I definitely don't need that," I said. "But being with you? That seems to be just what I need right now," I said.

Derek's expression didn't change. He was still gazing at me, tenderly searching my face. "You sure?" he asked finally. "Because I don't think I have the strength to turn you down a second time."

"It's taking all my courage to ask again," I admitted. "At least this time, I'm sober. And I'm really not looking for anything more than a way to get my mind off all this. For tonight anyway."

"Well, I plan to blow your mind, so I guess we're on the same page."

Going to bed with my teenage crush in my childhood home felt like more of a threat to my psyche than I could stand at the moment, so I followed Derek to his house. The grown-up me ached for some physical comfort, some relief and release, a break from thinking about my parents and my past and my path forward from here. Just for one night, I wanted to be in the moment, to forget about everything and everyone making demands of me.

When Derek opened his front door, I fell gratefully into his arms, repeating our first kiss with all the same intensity and promise and yearning. This time, he didn't pull away. With a heightened focus and awareness that I couldn't remember ever experiencing before, I felt the heat of his body, breathed in the delicious fragrance of his neck, stared at the smooth flawlessness of his skin, listened to the sweet murmured compliments he left in my ear, tasted the desire on his lips. We collapsed onto his bed, both of us trembling, both of us sensing how absolutely right this felt.

Later, on those clean, crisp sheets, with Derek's arm slung across my stomach, I fell into the deepest, most satisfying sleep I'd had since my father's funeral.

Back at the Harding Street house, I struggled to readjust to the realities of my family's current circumstances. Julie was still unconscious, Trip was still healing, Henry and Michael still needed help, the house still needed to be cleaned out. Spending the night with Derek and having him cook me breakfast—

with truly amazing coffee—had blissfully taken my mind away from these facts. But now I needed to refocus, re-energize, and get busy.

Aunt Elaine and I had finished with the desk in Paul's room and I had done most of the dresser drawers. Every time I thought about what room or closet or piece of furniture to tackle next, I remembered how I hadn't finished Paul's closet yet. And every time, I told myself I wasn't ready to look at that shoebox again. It weighed so heavily on me, nearly crushing me, the knowledge that I had let my mother down by not being able to find those shoes and take them to her, denying her last request, and I just couldn't face that reminder of my failure. I would also never know how the box ended up in Paul's closet.

Things had changed now, however. I had some new information about my mother, information that altered everything I thought I knew about her. When I first figured out what Trip's blood type meant, I focused all my anger on Paul, on how he had taken such a cruel revenge on my mother. How his actions had affected all of us, the whole town, not just her. And how Trip had absorbed the most impact without even knowing it. Paul had somehow discovered a secret he seemed to be the only one to know, a secret that made him so angry and jealous he was willing to bring his whole world crashing down.

But somebody else did know. Mom knew. She had an affair. But that was the only fact I could really know for sure. If Trip had a different father, then my mother had slept with someone else during her marriage to my father. I had no idea who. Or why. Or for how long. And it wasn't even clear that she ever knew that her husband hadn't fathered her son.

I tried hard to remember the year before Trip was born. GrandMom had just died. Paul was spending all her money. I was barely seven years old. Even if there had been clues at the time, I would have been much too young and naïve to pick up on them. If this affair had gone on for any length of time, surely I would have noticed something. Then again, maybe not. I hadn't paid all that much attention to what my mother did while I was at school. As long as my clothes were clean and my meals got to the table and she lavished praise on me when I thought I deserved it, I took her for granted. Maybe it had been easy for her to keep it a secret. Maybe Paul failed to pay attention to her, too. The more I thought about it, the more she seemed like a complete stranger to me. I began to feel like I had never really known her at all. This new knowledge I had raised so many questions, and the only people who could give me those answers were dead.

I wondered suddenly whether the shoes had something to do with Mom's affair. I remembered how they seemed to make her feel pretty, how her step was livelier when she wore them. She stopped wearing them because Paul took that feeling away. And that was just a year or so before she got pregnant with Trip. Maybe someone else had been paying attention, someone who noticed her because of those shoes, or someone who knew how to make her feel as special as the shoes did. Maybe that was why she had kept them all those years. And why she had asked for them that last day.

And yet, the box was in Paul's closet.

It felt like there was a jackhammer in my chest as I rushed into Paul's room and flung open the closet door. With all his clothes gone, the shoe box was immediately visible, no longer hidden on that back shelf. I reached for it with both hands.

As soon as I lifted it, I knew it didn't contain shoes. It was too heavy, and I could feel the contents shift; with a soft, scraping thud, they slid to one end. I was about to get answers, but I was no longer sure I wanted them.

PART FOUR

1974 – 1978

20

For weeks before Aunt Elaine and Uncle Ron's wedding, I would sneak into my closet, carefully unzip the garment bag protecting my junior bridesmaid's dress, and just stroke the silk ruffles on the skirt. The fabric was so delicate and soft and smooth, the color the prettiest sky-blue shade I could imagine, the style so reminiscent of all my best princess daydreams, that I was already dreading the moment I'd have to take it off. This wedding was going to be the best day I ever had. And the dress was only the beginning. I had pretty shoes dyed to match! With bows on the toes! And high heels! And I was going to get my hair done at the salon with Aunt Elaine and her best friend, the maid of honor. As "only" the flower girl, Julie was too young to merit this privilege. And she didn't even realize how much fun it was going to be. Whenever I talked about getting my hair done, she responded, "I like my hair like this," shrugging and swinging her ponytail and glancing in the mirror. "I would look silly with it all teased up all over the place." Too bad it was summer and Allison was away at camp. I really wanted her to be excited with me. I hoped I would have plenty of pictures to show her when school started.

After the rehearsal dinner, my father and some of Ron's friends took the groom out for drinks, but my mom brought Julie and me home early so we could get some sleep. But I hardly slept a wink; that's how excited I was. As soon as there was light outside the window, I crept out of bed as quietly as I could since Julie was still sleeping. I checked on the dress and shoes in the closet. I looked in the drawer for the new training bra that I hardly needed, but that somehow seemed both absolutely necessary and glamorous as soon as I put the dress on.

It was the longest, most torturous morning of my whole life, waiting until it was time to go to The Magic Looking Glass Beauty Parlor for my appointment. When I walked into the salon, greeted by the damp warmth of hair dryers, the heady floral fragrances of shampoos and conditioners and setting gels and hair spray, and the tinny music playing on the radio, Aunt Elaine was already under the huge hood of the hair dryer with high, round curlers framing her face. Her friend Debbie was getting her hair shampooed, an unimaginable luxury I was about to experience for myself. Elaine waved her freshly French-manicured fingers at me, and I was glad my mom had insisted on buffing and filing my ragged, bitten, dirty fingernails into something sort of presentable.

"Hi, honey!" Aunt Elaine called too loudly because she couldn't hear herself above the dull whoosh of the hair dryer. "Have a seat. You'll be next, after Deb."

I hopped onto a bright pink tufted vinyl chair under a row of dryers, making the cushion squeak. I ran my hands along the chair's cool, shiny chrome arms. I thought it must be the most comfortable seat in the whole world.

Leaning back with her hair in the giant sink, Debbie asked Aunt Elaine about where she and Ron were going to live. "I moved most of my stuff into Ron's apartment in the city," Aunt Elaine said. "But I hope we'll be out of there in about a year. We should have enough saved for a house by then."

"A house, huh?" Debbie said, sitting up as the shampoo girl wrapped a fluffy white towel around her head. "Thinking about lots of room for babies?"

"Oh, God, no!" Aunt Elaine exclaimed with an exaggerated shudder. "No babies for me. I love my brother's kids, but I'm not cut out to be a mother."

"Really? Does Ronnie know this?" Debbie asked. She tried to make eye contact with Elaine in the mirror, but Aunt Elaine turned her attention to me. Trained to be seen and not heard, I struggled not to react because I wanted to be privy to these grown-up conversations. I was afraid if she thought I was listening too closely, they wouldn't talk at all. I cocked my head just a little to one side as if I was simply mildly curious about her answer.

After a second, Aunt Elaine smiled. "Oh yeah," she said breezily. "I think I told him on our second or third date that I didn't want to have kids and that he shouldn't pursue me any further unless he felt the same way. And here we are, two years later, getting married."

Debbie still seemed a little skeptical. "What about Ron's parents? How do they feel about being denied grandchildren? You do know you're going to get a lot of pressure from them, right?"

"I'm kind of used to dealing with pressure from parents," Elaine said, her face darkening in a strange way. "I stayed single this long in spite of my mother. I got a master's degree in spite of my father. I can handle Ron's parents."

All this information crashed its way through my almost twelve-year-old brain. I did know that, at age thirty-two, Aunt Elaine was older than most brides; in fact, being over thirty at all made her seem absolutely ancient to me. Still, I felt a little protective of her, and I hated my father's jokes about her. Whenever she babysat Julie and me, my dad would suggest we play cards. "Just not Old Maid. Aunt Elaine is too good at that." It was such a dumb joke, but it made him laugh every single time.

I also knew Aunt Elaine was really smart, that my grandfather had been pleased and proud to pay to send her to a prestigious New England girls' college. It was also a family legend that he had been quite frustrated with her four years later when she came home with a degree and ambition instead of a fiancé. I didn't realize she'd gone on to earn a master's degree. Why would she want to stay in school that long? She had to know she wasn't going to run Cutler Enterprises, no matter what. My father was the one my grandfather had groomed for that, not Elaine, and he had taken over when GrandDad died.

What I knew about Aunt Elaine working at the family business was what I had heard in snatches of conversation over the years. Her arguing with my dad when she told him she'd taken another job: "We can't work together anymore, Paul! I just can't take it, the way you correct me in front of everyone, how you comment on which customers are single and maybe I should flirt with them. It's unprofessional, and it's not funny."

My father's disdainful response: "Construction materials is a man's business, Lainey. If you want to be in charge, find something in fashion or cosmetics or something."

My mother explaining to her friend, when she thought no one else was around, why Elaine didn't live in town anymore: "He never took her seriously, always teasing her and calling her by the nicknames he used when they were kids, and if he could make a joke at her expense, of course, he never passed up that chance. You can imagine how it all made her look to the other executives. And you know how Paul is, always so sure he's right about everything."

Aunt Elaine liked to talk to Julie and me about her life as a "career girl" and how we could do that, too, if we wanted. We loved spending time alone with her because she always gushed over how well we were doing in school and told us how proud she was and how important it was to keep our grades up. "Going to college and getting a good job means having your own money, and the freedom that comes with that, well, you just can't beat it," she liked to say. Nobody cared how much she spent on clothes, shoes, and jewelry! Her life seemed so glamorous to me. I loved my mother, and she seemed quite happy not to have a job. But I loved Aunt Elaine, too, and her life was the one I wanted.

Even so, the news that Aunt Elaine didn't plan to have

children was shocking. Who didn't love babies? I remembered how excited and thrilled my mother had been to learn she was pregnant with my little brother. All her friends made such a fuss, telling her how she was positively glowing with happiness. I had a hard time imagining that a woman wouldn't want that. Maybe I had just figured that Aunt Elaine was only working till she got married. Wasn't that what most "career girls" did? Suddenly, all my perceptions were turned upside down.

I heard Aunt Elaine say, "Hey, Madeline, are you okay?" She lifted the hair dryer to lean forward, frowning as she studied my face. "You looked so happy when you came in, but now you look like you might just break down and cry. What's the matter?"

I shrugged, not sure how to explain what I was thinking. "Oh, I bet I know," she said with a grin. "You were kind of looking forward to having some cousins, weren't you? Maybe a couple more little kids to boss around someday? I probably shouldn't have dropped that news on you this way. Sorry about that." She patted my knee a couple of times, then left her hand there to give it a squeeze. "I've known for a long time that I wouldn't make a very good mom. Not like yours, anyway. And every kid deserves a really good mother."

Now, I was totally confused. Why would she think she wouldn't be a good mother? She was funny and pretty, and she knew all the best games. "Look at it this way," she said. "There won't be anybody but you and Julie and your brother with any claim on Cutler Enterprises. Maybe I'm too selfish to have my own kids, but I can do this for you. You guys can run things the way you want to. You can be the big-time lady executive I never got to be. I know you'll do great things because you're so smart."

By telling me how smart I was, it seemed like Aunt Elaine was trying to pay me a compliment and make me feel better. But I already knew I was smart, and honestly, that didn't really seem like such a great thing to an awkward girl about to enter junior high school. The boys paid attention to the cute girls, not the smart ones. Today, of all days, I wanted to be pretty. I wanted everyone in the church to think about how grown-up I looked. I sure didn't want anyone looking at the junior bridesmaid and thinking, "Wow, doesn't she look smart?" But I also knew that today was Aunt Elaine's big day (that was what Mom kept saying to my father), and she had other things to think about besides my feelings. So, I swallowed hard and smiled back at her. "Okay."

Her hand still on my knee, she gave my leg another squeeze and a little shake. "Good. Now let us see what Miss Helen here can do with that beautiful hair of yours, huh?"

Getting my hair washed and styled and even being allowed to wear a little bit of blue eye shadow and some lip gloss was so incredible and exciting that it pushed the questions about Aunt Elaine and motherhood and having a good job out of my mind, at least for a while. The wedding ceremony was beautiful, and I did my part perfectly. Julie worked pretty hard scattering the flower petals evenly without bruising them or creating too big a pile in one place. I was relieved for both of us. Our father had spent the last few weeks entering rooms humming the wedding march and stepping as if he was walking down the aisle, especially if he knew Julie and I were watching. "Let me see you do it, just like this, so you don't shame us all," he kept saying.

As great as the wedding itself was, the reception was a million times better. I had never been right in the middle of such a huge grown-up party before. Laughter, music, and the clinking of crystal. Brightly colored fancy dresses and big, beautiful centerpieces. The mingled aromas of food, booze, flowers, aftershave, perfume, and cigarettes. Hugs and kisses and handshakes. I tried hard to absorb it all, hoping I would never forget a single detail. The best part was that I got to sit at the head table with the rest of the bridal party, away from my parents, far from my father's critical gaze. I didn't have to hear him breaking down my manners or telling me to eat everything on my plate even if I didn't like it. I was giddy with the freedom I'd been given, and I wanted this night to go on forever.

When Aunt Elaine and Uncle Ron took the dance floor for the first time as man and wife, the band playing "Time in a Bottle," I couldn't take my eyes off them. She looked so gorgeous and so happy. And he was clearly so proud and so in love. As I watched, Uncle Ron's father politely cut in to dance with his new daughter-in-law, so Uncle Ron guided his mother out to the dance floor. As other couples began to join them, I smiled to myself, thinking about how someday I would be out there, too, with my future boyfriend and eventually with my own groom. I imagined how it would feel to rest my arm on this as-yet-unknown handsome man's strong shoulder, to let my delicate hand get lost in his big, strong one, and to become aware of his touch at the small of my back. Would it be more romantic to stare into his eyes or let his cheek rest against mine? Maybe start out with eyes locked, then melt into a cheek-to-cheek snuggle for the rest of the song. What song would be playing? What would I be wearing? I was thoroughly enjoying creating this vision of my future as the music made me sway gently in my chair. Until I felt someone pinch my shoulder.

"Come on, Madeline, I'm going to teach you how to dance."

My father was about to ruin my fantasy. I did not want my first dance ever to be with my own father! In my panic, I glanced around, trying to find my mom, hoping she would come to my rescue. Shouldn't she be dancing with him anyway? I couldn't see her anywhere, so I turned back to my father's expectant face. "No, thank you, Daddy," I said brightly. "I'm okay just watching."

"You need to learn how to dance," he insisted, taking hold of my arm and trying to lift me out of my chair. "Dancing is how girls learn to figure out what a man is going to do before he does it. Besides, I'm the best-looking guy here. You should want to be seen with me."

"No, really, Dad, I would rather just watch," I tried again, still hoping I could pull my arm free and stay in my seat. But his grip was strong.

He looked down at me, his face set with determination and his joking manner quickly dissolving into anger. My heart began to pound because I knew that look. He got it whenever he thought I was not obeying him unquestioningly. When he spoke, I heard the edge of controlled fury in his voice. "Madeline. You do what I tell you." His hand tightened around my arm, and he pulled a little harder.

I panicked. All these people watching me dance with my father would suddenly see me as a little girl again, not as a young lady mature enough to choose her own dance partner. The perfect vision that my imagination had carefully crafted just moments ago was in tatters. My own father was going to teach me how to dance, in front of everybody. Even worse, I felt like I might start crying, and that would ruin the first makeup I had ever been allowed to wear. It was all too embarrassing and frustrating and maddening for words.

Once on the dance floor, my father turned to face me, grabbed my left wrist, and jerked it up to his shoulder. Then he took my right hand in his and roughly bent my arm. "Relax," he insisted, narrowing his brown eyes. His face was still clouded with anger because I had initially defied him, and he could still feel my resistance. "Now, follow my feet," he instructed. "I'm going to lead you."

I looked down at his feet and my own delicate blue shoes. I managed to follow his first few foot movements, but then he went to turn, and my foot landed on top of his. His grip on my hand was tighter than it needed to be, almost to the point of being painful. His jacket smelled of cigarette smoke, and on his breath were the remains of who knew how many martinis.

Instead of beautiful and adored, I felt awkward and nervous, even a little nauseated.

"We're just going in a square. One, two, three, one, two, three," he said impatiently. "Look at my face, not at my feet. It's not that hard."

I kept trying to follow along, but either I was leaving my foot where he would step on it, or I was going in the wrong direction, where it seemed like I was trying to get away. When that happened, he sighed with exasperation and reminded me that dancing was supposed to be easy.

"You're almost twelve years old already, Madeline," he was saying. "It's time for you to know how to dance."

By the time the song ended, my lovely blue shoes were hopelessly scuffed with the black marks my father's shoes left behind every time I stepped wrong. I'd been fighting back the tears the whole time, and I tried to avoid looking at my father's face. Luckily, the band began playing a faster song, so I let go of my father's hand and turned to leave the dance floor. But he held on to my arm.

"Madeline. You say 'thank you' to your partner at the end of a dance," he said sternly. "Remember your manners. Always."

"Thank you, Dad," I managed to say before I turned and fled. The tears in my eyes clouded my vision, and I stumbled like a clumsy ox at the edge of the dance floor. Horrified at how awkward I was sure I looked, I tried to right myself and regain my grown-up posture and composure. But the high heels I wore betrayed me, and they gave way underneath my unsteady feet. The next thing I knew, my face met the elaborately patterned carpeting, and I felt the sting of a brush burn on my chin. One of my ankles ached above those traitorous shoes. And the only sound I could hear was my father's laughter.

"Jesus Christ, Madeline," he chuckled from where he stood, still on the dance floor. "Did you have a good trip?"

Trying to keep my eyes down so I wouldn't meet anyone's

gaze and give away my utter humiliation, I carefully got to my feet. I had managed to tear the ruffle away from my beautiful blue dress, and when I touched my burning chin with my delicate white glove, it came away with a streak of blood on it. The weight of the past few moments landed on my shoulders with such a heavy thud that I seemed to be unable to move under such a huge and crippling burden. I didn't dare to even try to overcome it. I knew my face was fiery red, and the tears were falling unimpeded, but I couldn't make myself take a step. Until I heard my father's voice again.

"Well, don't just stand there. Go clean yourself up."

Taking my first careful steps with my eyes glued to the floor, I realized Aunt Elaine had come over to see what was going on. "Oh no, what happened?" she asked.

Still laughing, my father answered, "This little Mad Dog ran off, chasing her own tail, and she fell. She made a mess of herself, and she needs to go clean up."

"I'll go see if I can find Ginny," Aunt Elaine said. "Maddie will probably want her help."

"Oh, hey, Elaine?" my father called after her. "I just decided I better keep Mom's ring. The way things are going for Madeline, it might be the only one she ever gets." He found that impossibly clever and hilarious, and the last thing I heard before the ladies' room door closed behind me was that cruel cackling.

21

"I hope he behaved himself," Mrs. Dunn smiled, pressing a crisp ten-dollar bill into my palm. "I know he can be a handful."

"Oh, no," I replied. "We had a really fun day, right, pal?" I reached out to ruffle the damp brown waves on Jamie's head. The three-year-old was indeed a handful, but spending the afternoon at the pool tired him out, which made him a lot easier to babysit. He leaned against his mom's tanned leg, his arms held straight out from his chubby little body by the bright orange inflatable water wings he still wore. He refused to take them off, insisting he wanted one more dip.

Still wearing her white tennis dress and visor, Mrs. Dunn bent down to pick up her chlorine-scented son. "Thanks again for watching him today. Knowing he was with you, I could really concentrate on my game. That doesn't mean I won, of course, but at least I'm getting better." She tilted her head toward the tennis courts. "Hey, I think your sister was playing a match when I finished up. This late in the day, that would be the final, for the championship, right?"

No doubt, I thought. Julie started taking tennis lessons just last summer, and she was already the best player in her age group. Lots of the other ten-year-old girls lobbied to be her doubles partner in this tournament, but she opted to play as a single. "I couldn't stand it if I let somebody else down," she confessed to me.

Jamie was already dozing off against his mother's neck, so I waved goodbye, slung my beach towel over my shoulder, and started my walk home. Approaching the tennis courts, I knew that it was indeed Julie playing. Even if I hadn't been able to see her long brown ponytail or the colorful new tennis skirt she and Mom picked out for this tournament, I could hear the distinctively determined grunt she let out just before every thud of her racket on the ball. All the other kids who played in the tournament watched intently from the adjacent court or behind the chain link fence. "What's the score?" I whispered into the crowd just as Julie's opponent rushed the net and the return lob sailed past her.

"This is match point," someone replied, also in a whisper. Noticing the admiration in the voice, I glanced over at a boy I recognized from Julie's class. He didn't seem able to take his eyes off my sister as she confidently bounced the ball before her serve. "If Julie gets it, she wins."

I held my breath, watching Julie toss the ball above her head and then smash it with an aggressive pong against her racket strings. Her opponent was ready and slammed it back at her. But Julie was ready, too. I heard her grunt as she swung through a two-handed backhand return. Again, her opponent returned it easily. This time, though, Julie hit the ball with less force, and it arced just over the net and dropped daintily on the other side with a muffled thump. A moment too late, her opponent realized what had happened. She didn't get to the ball in time. In rapid succession, she yelled, "No," Julie yelled, "Yes!" and all the spectators broke into cheers. From behind the fence, I watched as Julie's friends rushed onto the court and mobbed her with excited hugs. I'd never get anywhere near her, so I turned to head home.

After I showered off all the sticky suntan lotion left from an afternoon at the pool, I made my way down to the kitchen to help Mom get dinner ready. While I pulled the husks and silk from the late summer corn on the cob, I told Mom about all the funny things Jamie said and did while we swam. "I must have caught him jumping off the side a million times," I laughed. "He loves that."

Just as I finished shucking the last ear, Julie burst in, waving her trophy. Mom had asked me if I knew how she did, but I shrugged and said I didn't. I thought Julie would want to tell the story herself. She could hardly contain her excitement, giving Mom a blow-by-blow account of every match she played.

"I had to play Patty in the final, and she's so good!" Julie exclaimed. "She's been playing forever, and I just started! I was so nervous. She won the first point and then the second, but then I started winning, and she started making stupid mistakes and finally, I just got to match point, and that was it!"

Over dinner, Julie breathlessly told the whole story again for our father. He asked a lot of questions. Who were her opponents? How long had they been playing? Who won the tournament last year? Were there any more tournaments this year? He nodded and smiled when she answered, confirming that his daughter was developing her tennis talent faster than the other kids.

Even though I was listening, I focused more on enjoying my mom's special barbecued chicken. The satisfying smell, the sweet heat of her homemade sauce, the sanctioned wickedness of eating with my fingers all made this dish my favorite of her summer recipes. I figured I could tell Julie later, alone, that I had, in fact, seen her last two points and I thought she played really well.

Suddenly, my father turned his attention to me. "Did you play in this tournament, Maddie?"

I looked up, surprised. He leaned back in his chair, arms crossed over his chest, his head cocked to one side, waiting for an answer. Across the table, Julie's face fell, and her shoulders slumped. Her accomplishment should have been enough to keep her in the spotlight for a whole dinner, at least.

"No, of course not," I said. "I don't like tennis, and anyway, I promised to babysit for Mrs. Dunn so she could play."

"Maybe you'd like it better if you let Julie here give you some pointers. She could teach you. Or I could." Dad reached for another ear of corn and began buttering it slowly, never taking his eyes off me.

"I took lessons from the pro a couple of summers ago," I said, looking down at my plate, breaking eye contact with my father. Had he forgotten that he did try to give me some pointers? That he ended up yelling at me because I tried to tell him that the serve strategy he was teaching me directly contradicted everything the pro said. That I had stormed into the house after just half an hour of his pointers. "I just didn't think it was much fun, that's all."

"You're right, it probably isn't much fun getting beaten by your little sister," Dad chuckled.

I desperately wanted to remind him that he was the one who took away the fun. Instead, Julie bravely jumped back into the conversation. "We never played against each other, Daddy. I started last summer when Maddie had already quit lessons." I could tell by the way she was sitting with her shoulders tightened up near her ears that her hands were clenched in her lap.

"Hmm, so you got really good in a single summer, and Mad Dog gave up." Dad shook his head sadly, still holding a glistening, steaming ear of corn between his hands. Turning to Julie, he said, "I'm really proud of you, JuJuBe. I'm sure you're going to keep winning because you have a natural talent, and you work hard."

He took a few bites off the cob and chewed them slowly. I glanced at Mom, who was quietly feeding Trip at the other end of the table. She hadn't said much since we sat down, letting Julie tell her story, glowing with pride as she talked. Now, Mom's attention seemed to be focused on Trip, but her jaw was clenched in frustration. Like me, she knew exactly where this was heading.

"I guess we're going to have to figure out a different sport for you, Mad Dog," Dad said, finally lowering the corn cob away from his face. "What do you think? Do you want to try golf? Or softball? There must be *something* you could be good at."

My face was burning. I was hurt, angry, and humiliated. Why was he doing this to me? Instead of answering, I stared at the greasy chicken bones in front of me while under the table, I furiously wiped my fingers on my napkin.

Mom finally broke the silence. "Paul, honey, Madeline is good at lots of things. They both are. It's just that Maddie doesn't like sports, and Julie does."

"Oh, yeah? What do you think you're good at, Mad Dog?" Dad watched me expectantly. The mocking look on his face told me he was ready to shoot down anything I said.

Not trusting myself to speak, I just shrugged. Anything I said would just fuel his teasing. So, Mom spoke for me.

"She's good at math and science. She reads all the time. You know she's one of the smartest kids in her class. And everybody asks her to babysit because she's so good with kids."

"Oh, okay. Well, when I build a case for Julie's trophies, I'll make sure I save a shelf for all your babysitting awards." Looking at Julie, he comically rolled his eyes. In spite of herself, she let out a giggle, then clapped her hand over her mouth.

I couldn't believe my ears. She laughed at his joke! Now that she had encouraged him, there would be no stopping him. How could she?

Then I realized he was right. Nobody really cared if you were good at something as unimportant as babysitting. And being good at math or science was hardly any big deal either. The school had a math tournament once, but we competed in teams, and mine didn't win. Even so, I don't think the winners got any awards. Nope, nothing with my name on it in that trophy case.

Fighting back tears, I put my sauce-stained napkin on the table with a little more force than I should have. "May I be excused?" I muttered, still not looking up.

"Good idea," my father answered. "Let's you and me go outside and have a tennis lesson."

"I don't want a tennis lesson," I protested, knowing even as I said the words what was coming. I felt sick to my stomach, but I was pretty sure that even throwing up wouldn't get me out of this "tennis lesson."

"Come on, I'll give you the same pointers I gave your sister. We can make you as good as she is."

I hesitated again, trying to think of another way to get out of this. It was enough to make him angry. "Madeline. Do what I tell you."

For the next hour, my father threw tennis balls at me, made me chase the ones I missed, and angrily repeated the instructions he didn't think I was following, all with increasing volume. He yelled when I hit a ball too hard or not hard enough, when I didn't follow through, or when my backhand shots skittered sideways. "Come on, Mad Dog," he sighed. "I'm giving you easy shots. A baby could return them."

As I bent over to pick up yet another ball I had missed, I mumbled, "Well, why don't you throw some balls at Trip for a while then?" When I looked up, my father stood over me, glaring into my face. He leaned closer and grabbed me roughly by the chin, forcing me to look right at the fiery rage in his eyes. Through tightly clenched teeth, he said, "Don't you ever talk back to me again." Then he stood up, took a few steps back, and said, "Now get in the ready position, like I showed you."

To avoid his stare and keep him from seeing the tears in my eyes, I glanced at the house, where I saw Julie watching from the kitchen window. The light was on in Trip's room, but I couldn't see my mom.

As the sun went down and the fireflies lit up the dark, the

mosquitos began to swarm onto my sweaty arms and legs. I was exhausted, bruised, and demoralized, not to mention itchy. Still, we kept going until it was so dark that all I could see was the bright fluorescent yellow of the tennis ball coming at me.

Finally, my father admitted defeat. "Yeah, I guess you're really not cut out for sports, are you?" He shook his head in disgust. "Go on inside."

I made sure I was in bed before Julie. I pretended to be asleep when she came in, and I said nothing to her.

22

I approached the midterm exams in the first semester of my junior year with outright terror.

Not only was junior year the most important one, with colleges scrutinizing everybody's grades from that year, but I also had the added pressure that came from my father. Long before I started high school, I had heard it over and over: Grades are everything. Every chance he got, he drilled that into my head, and if he thought for a second that I'd somehow forgotten and, God forbid, brought home a B, he was merciless.

So, for a solid week in November, I did nothing but study. If I wasn't at the library, I was in the room I shared with Julie, the door closed, unless I needed to yell at Trip or Julie for making too much noise and distracting me. Even though math was always my best subject, my trigonometry teacher, Mr. Hawkins, had a well-deserved reputation for toughness. Tall and intimidating, with a withering gaze that cut down students who thought they were smarter than he was, he didn't have a compassionate bone in his body. His were the hardest tests, everyone knew. And while he was incredibly demanding, a good grade in his class guaranteed a good letter of recommendation when college applications were due. I wanted and needed that really badly.

Every night, I reviewed my trig notes carefully. Read over every chapter till I almost knew the text by heart. Retook the tests we had done so far. I was having fitful dreams about sine and cosine and tangent and acute angles. As hard as I was working, my father found reasons to come into my room once or twice a day. To check on me. To supervise. To find something, anything, to criticize.

"What are you working on?" he asked, standing behind my desk chair, reaching for the carefully organized notes spread out in front of me.

"Trig," I answered, not looking up. "Can you please leave my notes alone? I have them organized exactly the way I want them."

Knowing he was smirking as he replaced the papers he'd picked up, I waited for him to say the thing he always said, no matter what I was studying. The standard line designed to tear down any confidence I may have built up, to make me think I had almost no hope of ever truly understanding the subject: "Trig is easy. I always got straight A's in that class. Don't you want my help?"

"No, thank you. I do better when I study alone."

"You should let me help you," he insisted. "You're obviously not getting it since you have to study it so much. It's not too hard for you, is it?"

If I recounted this conversation to anyone and tried to duplicate the mocking tone my father's voice took on when he asked these questions, they would say I was exaggerating. That it was nice my father cared so much. And why wouldn't I want help? "It's not too hard," I said, finally turning around in my chair to look defiantly into his eyes. "I can handle it. I study so much because I want to be sure I'm prepared, that's all."

"If you say so." He stood watching me for a long minute before he left the room. "Your mother will need your help with dinner pretty soon."

The next morning, I complained to Mom about the pressure my father put on me. "He keeps interrupting me. Then, he makes me so mad it takes me forever to get my focus back," I whined over breakfast.

"Oh, Maddie," Mom sighed. "Your dad is really proud of you, of how well you're doing in school. He wants to be able to say he had something to do with it. He wants to brag about you and tell everybody how smart you are and that you got it from him. Your success builds him up."

Frustrated that she didn't understand, I pushed myself away from the kitchen table. "I should get a little more work done before I have to leave," I muttered.

I had midterms in French, chemistry, and history, too, but I felt way more confident in those subjects than I did in trigonometry. At the end of midterm week, I was pretty sure I had done well enough to get the A's my father expected to see.

On the day before Thanksgiving break began, most of the teachers knew the students' attention was elsewhere: upcoming travel, the beginning of the Christmas season, football games, Black Friday sales, and a few precious days of freedom. They usually chose this day to return our graded midterm exams and review them.

In my first-period French class, I sighed with relief to see the A and the "Très bien, Mademoiselle," written across the top of the page. History was next. One of my best subjects ever since elementary school. In fact, most of the American history we were studying was basically a review, at least for those of us who had paid attention the first time around. Even so, I was happy and again relieved to see that I got another A. I was, however, preoccupied while Mrs. Bender reviewed the answers. My third-period class was trig, and the suspense was killing me.

The tension in the room was thick as my trigonometry class assembled before the late bell rang. As Mr. Hawkins stood by the open classroom door, looming over us as we walked in, he wore his familiar knowing expression, realizing that we were all nervous and he had the power to make or break each one of us.

"Come in and take your seats quickly," he said. "We have a

lot to get done today."

He was met with mild groaning. Oh, great, we were all thinking. We're not just getting our midterm exams back, we were going to do actual work today, too? And that probably meant homework over Thanksgiving break.

Mr. Hawkins walked to the front of the classroom. "Based on all that groaning, I assume you thought you'd be getting your midterm grades today. I have good news and bad news, then. The good news is, you're right. I will be giving you your tests back. The bad news is, you have to wait till the end of class. I don't plan to review the exam with you or give you the opportunity to argue about your grades. So, let's open up our books and get started."

All through class, my heart pounded. He knew someone would want to argue about their grade. Of course, I assumed that someone was me. What had I done wrong? Would I be able to explain away a mistake, to show that it really wasn't one? Could I argue a B up to at least an A-minus?

It was the longest class I had ever endured.

Just before the bell, Mr. Hawkins wrapped up the lesson, then strode purposefully to his desk. Without another word, he began walking through the aisles, dropping papers in front of anxious students, some people struggling not to react and some unable to conceal their joy—or disappointment. Occasionally, he would sigh or shake his head at one of my classmates. Knowing Mr. Hawkins, however, that might mean the kid had done really well. Then again, it could also mean, "Sorry, but your life is pretty much over." My heart continued its pounding, and in sympathy, my palms began sweating as well. Finally, Mr. Hawkins stopped by my desk. He took one last look at my test paper. And nodded. Then smiled. He turned the paper towards me, then laid it carefully on the desk so I could see the A circled in red. Sweet relief flooded through my whole body.

After that, I sailed through my gym class, then lunch

period. In the afternoon, I spent my English literature class only half listening to a discussion of *King Lear*. Still basking in the sweet relief of an A in trig, I allowed myself to relax a little after an intense week of studying, knowing it had paid off.

My last class of the day was chemistry. The teacher, Mrs. Gorsky, reminded me of a bird—a tiny woman with a high chirping voice and a nose that was noticeably beak-like. When she put on the safety goggles, it was hard not to think of an owl.

"Yes, yes, I know I'm the only thing between you and your Thanksgiving break," she sighed as she herded us all into the chemistry lab. "But we are still having class here, so let's get settled." We perched on stools and stowed our books under the lab tables. I took out a notebook and pencil, ready to take notes on whatever she was going to teach.

"We're going to spend this class period going over your midterm exam," Mrs. Gorsky told us. "I didn't think I made it a difficult test, but a lot of you seemed to have trouble with it. So, let's review."

She walked us through each question, pointing out the important aspects, the things she expected us to have down pat by now. It all sounded familiar, and I was pretty sure I knew all that stuff reasonably well. But if my classmates were struggling, it was okay with me if we spent some class time on review.

"Okay, now you know what the answers should have been," Mrs. Gorsky said as she hopped off her stool, exams tucked in the crook of her elbow, and began moving through the lab, handing each student a paper. Passing me, she paused. "We should talk after class," she said softly, for only me to hear. Then she handed me my test, with a red C-plus in the top right corner.

My cheeks began to burn, my vision clouded with the stinging tears that sprang to my eyes, my hands started trembling, and the dull roar of defeat boomed in my ears. How could this have happened? How could I have let it happen? Blinking hard and fast so I could see clearly, I looked at my test. I knew every answer as Mrs. Gorsky reviewed the questions. I couldn't possibly have gotten so many wrong. And yet I had.

In my head, the excuses began to form right away. I grasped for something, anything, that would make this all right. I was tired from so much studying. I spent so much time on my trigonometry exam—which I got an A on, by the way—that I neglected chemistry. It had been the last exam that day, and my brain was just fried. But there was not a single rationalization I could offer that would satisfy my father. He was going to make a federal case out of this C, and that was the thing that nobody would ever understand because he wasn't *their* father. They couldn't possibly know what things would be like at my house when he found out about this.

Whatever Mrs. Gorsky talked about for the last few minutes of class, I didn't hear it. At last, the final bell of the day broke into my consciousness, and I tried to quickly scoop up my books and papers and race to my locker. I kept my head down so no one would see the tear streaks. But Mrs. Gorsky headed me off. "Maddie? Can you stay a moment?"

Already at the door, I sighed and turned around to face her. I was suddenly aware of the caustic chemical smell in this classroom. As it mingled with the adolescent aromas of deodorant and perfume and hair spray while my classmates hurried past me, I felt overwhelmed, unable to breathe. I hugged my books a little closer to my chest, as if they would somehow shield me from whatever lecture I was about to get.

"I won't keep you long," Mrs. Gorsky began, looking sympathetic. "But I wanted to know what happened with this test. You seemed to have a better grip on the material than your test demonstrated."

I shrugged. It was easier not to speak.

My silence hung for a moment as she studied my face.

"Well, as I said, it turned out to be a tougher test than I thought, and lots of people didn't do very well. You can bring up that grade. An A for this class is still very possible. I don't want you to get discouraged. Okay?"

Hoping my voice wouldn't give me away, I managed to squeak out, "I'm not. Discouraged, I mean. Thank you."

"You're welcome," Mrs. Gorsky smiled. "You can always come by after school if you need a little extra help."

I nodded and took a step toward the door.

"All right. Have a happy Thanksgiving. I'll see you next week." I was dismissed, and I couldn't get out of that lab fast enough.

And yet, I didn't want to go home either. There was no point in hoping my father wouldn't ask about my midterm exam grades; he had already been harping on the subject for days. "You haven't gotten your test grades yet? Why not?" he kept asking, as if it was my fault, as if I had some control over how long it took a teacher to grade an exam. I had held him off by saying it probably wouldn't be until the last day before break. How stupid I'd been!

At my locker, I looked around desperately for someone, anyone I could talk to, just to stall. Almost frantic, I tried to think of somewhere I could go, some friend who might invite me over, or someplace I could just hang out, the way the other kids seemed to. But the few other students still milling around ignored me, and I really had absolutely no idea where they might be going after school. Even if I did, I couldn't just show up there. That would be weird.

With no other options available, I walked slowly home. Still clutching my books against my body, I kept my eyes on the sidewalk, oblivious to the beautiful, unseasonably warm, late autumn afternoon blooming all around me. The tremors I could feel deep in my chest and that horrible stone of dread settling heavily in my stomach made it hard to move my feet or think about anything but the reaction I was going to get from my father. When I came in the kitchen door, Mom was at the table, up to her elbows in flour. She was working on the pies for Thanksgiving. Julie sat opposite Mom at the table, happily stirring a large bowl with a wooden spoon.

"Hi, sweetie," Mom said to me with a big smile. "I'm so glad you're home. I really need your help." Then she noticed the expression on my face. "Uh oh. What happened?"

"Nothing. I'm fine," I said, too quickly, too sharply. "What do you need help with?" I didn't want to talk about it, especially in front of Julie.

"You're really good at rolling out the pie dough," she said, still looking at me, a slight frown creasing her brow. "Could you do that for me?"

"Okay. Just let me get my coat off and put my stuff in my room."

"Maddie, are you sure you're all right? You look like you've been crying." Mom followed me to the stairs, but I refused to talk or even turn around. "Maybe you'll feel better if you talk about it."

"There's nothing to talk about. I'm fine. I'll be right back." In fact, I did want to talk, to sob, to rant, to rage. If anyone could make me feel better, it was Mom. But I wasn't going to do any of that with Julie around. And I knew that even Mom couldn't cushion the blow my father would deliver when he found out.

I tore through the house to my room and dumped my books on my desk. Even here, I was still trembling, still on the verge of tears, still feeling like my world had come apart at the seams. "It is just one C, a C-plus even," I tried to tell myself. "Almost a B. It shouldn't be that big of a deal. You did really well in everything else. You can still get an A for the class. Why are you taking this so hard?"

I knew perfectly well why. Because my father would never let me hear the end of it. His teasing would be relentless. He would talk about it every day, at every meal, and pound it home that I was less than perfect and I might as well be a complete failure. And I wouldn't be able to go to school to escape him. My only hope was that he would forget about my midterms in the midst of all the Thanksgiving preparations.

Back in the kitchen, I rolled out pie dough while my mother and Julie kept up their banter about all the cooking that was about to happen. I focused on getting the dough smoothly and evenly into the pie plates, and I pushed them toward Julie so she could add the filling. I didn't contribute to the conversation about who liked marshmallows on the sweet potatoes. Who would want the drumstick. What to wish for on the wishbone. When we would put up the Christmas tree.

At last, Mom sighed and said, "Well, I guess I'd better start on dinner for tonight. You girls set the table, please." While I laid down placemats and napkins on the table, Julie followed behind me, carefully arranging silverware at each place. I was putting the salt and pepper shakers in front of my father's place when Julie said as if she had just thought of it, "Hey, did you get your midterm grades today? I got mine. Dad's been asking about that all week. I can't wait to tell him I got all A's and get him off my back."

I stared daggers at my little sister for a long moment. "Thanks for bringing that up," I hissed finally. Julie was just a freshman. Her classes were easy. I knew because I had sailed through them two years before. Before honors classes. Before expectations were ratcheted up so high. Before every grade was a life-or-death matter. Before my only goal became getting out of Graverton.

Now, not only was my father going to berate me for a C in chemistry, but he was also going to be able to hold Julie up as a shining example of how easy it is to get straight A's. I was doomed. Without another word, I left Julie to finish setting the table alone and retreated to our room. There, I curled up on my bed, trying to think of ways I could get out of dinner. There were precious few alternatives. I could say I wasn't hungry or I didn't feel well. But then Mom would make a fuss, and

I might not be able to leave the house at all over break. I could say I'd been invited to a friend's house, but who would believe that? What friend? Where does she live? When will you be back? I had no escape.

My father was almost always home by six o'clock. I heard him come in, but I stayed in my room until Mom called me to the table. When I came into the dining room, Mom was putting a platter of spaghetti and meatballs on the table, and Trip was already sitting at his place, gazing hungrily at the food. At the head of the table, my father and Julie were locked in a hug. He was smiling and saying, "I'm so proud of you, JuJuBe. My little girl is smart, just like me." Seeing me, his smile changed ever so slightly, but enough for me to notice that instead of pride, his expression had morphed into gleeful anticipation. "And where have you been? Everybody's been asking about you." I slid into my seat without answering.

His smile didn't fade as he pulled out his own chair and made a great show of sitting as if it were the first time he hadn't been on his feet all day. Still looking at me as he spread his napkin over his lap with a flourish, he said, "So your sister tells me she got A's on all her midterm tests. How did you do?"

"I got an A on my trig exam," I ventured, taking the spaghetti platter from Mom, who beamed at me proudly.

She said, "That's the one you were worried about, right? Good job."

As I was serving myself, my father interrupted. "Madeline, you are making a mess. Set the platter down and use two hands." When I had enough spaghetti, I handed the plate across the table to Julie. She avoided eye contact with me.

"I should hope you got an A after all the time you spent on it. What about your other classes?"

"A's in French and history," I mumbled, twirling some of the pasta onto my fork. This was one of my favorite dishes from my mother's kitchen, but I was having a really hard time swallowing. Chewing carefully, I mumbled, "I got a C-plus in chemistry."

"How many times do I have to tell you not to talk with your mouth full?" my father demanded. "You got a what in chemistry?"

I whispered the words again, and even though I said them as softly as I could, it sounded to me as if they echoed loud and long throughout the room, followed by a deafening silence.

"A C? How could you get a C in chemistry?" And so it began. "Chemistry is so easy! Acids and bases and solutions. You just do experiments and write down what you think will happen, and then you watch what happens and write that down. A baby could do it."

"There's a little more to chemistry than acids and bases," I said, not even trying to keep the impatient edge out of my voice. "And experiments are a lot harder than that."

"You just have to be able to follow directions. Measure stuff into test tubes, hold it over the Bunsen burner, make sure it doesn't blow up. Can't you follow directions by now?"

"This was a test, not lab work. It's not baby stuff; it's hard. Anyway, it was a C-PLUS, so it isn't that bad. I can still get an A for the semester."

"Oh, chemistry is hard for you, is it? Why didn't you say so?"

"It's hard for everybody, not just me," I said defensively. "My teacher told me most of the class did badly. And I can bring my grade up by the end of the semester."

"Can you?" He was still smiling, but his voice took on a different tone, one that I was all too familiar with, one that put me on alert but never fully prepared me for what was to come.

Over the next few days, my father took every opportunity that presented itself, and created a few on his own, to remind me and everyone else that I didn't have straight A's for the term.

When Aunt Elaine and Uncle Ron came for Thanksgiving dinner, they heard all about it. When Mom took Julie and me Christmas shopping, my father asked if I was sure I should go. Shouldn't I be working on my chemistry homework? When he was mixing himself a cocktail, he said, "Hey, Mad Dog, watch me. See how easy it is to measure and mix things carefully? That's how you do it when you do chemistry experiments."

By the time Thanksgiving break was over, I was dying to get back to school.

Once at school, I was torn between wanting to get into the Christmas spirit and needing to make sure my grades didn't slip even a little. It was pretty stressful, but eventually, the holiday spirit took over. After all, I'd always loved Christmas, the carols, the shopping, the specials on television, the cookies and candy, the decorations, everything. And my father stopped harping on my chemistry grade.

In fact, his whole demeanor changed, mostly because he liked Christmas, too. He played Christmas albums on the stereo, he wanted to ride around town to look at Christmas lights, and he took Trip to visit Santa. He even decided we should have a Christmas Eve party at our house, something we'd never done before.

"You kids can invite some of your friends if you want," he suggested. "We'll make it an open house. People will stop by for a little while or a long time, and we'll just have hors d'oeuvres out."

Around dinner time, our house was full of people. My parents' friends, the neighbors, Aunt Elaine and Uncle Ron, and some of the other executives from Cutler Enterprises. As I helped my mom fill another tray of my father's favorite shrimp puffs to take to the table, Julie came into the kitchen.

"Daddy's looking for you," she said to me. "He sent me to find you."

I looked at my mother with the question in my eyes. Why? But she didn't seem to know either and said, "Go ahead, honey.

I'll finish up with these trays and be right behind you."

Instead of the fun, festive Christmas spirit I had felt just a few minutes earlier, a heavy sense of dread and anxiety loomed over me now. What did my father want with me? What was he going to do with all these people here?

I found him in the living room, with all our guests gathered around him, seemingly waiting for me. "There she is!" he cried out as everyone turned to look at me. Any casual observer would think he was smiling at me in a proud, fatherly way. But what I saw in his face was that half-sneer, that self-satisfied grin, that I-am-about-to-get-you-good look I knew so well.

My stomach felt as knotted and tangled as a pile of holiday ribbons in the middle of the floor on Christmas morning. As he waved me closer to him, he began his speech. "So, my daughter here got her midterm grades right before Thanksgiving. It's her junior year, and we've got to be thinking about colleges now, right, Maddie? So now that I know how you're doing in school, I thought I should get you something special for Christmas. Here you go, Mad Dog. Open it."

With a flourish to impress his audience, he handed me a flat rectangular box wrapped in festive paper with elaborate bows. I stood holding my gift, looking into his eyes and silently pleading with him not to do this to me. Whatever was in that box, it was not "something special" to reward me for good grades. That I knew for sure. I wanted to run out of the room and throw the unopened present into the trash.

"You heard me, Madeline. Open it. Everybody's waiting." My father took a drag from his cigarette. "Go on."

Suddenly eager to get it over with, I pulled hard on the ribbon until it broke, and I tossed it to one side. Then I ripped right through the elves and Santas on the wrapping paper to reveal the words on the box beneath.

My First Chemistry Set.

A little blond, blue-eyed boy and a little dark-haired girl with perfect, straight white teeth looked ridiculously happy to be playing with kid-sized plastic test tubes and tiny beakers that held brightly colored liquid. There was a little yellow funnel and some long blue sticks for stirring. Hours of educational fun! the box declared. Dozens of experiments to perform!

My father had played practical jokes on me before, so I don't know why I was so surprised and hurt. He'd just never come up with anything quite so cruel or done it in front of so large an audience. The worst part was I found myself on the verge of tears yet again. It was just so mean. Humiliating me in front of everyone! On Christmas Eve! I was completely crushed.

"Don't you like it? I thought it would help. You did say chemistry was hard," my father said as he blew his cigarette smoke into my face. The awful smell hung in the air. He looked at our guests with mock confusion, eyebrows raised. "I don't think she likes it. I just wanted to make sure she didn't fail the class."

"Oh, Paul," was all my mother could manage to say.

Without looking at my father, I set the box under the tree and fled to the kitchen. My intention was to get myself something to take to my room, where I would stay for the rest of the night. "Oh, hey, Mad Dog, while you're in there, grab me another beer, will you?" I heard him call after me. "Or better yet, mix up some martinis. That's like chemistry. It'll be good practice. And if you do flunk out of high school, you can always work as a bartender!" At least I was alone in the kitchen, where no one could see me shaking with anger and frustration and despair. Someone turned the stereo back up, so I could no longer hear the conversation in the living room. He was probably laughing and telling his friends I couldn't take a joke.

Finally, with a deep breath, I brought the sobs under control. Just a year and a half to go. Then I'd be in college, gone from here, away from my father.

PART FIVE

1998

23

Dear Ginny,

I wish there was some way I could reach out to Paul and ask him why he doesn't appreciate you. You are beautiful and kind, intelligent and compassionate, nurturing and loving. I hate that your affection is wasted on someone who can't see that. You told me the story of your courtship with so much longing and wistfulness I can see that you want to return to that state in your marriage. It's so hard for me to watch him when we are all together, belittling you in his subtle way that everyone else seems to find so funny, but I can tell it hurts you. I wish I had the guts to speak up for you.

But if I were to say anything to Paul, it would seem suspicious. Why would I notice how another man treats his wife? Why would a friend (a male friend at that) be so familiar with the workings of your marriage? Why would I care so much about your feelings? Our friendship would be exposed, in danger. Nothing we've done breaks your wedding vows or mine, of course, but I don't know if your husband or my wife would see it that way. So, I watch silently and hope that our meetings and correspondence help in some small way. I know it helps me.

I wonder if Paul knows what a good job you're doing with your daughters. They are both lovely. You tell me how well they are both doing in school, how smart they are. I can see for myself how pretty they are. I know you say they don't look like you, but I can see you in both of them. They seem very happy, which I think is the most important thing at their age.

Can we have lunch again sometime soon? I prefer to talk with you in person, to get immediate answers to my questions, *to see your face when you respond. One lunch every few months doesn't really seem like enough, but I know it's what you can give me at this point.*

Let me know when you are free.

J.

So there it was. Proof. An answer. My mother had had an admirer. It didn't sound like she had been unfaithful as of when this letter was written. There were about twenty, maybe twenty-five, letters in this shoebox, all addressed to Virginia Burton at a post office box in Brockport, a town a few miles away and even smaller than Graverton. The date on this first letter was from 1969, a couple of years before Trip was born, around the time she bought those wonderful shoes. The fact that she set up a post office box in her maiden name told me she had taken pains to conceal this correspondence. She must have replied as well.

And now, so many more questions tumbled over each other, trying to get to the front of my mind. How had this affair begun? How long had it gone on? Where had they met? How had they arranged for this correspondence? When had she decided to give "J" more than her company or more than correspondence? What had made her fall off the fidelity wagon? And just who was J anyhow? My parents had lots of friends, and many of their names started with J—Johns, Jims, Jacks, Joes, and even a couple of Jeffs and a Jake, if I remembered right. And those were just the people I could think of off the top of my head after all this time. J could easily be someone I had never even met. But it did seem like he lived here in Graverton, or at least he had in 1969. Who could he be? So many questions. I hoped the rest of the letters contained some answers. Carrying the box to my old bedroom, I felt the same childishly guilty exhilaration I used to experience when I was doing something forbidden, like stealing a cookie right before dinner, reading under my covers long after lights out, or lifting a ten-dollar bill out of Paul's wallet. Even though there was no risk of getting caught now, I still felt very nervous. What would I find in this box, in these letters? Was I ready to know the truth?

Dear Ginny,

I saw you walking in the rain a few days ago. I think you were on the way home from shopping. I wanted to honk and wave and say hello. I wanted to stop you and talk to you, to look into your eyes, to hear your voice, even for just a moment. I didn't because I'm so clumsy and tongue-tied unless it's just you and me. I'm afraid my feelings will quickly become apparent to anyone who might happen to see. I worry that it shows in my face. And I am not yet sure how to define our friendship. So all I did was slow down and take a good look at how pretty you were in that blue raincoat, the damp air making your hair even more curly.

You should know that I don't just admire your physical beauty. You have a beauty of spirit that draws me to you and makes me want to engage you in conversation just so I can be close to your warmth and grace. We had that lovely lunch together as friends, in which we learned how much we have in common. It did help to talk—you are so understanding!—and I really look forward to having that chance again.

I hope we can see each other again soon. I know you don't believe this, but it is enough for me to spend time alone with you. That is how good you made me feel that day, how much I covet your attention. Please tell me where we can meet and when.

I look forward to your answer.
J.

I smiled in spite of myself. Yes, my mother was very pretty. I liked knowing that someone else had noticed, had tried to make her see it for herself, had laid out all the reasons she was beautiful. Someone wanted to build her up instead of tearing her down.

At the same time, it broke my heart to realize how badly she needed someone to say those things to her. I remembered watching her put on that blue raincoat whenever it looked like rain and being so envious of the color and the flattering style. I doubted that Paul had ever told her she looked nice in it. I remember him commenting on my raincoat, though. In those days, I wore a bright yellow shapeless hooded slicker that Mom bought a size too big so I could "grow into it" and make it last more than one season before handing it down to Julie. My father had often said it made me look like a walking banana and always offered to help me peel it off. When it came time for me to buy a coat for the rainy days in Seattle, I shopped for a stylish one like Mom's, remembering how she could look so pretty even in the pouring rain.

Dear Ginny,

You're right. Divorce is becoming more socially acceptable, even fashionable, these days. It's just that it's not acceptable to me. I know how it would affect my children, and I can't do that to them. There is still some stigma attached to divorce, and I don't want to go through it or put my kids through it. You may be thinking that I'm afraid of my wife getting all my money if I were the one to end the marriage. I have to admit, that is a consideration. I worked hard to get where I am, and I don't want to lose everything. So, I continue to try and make it work.

You said you had your reasons for not getting a divorce from Paul. I think I can guess: money is an issue for you, too. You married into a rich family that has a lot of influence in this town, and it has worked to your benefit in a lot of ways. You live in that beautiful house, and you want for nothing. You have two beautiful daughters, and they are having a happy childhood. Most people around here appreciate the jobs that Cutler Enterprises provides, and there is a lot of respect that comes with that. It would be hard to give that up.

But I also think there is another reason. Paul is mean. Most people who know him think he's very funny, that he has a great sense of humor, that he's just a wisecracker. But anyone who paid close attention to his jokes would see the cruelty in them. I think you think he would be vindictive if you tried to leave. And with his influence in Graverton (and his mother's, for that matter), that could make things very hard for you. So, I think you think your best option is to hang in there.

So, we both feel trapped in our marriages. Believe it or not, it does help to know that there is someone else feeling like I do. And it is helping me to write to you. I hope it can continue.

Fondly,

J.

What J had written in this letter didn't surprise me. In fact, it confirmed what I had always suspected, long before I knew about this affair. Even if my parents' marriage hadn't been a particularly happy one or had gone through rocky periods, my mother would never have considered a divorce. Partly because she took those wedding vows seriously, partly because of "how it would look," she stayed with Paul and did everything she could to cope. However, J had touched on another reason. My father didn't like to lose, and he would have made it very hard for her to go. I wondered if either of them ever figured out just how right they were, how truly vindictive Paul could be.

I made mental notes of the clues to J's identity contained in this letter. He was married, too, with children. And he had some measure of wealth. Clearly, J and his wife moved in the same social circles, attended the same parties and events, knew many of the same people as my parents. Still, it could be almost any one of my parents' friends.

Dear Ginny,

Thank you for telling me the story of your first date with Paul. Of course you fell in love with a handsome man who made you laugh. Of course you were flattered by his attention. Of course you knew that marrying into the Cutler family would be a welcome break away from your own working-class roots. It sounds like your marriage made you very happy in its early years.

I think I'm a little sad for you, though. Your story tells me that Paul knows how to use his sense of humor in a gentle and loving, even self-deprecating way, that he didn't always give his jokes such a cruel bite. I wonder why he lost that. What made him start wielding his wisecracks like they were weapons? I have heard him joke about his friends behind their backs, and it makes me curious what he might be saying about me when I'm not around. You're definitely not the only one on the receiving end of his jokes.

I enjoyed telling you our story, too. You're such a good listener, and your questions made me remember details that had slipped away from my memory over the years, things about my wife that I had forgotten, reasons why I loved her then and still do now. My marriage was happy in the beginning, just like yours. I have high hopes that it can be again, as long as we both remember the good things. We have drifted apart slowly in so many small ways that neither of us noticed until there was this chasm between us. I think that happens to a lot of people, and lately, the trend is to just stop working at it, to say, "Oh, well," and just get a divorce. You might be surprised (or maybe not) how many men in our social circle joke about trading in for a newer model. I never know whether to take them seriously.

In any case, you and I have both said we don't want to give up on our marriages. So, let's keep talking and helping each other try to find our way back.

J.

I knew my parents' first date story well: when my mom was working her way through college by waiting tables, and Paul stopped by the diner with some friends late one night, just before closing. All four of them noticed the pretty blond waitress with the breathtaking gray eyes, but my father was the one most smitten. He did his best to make her laugh with questions about the menu.

"I would become a vegetarian, but I think it would be a big missed steak."

"Do you have escargot? I don't like fast food."

"I would tell you another vegetable joke, but they are all too corny."

He still told some of those corny jokes when I was young.

The way the story went, my mother was exhausted at the end of her shift and really not in the mood for comedy that night, especially since these clowns were keeping her at work even later than normal. But, in the name of keeping her job and getting a good tip, she swallowed her annoyance and gave the young men her brightest smile, filing away the one-liners because they would make a good story to tell her friends later.

"He was memorable even before he left me a huge tip," Mom would say.

The guys knew they had failed to impress the pretty waitress, but three of them were happy just to have gotten a late-night cheeseburger and shake. Then there was Paul, the one who didn't like to lose. He had to go back to that diner to see that waitress again and find a way to win her over. When he related the story, he liked to say, "Hey, the food was really good at that place. I thought maybe she was doing some of the cooking, too. But now I know why they had her waiting tables instead of working in the kitchen," punctuated by an exaggerated eye roll. Mom always responded by laughing, playfully slapping his arm, and saying, "I cook even better than that guy at the diner!" He'd give her a quick kiss and then, with eyes wide and a comical look of fear on his face, shake his head behind her back.

No matter how he really felt about the diner food, he kept returning to the place, always sitting at my mother's table, always joking with her, always leaving a big tip. Finally, it was enough to get my mother to agree to go on a date with him. Her only condition: they couldn't go to a restaurant. "I've already heard all your diner jokes. Use all that creativity and imagination and come up with something different and fun," she challenged him.

At this point in the story, Paul would grin and describe the carnival he took her to: "Rickety rides where she would have to hold my hand because she was really scared, silly games where I could show her how strong I was, and very cheap food. It was perfect. I still take all my first dates there."

He also liked to brag about winning her a teddy bear. "Threw that baseball right through the stack of milk bottles. The bear was so big it almost didn't fit in my back seat." Once, I asked Mom what ever happened to that bear. "Oh, I kept it for a while, but every time I looked at it, it just wasn't as cute as I remembered," she sighed. "Then I think it got a tear in it at some point, and all the stuffing started coming out. It just fell apart, so I got rid of it."

My parents didn't talk much about any other part of their romance. I knew that when they met, Paul had already graduated from college and started working for his father, while my mother still had two years of school to go. Paul tried to convince her to marry him instead of getting her degree, but Ginny stood firm. She wanted to finish what she started. Their wedding, which Paul's parents paid for because my Burton grandparents could hardly afford the lavish event the Cutlers wanted, took place less than a month after my mother graduated.

I wondered if there were elements of Paul and Ginny's romance that J knew about and I did not. Maybe Mom had shared those stories with me, and I had forgotten them or just not paid attention. She must have talked to her friend about Paul's nature and its evolution from warm and witty to stinging and sarcastic. Would she have shared those things with me if I had been listening? The possibility nagged at me.

Dear Ginny,

I'm sorry you couldn't meet me last week. The girls are your priority, as they should be. I hope Maddie and Julie are feeling better. Chickenpox is just as miserable for parents as it is for kids, especially when you have to keep a child from scratching that miserable itch. When my daughter had it, I kept saying I wanted to buy stock in the calamine lotion company, my wife was going through it so fast. One of the things I admire most about you is that you are such a good mother. Your daughters are very lucky.

I wanted to tell you that I took your suggestion and planned a special night out with my wife. I'm going to take her to dinner at the place where we had our first date, and there's a classic film festival in the city where we can see a movie from those days. It won't be A Star Is Born, which I'm pretty sure is the first film we saw together, but I'm hoping whatever we see will stir the right memories. Wish me luck. I should have lots to tell you when we meet again.

J.

Now, I had chills. I remembered having chickenpox when I was little. I had itched furiously, and Mom had been so patient in trying to keep me from scratching. Using a mountain of cotton balls, she gently dabbed that smelly pink stuff on each one of those angry red bumps on my face, arms, and chest.

But what gave me such a jolt about the memory of chickenpox was that I also recalled watching *20,000 Leagues under the Sea*, the Kirk Douglas version, on television. I was wrapped in a blanket on the living room couch, snuggled close to Mom, even before the scary giant squid part. During commercials, she told me about James Mason.

"He plays the villain in this movie, but look how handsome he is." She whispered, as if we were actually in a movie theater. "He's such a good actor. The same year as this movie, he was nominated for the Best Actor Oscar for another movie called *A Star Is Born*. That's not really a movie for kids. But it's pretty good. So, maybe we'll watch that when you're older."

I remember being a little puzzled about her obsession with this James Mason guy. He was kind of familiar, like maybe I'd seen him before on some TV show that I couldn't really recall. But Mom seemed kind of preoccupied with him that night. Being sick, I was kind of sleepy, so I tuned her out to pay attention to the movie until I dozed off.

In the past, whenever I thought about that time I had chickenpox, I only remembered how miserable I was, how frustrating it was not to scratch, how sad I was about missing the chance to be outside playing. I hadn't given much thought to my mother staying by my side the whole time, nor had I considered that she might be giving up anything.

Dear Ginny,

I understand why you feel like you can't get away for lunch for a while. I'll wait and be satisfied with getting your letters. However, I think you may be overreacting to Paul's teasing in this case. His comments about your new shoes and how much they cost don't necessarily mean he's paying closer attention to your household budgeting or how you allocate the money he gives you. On the other hand, if you're uncomfortable spending your cash, I can pick up the tab when we have lunch. Nobody keeps track of my expense account. It's one of the biggest advantages of being an executive.

If we had gotten together, I could've told you about my date with my wife. In spite of my careful planning, it didn't go very well. Back when we were dating, it seemed to me that she ate her meals with pleasure, enjoying her food, unconcerned with calories, fat, cholesterol, or weight gain. As much as she liked being out at a fancy restaurant—she commented several times on the "ambiance" and what good things she had heard about the place—she refused to order anything more than a salad. And she just nibbled at it. I was a little angry and frustrated that she wouldn't have an actual dinner at such a nice place. But she simply declared that she was on a diet, and that was that.

At the classic film festival, we saw *To Catch a Thief*, which is still good even if you've seen it several times. On the way out of the theater, I said something about wishing we could have seen *A Star Is Born*. She asked why. Apparently, my memory is faulty, and that's not the first movie I took her to after all. I could have sworn it was, but she was nearly in tears, insisting it was not. So, in spite of my efforts to be romantic, she ended the evening upset with me. And now she is barely speaking to me.

Now, do you understand why I wanted to see you so badly? I would love your advice about what I should do now.

J.

Oh, those shoes again. Something that made my mother feel so beautiful, so happy, had broken down into something that instead made her so unhappy and even paranoid. No wonder she stopped wearing them. No wonder she kept J's letters in this box. What happened to the shoes themselves, I wondered. Did she throw them away? Would she have put them on one last time, for one last dance around the room, before she let them go? I tried to picture her with a sad smile, looking at her feet, turning them this way and that as if she were trying on the shoes for the first time. Maybe even looking at herself in the full-length mirror in an attempt to reimagine the young mother who had delighted so much in that frivolous splurge. When did that woman disappear? How did I fail to notice her happiness slipping away?

Paul teasing her about the shoes seemed to have had a somewhat sinister undercurrent for Mom, too. Not only had he given her grief about how much they cost, but she had begun to worry that he was suspicious of how she spent her money. Was she being paranoid? Had Paul really started paying that much attention to her budgeting? In my memory, Paul was the one who spent lavishly. I always thought of Mom as the frugal one, based on her own childhood in a family with never quite enough. That's why those Ferragamo shoes were such a wild departure for her. It could be that's exactly what triggered Paul's suspicions, too.

Dear Ginny,

While I love being able to put my thoughts in writing to you, it's just not the same as talking to you face to face. You are kind and understanding, and looking into your eyes makes me even more eager to share my feelings with you. There are few friends I can talk to about how difficult things are, but knowing that you understand and you are having some of the same issues really helps.

That's why I took a chance on reaching out to you in the first place, and I'm glad I did. I was afraid I was overstepping the polite boundaries of our social circle, but I've noticed that you look so unhappy lately. Every time I see you, you're trying hard to smile, to keep up a brave face. I don't know why it's not plain to everyone else that it's an act. You are so clearly hurting, and the reason is so obvious, as is the reason you can't do anything about it. I just hope our correspondence will help you as much as it has been helping me.

That doesn't mean I don't want to see you. I do very much. I will be happy to meet you whenever and wherever you can. Just let me know, and I will be there. In the meantime, write to me whenever you want. I will always be listening.

J.

So much in this letter was devastating. The thought of my mother putting up a wall of courage and hiding her heartbreak behind it. The realization that someone I didn't know had not only seen and acknowledged that wall, but had also decided to try and tear it down. The slow, creeping realization that I had stood outside that wall my whole life and never bothered to try and see what was behind it.

I began to feel as if my mind and heart were both bursting at the seams, full as they were of new upsetting information and new unanswerable questions. I couldn't read anymore tonight.

Things started happening really fast after I found those letters. I spent my free time cleaning out the house with an almost violent energy and purpose that drove me so I wouldn't think about what I learned by reading J's letters. Every morning, I just kept telling myself that the sooner I finished all this, the sooner I could be rid of the house and the memories and never look back. That this story I had just discovered did not and should not have any effect on me or my life at all. My parents had both made their choices, and they had both lived with the repercussions. By leaving town, I had gotten myself free of them, and I didn't intend to shoulder the weight of that burden now.

After the days I spent frantically cleaning the house, in the evening, I would find myself making my way to Derek's house more often than not. He cooked delicious dinners for me and told me how his restaurant plan was shaping up. We never talked about how anxious I was to leave Graverton or about what I read in the letters I found. We didn't discuss what would happen when I finally went back to Seattle or whether I'd be around for his restaurant opening. We just made each other feel better in the moment.

On the nights I stayed home, I took the shoebox to bed with me to read more of J's words to my mother, the comfort and compliments and encouragement and consolation she seemed to crave but never receive from my father. Every so often, J would mention an event that jarred a memory loose from the cobwebbed recesses of my childhood. That time Frank Nichols was pulled over for drunk driving after a party my parents' whole social circle had attended. When a woman ran for mayor of Graverton, almost unheard of at the time, and her campaign was a colossal failure. A fire that destroyed Brockport High School and the rumors, never proven, that it was started by a rival high school's football team to force a forfeit in the game that would determine who represented the division in the state championships. My mother had talked to her friend about all these things over lunches and in secret notes. From what I could gather from his half of the correspondence, they had been lively and engaging discussions. She'd had opinions and perspectives, theories and thoughts, but I had never heard what they were. I'm pretty sure I know why she didn't bring up her opinions at home. I remember my father laughing till he cried when he heard about Valerie Glass declaring her candidacy for mayor. Something about how the hat she would throw into the ring would be wide-brimmed and floppy and covered with flowers, probably bright pink. For some reason, his own joke had struck him as enormously funny. It only made him laugh harder when his seven-year-old daughter had spoken up in the woman's defense, saying there was no reason to believe she wouldn't make a fantastic mayor.

"Oh, Madeline, please stop," he had said, wiping the tears from his face. "You're making me laugh so hard I might hurt myself."

I remember kind of wishing he would.

But I have no memory of my mother saying anything on the topic, just listening with a passive face as Paul belittled Mrs. Glass for even thinking she could compete in the race. When he ranted that the Brockport police should be trying harder to find the real culprit behind that fire instead of harassing some innocent teenagers. When he declared that anyone who thought Frank Nichols had a drinking problem probably had one themselves. Mom never said a word. Or if she did, I wasn't listening. I wished I had asked for her opinion more often, found out her perspective, listened to her reasoning. It made me very sad to realize I had no idea what she thought about any of these things.

Now, alone in my childhood bedroom, I was finally getting to know my mother. With tears stinging in my eyes and a tightening in my throat, I read a third-party account of a life I never knew she had.

"... Frank may be lucky he was caught before he got home. You raise a really good point, and I wonder if you're the only mother who thinks of the babysitters getting driven home by fathers like Frank who have had too much to drink."

"... I guess it remains to be seen whether women will really begin to have an impact on the political landscape, locally or nationally. I like the way you think about how a woman's intuition and perspective could get more things done. Maybe Shirley Chisholm was just ahead of her time."

"... As a former high school football player myself, I understand the passion that might drive a boy to commit a crime in the name of helping the team. That doesn't excuse it, of course. And I understand your concern about what it says that football is that important to the team, the students, the town, and the whole region. It does seem to have gotten out of control on some levels. Yet, I still think team sports are pretty important ..."

I read voraciously until I got to the one letter that ultimately confirmed my theory—that my mother's close friendship with J had become something much more.

Dear Ginny,

It should not have happened, but I refuse to say I'm sorry that it did. This has been building for a long time now, this undeniable attraction between us. You know it as well as I do. We started as friends who just needed to talk to each other and see each other through a difficult period in our lives. I tried to deny to myself that I was starting to see you in a different light, as a woman and not just as a good friend. So, I take full responsibility for what happened the other night.

That said, I wish you would reconsider breaking off our correspondence. I understand why you believe it's necessary, that you don't think we can return to the place where we were, to go back to being just friends, now that this has happened. I would really like to try. Yes, there is a risk that it will happen again, but if we are aware, we can make sure it doesn't. I will miss you so much if we no longer have contact of any kind. I still need your friendship and understanding as much as ever. On the other hand, I know you will have trouble believing me when I say we can make sure it will not happen again.

It was lovely.

Thank you for the time you have given me. I'll have to make excuses to my wife about why we have to miss the social events where I might run into you because they will be too difficult for me to attend, at least for now. Know that I am thinking about you, and I wish you well.

J.

That appeared to have been the last letter he wrote or at least the last one she kept. For so many years, these letters had been hiding in that shoe box. Until Paul found them. As I sat on my bed, holding that last letter, I let my sadness and regret tumble over me. I murmured my apologies to Mom and even begged her for some sign, some help, something, anything, that would tell me what to do now. I fell into a dark and dreamless sleep and woke with no answers.

As I tried to speed through the process of cleaning out the house, things were moving quickly for Trip, too. His new lawyer managed to get his case separated from Julie's, and Trip jumped at the second settlement offer he got. With all that money, his gaze moved to bigger horizons, and all that nonsense about him keeping the Harding Street house and living here was forgotten. No, no, now he could pursue bigger ambitions, much bigger, he told me. He would make enough money, eventually, to resurrect Cutler Enterprises and return the company and the town to its former glory. This money was the break he'd been needing!

I heard all this over dinner, which I cooked, in the kitchen on Harding Street. With his bruises mostly gone, broken bones healed, and stitches removed, he was out of the hospital and on his way to bigger, better adventures. He came to say his goodbyes and to make sure he had everything he wanted out of the house.

"As soon as I had that check in hand, I told my boss I was out of there," he told me. "And then I told my landlord the same thing. The bastard kept my security deposit, but I don't care. I don't need it."

"So, where are you going?" I asked.

He was headed to New York City, he declared, now that he could afford to live there. He had a college buddy who would let him crash on the couch while he looked for his own place. All I could do was hug him (carefully, since some of his bruises were still tender) and wish him luck, even though my heart was breaking for the disappointments he was going to slam up against before he knew it.

For his part, Henry decided to take Anthony Marossi's advice and reject the first settlement offer. He had a much stronger case: a pregnant woman, still hospitalized, still unconscious, possibly unable to walk or worse, and in constant danger of losing her baby. A young son who didn't understand having to be away from his mother. A father who would eventually be caring for all three of them on a teacher's salary. The other driver didn't have much money himself, but he was well insured, and Anthony seemed certain that they would pay more to stay out of court.

And then the case took an even worse turn.

PART SIX

1981 – 1992

24

Mom stood in the middle of the room, hands on her hips, nodding with approval. Just a few hours before, it had been a cinderblock box with a cold linoleum floor, a bare mattress on an institutional metal bed frame, a wood veneer desk with a bright green plastic chair, all of it illuminated by a blinking, buzzing fluorescent light fixture and infiltrated by an unpleasantly musty smell, like wet cardboard. But Mom and I had worked tirelessly to unpack my clothes, bedding, curtains, throw rugs, a small lamp, and a few posters, and the difference was amazing. Thanks to Mom, everything—from the closet to the top of my dresser to the stuffed animals on my bed—was sparkling clean, organized, and tidy, ready for me to begin my new life as a college student. It looked cozy and comfortable, like a place I would happily spend the next nine months. There was even a wonderfully homey smell, probably from the familiar laundry detergent Mom used to wash all my new sheets. For the moment, I tried not to think about the hard work ahead of me, living up to the good grades and test scores that I brought from high school and that got me admitted to my first-choice college. Instead, I was looking forward to getting to know the other girls in the dorm—who knew nothing about me yet, nothing about my family, nothing about where I came from, nothing about what a weird crybaby my high school classmates thought I was—then exploring the campus and the town more closely, and really finally being on my own. Classes would start soon enough, and I'd have to focus on exams and term papers, but right now, I was too excited to think about how hard my course load might be.

"It's been a while since I had my own room," I said with a smile. "I think I'm going to like it."

"Do you think you'll need a fan?" Mom asked. "It could stay warm here well into October. And I don't think this building is air-conditioned. We could go into town and get you one if you want."

"I might, but I can get one later if it gets unbearable." I was still looking around the room, in awe of having my very own space again.

"Okay, if you're sure." Mom glanced at her watch. "I, uh, well, I guess my work here is done." She paused and looked around again. "If I get on the road now, I'll be home in time for dinner."

You mean in time to make dinner, I thought but didn't say out loud. Paul had opted not to come along on this trip, perhaps the most important one of my life. He had scheduled a golf game this weekend, saying he needed to work out a better deal with one of his suppliers and the guy loved golf, and that was, apparently, not worth giving up to see his oldest child off to college. I told myself that he had actually done me a huge favor. He would have found some way to ruin this day for me, to embarrass me in front of all these new people, or just to say something that would make me angry. Or worse, cry. At the very least, he would have tried to smoke in here, leaving his stench in this room for weeks. No, it was definitely better this way, but I resented him just the same.

Strangely, though, when Mom said she would be leaving, I realized with a jolt that I hadn't considered what it was going to be like without *her*. Sure, I had this fantastic vision of myself on my own, a college freshman with the world at my feet, without my father breathing down my neck all the time. I just hadn't thought about not having my mom, either. This dorm room wasn't likely to stay this neat and tidy without her. Even more than that, I suddenly knew how much I was going to need her encouragement, her reminders of my own abilities, her comforting advice. Sooner or later.

It brought me up short for a moment, trying to imagine her going back home without me. What her days would be like now. Would she spend her time differently, with only two kids at home? I really had no idea what she would do. And that was because I had no idea what she had done before.

When I looked at her, my mind still saw the beautiful, slender, blond woman who took me clothes shopping, who baked me special treats, who had to reach down when she cupped my cheek in her palm. Now we stood eye to eye, and I noticed the softly sagging skin under her chin, the deepening worry lines on her forehead, the dark spots spreading across her cheeks. This is the Mom I would remember when I got homesick or when I needed someone to build up my confidence or celebrate with me.

She stood in the middle of the room, studying my face with an expression of both sorrow and satisfaction. I knew she was proud of me, and I knew she would miss me. But I also knew that Paul, Trip, and Julie would keep her plenty busy even without me around. Her life probably wouldn't change nearly as much as mine. I didn't want her to worry, to have any concern that I wouldn't be fine, to have any reason to report anything even remotely negative to my father. Most of all, I just couldn't have her tell him I cried.

So, I broke into a big smile. "Okay," I said brightly. "I'll walk you out to the car."

"Don't forget to take your key," she reminded me, nodding her head toward the new university-mascot-adorned key chain on the dresser. "You'll need to make sure you keep the door locked when you're not here."

We made the walk to the parking lot behind the dorm without a word. She linked her arm through mine as if she wanted to hold on to me, however lightly, for just a few more minutes. Standing next to the now empty car that only a few hours ago held everything I wanted to have with me in my new life, we stood facing each other, neither of us daring to speak. Finally, I broke the silence.

"Thanks for your help," I said, gathering her into my arms, feeling the soft fabric of her blouse, breathing in the scent of Chanel No. 5, letting her silky hair fall against my cheek. "I really appreciate it, and I'm glad you were here." While I held her, I felt her silent tears falling onto my shoulder. Without releasing her, I said, "Please don't cry, Mommy. I'm going to be fine."

"I know you are, sweetheart," she said softly. "That's not why I'm crying. I'm so happy for you, starting off on this new phase and building your new life. But I can't help being a little sad, too. I mean, don't you feel just a little bit sad?"

"Of course," I replied, pulling back to look closely at her face. "I won't be seeing you every day anymore. That's going to be hard."

"I've been thinking about something somebody once said to me about turning points like graduations and such: The thing about milestones is that they don't just show you the way to something new. They also mark the journey away from where you've been."

"I get it," I said, nodding. "That's why you're happy and sad at the same time."

"Exactly." With one last long look into my eyes and that familiar, gentle hand reaching out to touch my cheek, Mom stepped back. "Go on back inside and make some new friends." Then she turned toward the car to unlock the door. By the time she looked again, I was walking away.

25

The ten o'clock service was nearly full, but I knew almost everybody. Same church, same people, pretty much my whole life. The dark wood pews, some with cracked seats, were more crowded than usual, with kids home from college like me. The kids were all taller, some of them wider, than they had been when every family in the congregation occupied their own pew. The fragrance of Easter lilies blended with candles, the organ played "Come Ye Faithful, Raise the Strain" as the processional hymn, and the ribboned Easter hats the matrons still wore dotted the sanctuary like colored eggs in a basket. All so familiar after twenty-one Easters here in this church. Would this one be my last?

After the service, as Mom, Trip, and I filed out with the rest of the congregation, I repeated the same phrases over and over: "Happy Easter to you, too."

"Yes, I am in my senior year ... Almost done ... Just a couple more months ... Computer science."

"No, I don't know yet. But I have a few prospects, so we'll see."

"She went to Fort Lauderdale with some friends for her spring break ... No, not this year."

"Okay, I'll tell him you said hello."

We arrived home to find my father sitting in the kitchen smoking a cigarette. From the look of him—unshaven, hair uncombed, not dressed—he hadn't been out of bed for very long.

"Happy Easter!" My mother greeted him with a kiss on his stubbly cheek. "It is almost noon, and I told Elaine we would be eating dinner around one o'clock. That means they could get here at any time, so you might want to go get dressed."

Without any other greeting or acknowledgment, he responded, "Did you let Madeline wear that to church?" At the sink, getting myself a glass of water, I turned to see my father still in his pajamas, frowning at me. Apparently, because of what I was wearing.

"Why wouldn't I? She looks very nice." Mom covered her own Easter outfit with an apron as she began the final stretch in her meal preparation. Forget the fact that I am twenty-one years old and nobody "lets" me wear anything anymore.

"She is wearing pants. To church. On Easter." Clearly, this was making him angry.

"It's a pantsuit. It's very fashionable. You should have seen some of the other kids in church. Jeans. T-shirts. She was better dressed than most people there."

"You guys? I'm right here. Don't talk about me in the third person."

"On Easter? What's the matter with you? The most important Christian holiday, and you thought it was all right to wear pants to church? If your brother can put on a jacket and tie, you can make an effort to wear a skirt." My father always fell back on his ideas of the way things should be, the way it has always been done. He hated it when anyone challenged his cherished norms, no matter how outdated they were.

"You don't even go to church! If it was so important, maybe you should've gotten up for the service." I put my empty glass in the sink. "But now that you mention it, I am going to change my clothes. And put on something comfortable."

In my room, I thought about putting my nightgown back on, just to spite my father. I also had some comfortable sweatpants with me. In the end, though, I decided it wasn't worth it to ruin the holiday dinner for everyone, so I put on a pair of jeans and a blouse. Not what Paul wanted, but also not obvious spite from me and still presentable. I waited till I heard

Aunt Elaine's voice before I went back downstairs.

While I brooded in my room, Mom pulled out all the stops on dinner. The smell was heavenly. The table was set with her best china and crystal and silver, and there was a bouquet of Easter lilies in a delicate cut-glass vase for a centerpiece. Feeling a pang of guilt that I hadn't helped at all, I resolved to clean up after dinner.

Aunt Elaine looked beautiful and stylish, as usual. She and Uncle Ron were in the living room, enjoying the drinks Paul had already poured for them. I saw an open bottle of white wine chilling in the silver wine cooler, so I uncorked it and helped myself. With my expression, I dared my father to say anything.

Mostly, he left me alone through dinner. He was busy bragging about Trip and how well he was doing on the junior varsity baseball team. Trip tried to tell parts of the story, to describe his own accomplishments, but Paul had the stage, and he liked the spotlight too much to share. No mention of Trip's grades. Aunt Elaine and Uncle Ron tried to stay on neutral topics, like the new leader in the Soviet Union and how cold the winter had been. I stayed out of the conversation except to compliment Mom on the dinner. She seemed pleased that we were enjoying it.

It was all pleasant enough. Until dessert.

"Hey, Madeline," my father began, addressing me directly for the first time since we sat down to dinner. "Tell your Aunt Elaine about your job interviews."

I was immediately suspicious. "What about them?" I asked.

"The Mad Dog here is going to make big bucks with this computer science degree she's getting," Paul said, referring to me not only in the third person again but also by the childhood nickname he knew I hated. "All these companies want to hire her and take her away from all this." He gestured around the dining room with his dessert spoon.

"Good for you, honey," Aunt Elaine smiled. "I always knew

you would break out in a big way. Who are you interviewing with?"

Since Aunt Elaine was the one who always encouraged me, always told me how great it was to have a rewarding career, I was eager to tell her about all the opportunities I was exploring. So eager that I let my guard down and started babbling like a brook after a hard rain.

"Lots of exciting things are happening in the tech sector," I said, "and there's so much opportunity. New coding languages are being developed. There is this new program called PageMaker that is going to revolutionize the printing and publishing industry. These Macintosh computers are really challenging IBM in the market. And, of course, there are computer games! It is really hard to decide what I want to do, where I want to focus. I do think the best opportunities are in software development."

"A lot of that is happening out west, right?" Uncle Ron asked. "Are you really thinking of moving so far away?"

"Yeah, the best jobs I'm looking at, they're all on the West Coast," I acknowledged. "I do have one possibility a little closer to here, but it's not as attractive. The money would be about the same, just not very exciting work." I stole a sidelong glance at my mother. She and I had talked a lot about where I would live after college. Or rather, I talked, and she listened without passing judgment or giving me her opinion. I knew she would support whatever I decided, but she didn't have to like it.

"I think you should take the job in Seattle," Paul put in unexpectedly. "If you get it, that is."

"You do?" I was very surprised.

"Based on what I'm hearing here, it pays the most and it will give you the best experience. For when you come back to Cutler Enterprises."

I laughed. "*When* I come back to Cutler Enterprises? Not in the plan, sorry."

Pouring himself another glass of wine, Paul said confidently, "You'll come back here, eventually, to live in Graverton. A few years somewhere else first to get some experience, and then you'll put all this computer know-how to work for our company." He was making declarations, not asking questions, not posing possibilities, not allowing for any uncertainty. Ever since Trip was born, all I ever heard was that the son was the successor, that Trip was the one who would take over. I couldn't recall a single discussion, ever, of me working at the company in any capacity. So, I felt more than a little ambushed.

"I don't think so." Even to my own ears, I sounded more like a thirteen-year-old girl trying to rebel for the first time and not like a confident twenty-one-year-old woman about to set out on her own. "I have absolutely no plans to live here ever again. I never have."

"What are you talking about?" Now, Paul laughed. "Of course you're going to work for me. You have an obligation to this family and to our business. You think I paid all that money for you to go to college so you could work for somebody else? You were an investment in Cutler Enterprises, and I expect a return."

"Where is this coming from?" I exclaimed. "You never said anything about this, ever before! You're always saying Trip will take over when he grows up. There was never any talk of me joining the company. Or Julie, for that matter. And I never wanted to!"

"It's a family business, Madeline. I assumed you understood that was the deal. I'll be in charge till Trip learns the ropes and takes over. With her accounting degree, Julie will watch over the books. I'll hang around long enough to make sure you make us modern with new computer systems. Then I'll retire. And keep tabs on you from the sidelines." Paul settled back in his chair, calmly sipping his wine and looking at me with his devious smile building at the corners of his mouth. "When I took out the loans for your last two years of college, I put them in your name. If you decide not to come back, you can pay them back yourself. I'll only pay them if you're working for me. So, you see, you have to come back."

"No, no, I do not." As I was saying this, I felt my panic rising, with the realization that Paul had devised such a diabolical way to force me to move back to Graverton just beginning to sink in. I couldn't do it. I wouldn't. I had never fit in here, and now that I had seen that there was a whole world out there, I was eager to find a place where I could. I looked desperately at my mother and Aunt Elaine, silently begging them to come to my rescue.

"Paul, you know she's not happy here," Mom said. "We need to let her live her own life. Somewhere she really wants to be."

"And since when has the Cutler family passed its business on to its daughters?" Aunt Elaine sounded disgusted. "I did want to work for our company, but Daddy groomed you for it all your life. And when I did try to contribute, you just made it impossible."

Paul laughed again. "You were the one who made it impossible, Lainey. You didn't understand that there could only be one boss. Madeline will know that. She knows I'm the boss. She's not going to be in charge anyway. She's just going to run our computer systems. You get that, right, Mad Dog? You know I'm the boss."

By now, I was breathless with fury and fear. It was absolutely unbelievable that he had never told me he expected this of me until now. And to threaten me with so much debt to force his will on me was just too much. How could he not have known that it would kill me to have to come back here? My rage roared in my ears, like a fire burning down everything I had worked so hard for, and I had no way to put it out. I almost didn't hear him repeat his last comment.

"Isn't that right, Madeline?" he repeated. "You know I'm the boss."

At that moment, my self-control disintegrated. An all-consuming sense of grief and gloom and outrage washed over me all at once, a tidal wave of doom that crashed into my life and drowned every last ounce of hope I ever had. Without even thinking, I grabbed my wine glass, stood up, toppling my chair behind me, and flung the goblet as hard as I could against the wall. The resulting shattering and the almost musical tinkling sound it made were strangely satisfying, if only for a moment.

"Whoa!" I heard Trip say, almost under his breath, with a hint of admiration in his voice. I had almost forgotten he was even in the room. Everyone else was silent, staring at me in disbelief.

"I'm sorry, Mom," I whispered, falling back into tears yet again. I fled from the dining room, slammed my bedroom door behind me like a spoiled teenager, and began throwing my clothes into my suitcase. Shaking with anger and frustration and shame, I cursed myself for letting Paul get to me, for losing my cool in such a destructive way, for not having an escape plan, for allowing myself to look like such a fool. I desperately needed to get out of this house, but I had nowhere to go and no way to get there, even if I did.

After a while, the bedroom door opened, and my mother entered. In a soft, sad voice, she told me, "I convinced Dad he should go out for a while, and Elaine and Ron have gone home. You need to come back downstairs and clean up the broken glass. Then I'll drive you to the bus station. You should get back to school."

"Mom," I began, but no other words came. I fell gratefully into her open arms, fresh sobs wracking my body all over again.

"Maddie, I can't believe you haven't figured this out yet," my mother said. "It's like I keep telling you. Dad thinks of you as an extension of himself. Whatever you accomplish, he feels like he accomplished it, too, because you're his daughter. Because he made it possible for you by giving you the best opportunities, sending you to the best college. He brags about you all the time. It's all about making everyone else jealous. You're the trophy he wants to show off, and it's hard to do that if you're a thousand miles away. He needs to keep you on his shelf."

"Even if it makes me miserable?"

"He doesn't see it that way, honey. He's happy here. He's been happy here his entire life, so you should be, too. In his mind, it's just that simple.

"I will admit, though, I had no idea what he'd done with your school loans. It does seem very unfair to expect you to pay back a loan you didn't even know about."

"How could even he do that?" I wailed. "Wouldn't he have needed my signature on something?"

"Oh, Maddie, you know how it is in this town," Mom sighed. "Everyone knows your Dad; everyone owes him something because of the business. I'm sure one of his friends at the bank let him get away with saying you would sign the papers later or something."

"I will pay it all back on my own, then," I declared, not really caring what it would cost me.

As soon as I got the job offer, I made my decision and moved to Seattle. I never looked back.

26

I didn't mind working late. In fact, I preferred the office when it was quiet, when there were no distractions. As one of the newest members of the team, I knew I was cementing my reputation as a hard worker. No one needed to know that I kind of enjoyed it, that I thought writing code was almost soothing, like solving puzzles. Once you got it to work, it felt amazing. What I liked best was that no one could tell me I had done it wrong, or it wasn't good enough. It worked, and that made it perfect, like a tiny victory every time. Also, it wouldn't hurt my standing on the team or in the company to have the work done when my boss arrived in the morning.

It was so quiet and I was so focused that the phone ringing next to my computer shattered my concentration, and I jumped a mile. It had to be a wrong number. Anybody who knew I was here would also know I wouldn't want to be disturbed. But it could also be a security guard checking to make sure I was still in the office and that I was all right. It was also possible a colleague working at home needed my help. Good for them to confirm that I was, in fact, still at my desk. So, I grabbed the receiver.

"This is Madeline," I said in my best professional voice.

"Hey, Maddie, this is your baby brother," I heard over some long-distance static. "I need a big favor."

"Trip? Geez, what time is it there? What kind of favor could you possibly need from me at this time of night?" I tried to ask more of the questions flooding into my head, but he interrupted me.

"I need some money," he said. "I'll pay you back. It's just

that I need it right now, or I'm in a lot of trouble."

"Okay, back up. What kind of trouble are you in?" Trip wasn't even sixteen yet. He should be home in bed, getting a good night's sleep for school the next day. At least, I thought he should be because that's what fifteen-year-old me would have been doing on a weeknight. Then again, it had been pretty clear for a while that Trip wasn't me. Whenever I called home, Mom had a story about Trip talking his way out of a failing grade or charming a new girlfriend or getting home late from a party. But so far, Trip seemed to have avoided any real trouble. If he was calling me from three time zones away and he couldn't go to our parents, this was huge.

"Oh, man, I really don't want to go into it right now," he sighed. "Can you just give a credit card number or something? I can explain it to you later."

"Are you crazy? You want me to just give you my credit card number without telling me how much you need or what it's for? Or maybe you think I'm crazy?"

"Come on, Maddie, you know I'll pay you back. Can't you just trust me for once? Would that really be so hard?" Trip started to sound angry. I couldn't believe it.

"Nope. Not going to happen. I know you think I have unlimited funds because I have a job. But it doesn't work that way. You have to know that it would be stupid of me to just give you a credit card number. So if you want my help, you're going to have to tell me what's going on." I leaned back in my chair, trying to feel confident that I had the upper hand in this situation. My brother was a master manipulator, something he was learning at our father's knee, so I had to be strong and not get sucked into a sob story.

"Look, I was just out with some of my buddies, that's all. We were having a little fun, and things got out of hand." He paused. "Some stuff got, well, sort of damaged, I guess you could say. If we just pay for it now, on the spot, then Dad won't have to find out. It's really not a big deal. Probably a couple hundred bucks."

"So, you and your friends are out after midnight on a school night, and you caused a couple hundred dollars' worth of damage? To what?"

I heard Trip heave a large sigh on his end. "They're waiting for an answer here. Can I have the money or not?"

"Not. At least not until I know more. What did you damage?"

"A field. Well, a yard. Outside of town. It just got torn up a little. And the fence probably needs to be fixed. The guy is making a big deal out of nothing. But he's being cool enough not to call the cops. Or Dad. As long as I can tell him how we're going to pay him back. So how about it? Can I give him your credit card number so he can charge the fence repair to me?"

Piece by piece, I learned the story. Trip's friend got a brand new driver's license, so a group of guys snuck out to go for a joy ride that included doing donuts in some poor guy's yard. And in trying to flee the scene when the lights came on in the house, they miscalculated where the opening in the fence was—and took out a few feet of it.

I had one more question, and I feared I already knew the answer. "So, why are you the one paying for the damage? Why isn't it your friend?"

Another sigh. Another pause. "He let all of us drive his car a little. I may have been the one who hit the fence."

Even though Trip was barely thirteen when I moved away from Graverton for good, I knew enough about his personality, his outlook, and his worldview to figure out exactly what happened. Likely, the whole adventure had been Trip's idea, right down to the donuts in somebody else's yard. I doubted if any of the other guys had even taken a turn driving the car. Trip had probably talked his way into the driver's seat with the same kind of guilt-laced charm he always used. I could almost hear him. "Don't you trust me? Come on, I'm a good driver. You know nothing is going to happen. We're not even on the road! What do you say? Let me have some fun."

I thought about what would happen if I said no. Trip might try Julie, but she had just finished school, and her first job didn't pay very much. She would say no for budgetary reasons. Then he would have to call our parents.

"Why didn't you call Dad?" I finally asked. "You know he would bail you out. He thinks you can do no wrong."

"Yeah, well, it's good for him to keep thinking that, right?" Trip replied. "And I would really owe you one. And you'd have something on me, something Dad didn't know about."

I hadn't thought of that. Maybe just a tiny little bit of revenge on Paul, knowing something he didn't. Knowing that Trip wasn't perfect. I was leaning toward yes, even before Trip went in for the kill.

"Plus, it would break Mom's heart if she found out."

He was right about that. Mom would be destroyed to know Trip had done something this stupid and destructive. She still thought of him as a mischievous little boy, not as someone who would damage property and put his friends in danger. If I could keep her from knowing this, even for a little while longer, I wanted to spare her.

"All right," I sighed. "Let me talk to the guy whose yard you wrecked."

"It's not wrecked," Trip protested. "It just needs a few repairs. Like I said, a few hundred bucks."

"Just let me talk to him."

The property owner was justifiably angry, but for some reason, he was also sympathetic. Probably had a relative working at Cutler Enterprises who really needed the job and, therefore, couldn't afford to cross the Cutler family. "I know they were just having fun," he told me. "Boys will be boys and all. But they did tear up a lot of sod and crash through my fence. Somebody has to pay to fix that."

I negotiated with him, promising to reimburse him for the repairs if he sent me the bills. "If I don't, you can call our father. Or the cops. But please give me a chance to make it good first."

I'm not sure why, but he agreed. Then I got bills totaling pretty close to two thousand dollars, considerably more than Trip's "few hundred bucks" estimate. When I told him how much damage he caused, he snorted. "That guy fleeced you, Mad. There's no way those repairs cost that much. He probably replaced the whole fence. You should refuse to pay."

Then I reminded him that he had promised to pay me back. "You said you were good for it, that I could trust you. Remember? So, when do I get my money back?"

"Well, I didn't know it was going to be two grand! Where am I going to get that kind of money? I'm telling you, you got taken. No way I'm paying, even if I could."

I considered threatening to tell our parents, but we would both know what an empty threat that was. Paul would laugh at me, saying I got cheated twice. He would probably be proud of Trip for getting out of the situation without paying a dime. Trip knew how much I wanted to avoid Paul's taunts. And Mom? Well, the heartbreak I had tried to spare her would be increased a hundred-fold, knowing what Trip was really capable of. She still had a blind spot where he was concerned. Still believed the best of him in spite of all evidence to the contrary.

In the end, the best I could hope for was that Trip knew he couldn't call me the next time he got in trouble. He had burned that bridge.

27

When he finished describing my promotion and all the perks it came with, the head of my department, my mentor and role model, looked at me with a fatherly smile. I sat in his office with a stone face, fighting hard to contain my emotions. I desperately wanted to be professional, to impress him with my calm, even as my heart pounded with pure joy. "You know, it's okay to be excited about this, Madeline. We're all pretty happy that we found the right person for this position in-house. And I know how much time you put in, how hard you worked. So, go ahead and take off a little early. Have a celebration. You can move into your new office tomorrow."

"Thank you so much," I said, risking a small smile as I reached for the hand he extended across his desk. "I won't let you down."

I managed to wait until I was out of the building to break into full self-congratulatory giggling, fist pumping in the air as I bounced along 4th Avenue. Even a chilly and dreary Seattle afternoon couldn't dampen my spirits. This was just so huge! When the company I joined right out of college merged with a competitor, most of my co-workers feared for their jobs, feeling threatened by rumors of downsizing. But I liked the new guy who took over our department. Ben was enthusiastic in his encouragement, quick to share credit for a success, and always reluctant to criticize. Under his guidance, I moved up in the merged company pretty quickly. And this promotion was another big jump in responsibility. And visibility. And pay. An office with a door! I wouldn't just be leading a team, I was going to be coordinating several teams. I knew I deserved it. I knew I could do it.

As I made my way home, I started thinking about the celebration Ben had instructed me to have. I couldn't wait to call Daniel. We hadn't been dating very long, only a few months, but the thought of inviting him to a fancy dinner, my treat, seeing admiration, maybe even pride, in his eyes, waking up on my first morning as a new Team Coordinator with him right there, I was practically trembling with excitement.

"Hi, Daniel," I began when I reached his office voicemail. "I know it's last minute, but I really want to have dinner with you tonight. Can you meet me at Elliott's? I have great news, and I want to celebrate. Call me."

While I waited for Daniel to call back, I thought about how much I wanted to talk to my mom. She would be excited for me. Ask all the right questions about what the promotion meant. Be impressed with the raise I got. She would even want to know about my new workspace. She would be proud, and she would tell me so over and over again.

Unfortunately, if I called Mom, I risked getting Paul. He was the one person I did not want to talk to. I started to think about what he would say: "So, you think they like you okay?" Or he'd want to know what had taken so long. Or why I wasn't leading the whole department by now. He would certainly ask about my new salary. And my bonus. And what I was going to do with all that money. In my head, I wrestled with responses to his jabs. I knew no matter what I said, Paul would try to find a way to diminish this accomplishment, to knock me down, to destroy my excitement. Yeah, well, I told myself, his opinion doesn't matter anymore.

As I looked through my closet for the most appropriate celebration outfit and the right shoes to go with it, Daniel called back. "I'm so sorry, but I'm going to have to take a raincheck," he said, his voice warm with genuine regret. "I'm on a deadline, and I can't leave the office till we finish this proposal. Make a reservation for Friday, and I'll toast you all night."

Knowing I would have a more appropriate celebration soon, I opened a bottle of my favorite wine, just for me. As I poured myself a glass, I decided to call home after all. If Paul answered, I didn't have to tell him why I was calling. I could just ask to talk to Mom. Then she could tell him.

I settled into my most comfortable chair and dialed the phone number I memorized when I was a little girl. It had been the number for 167 Harding Street since before I was born. It was unlikely to change as long as a Cutler lived in the house.

It was Julie who answered. She still lived with our parents, but she was rarely at home, spending almost all her time with her boyfriend, Henry.

"Oh, Maddie! It's so amazing that you're calling right now!" she exclaimed. "I have something so exciting to tell you! Henry and I are engaged! Henry's parents are here, and we're all having champagne. I wish you could be here, too."

"Oh, my God! That's wonderful! I'm so thrilled for you!" I jumped out of my chair. "What a great day it is for the Cutler sisters. I have some news of my own." Too late, I realized that I was talking over Julie as she said, "Dad wants to talk to you." She had handed the phone to Paul. "What'd you say, Maddie?" I heard him ask. "You have news? Is it about work? You didn't get fired, did you?"

"No, I didn't get fired," I said, unable to disguise the exasperation in my voice. "I was talking to Julie. Can you put her back on? Or let me talk to Mom?"

"If you didn't get fired, then what's your news?" Paul spoke a little too loudly, and I knew exactly why. Paul enjoyed teasing me even more when he had an audience. I could hear Mom asking him for the phone, but I could also picture him turning his back on her to keep the receiver away.

I wondered if I could just hang up on him, pretend the connection was broken. "This really isn't the time to talk about it. You're celebrating Julie and Henry. I'll just call you guys tomorrow."

"Come on, Mad Dog, tell me. What's the news?"

I should have said goodbye right then. I should have let the evening be about Julie and Henry. But old habits die hard, and even from hundreds of miles away, I was seized with the sudden urge to wipe that smirk right off Paul's face. So I blurted out, "I got a promotion today."

"Ooh, a promotion," Paul repeated, dragging out the words. "And more money, I hope."

"Yeah, I got a raise, too," I said, already regretting my admission. "Listen, you should go back to toasting the happy couple. Tell Mom I'll call her later."

"Well, wait. How much are you making now?"

I hesitated, but I knew he would ask every time I talked to him until I told him. And my vanity wanted him to know, to show him up. So I gave him the number.

Paul let out a long, low whistle. "Not bad. What was their initial offer?"

"What do you mean, initial offer? That's what the job pays. I knew that when I put in for the promotion."

"Oh, come on. A baby knows you don't accept the initial salary offer! You always negotiate. Always." The smirk had returned. I could hear it in his voice. "You could've gotten another ten, maybe fifteen grand, easy. Why wouldn't you negotiate for more?"

Well, that didn't take long. A minute on the phone with Paul, and I already felt defeated. The best achievement of my career so far, and still, he could zero in on the one thing I did wrong. As Paul lectured me about how executives always think a job candidate is a "sucker" if he doesn't ask for more pay, I tilted the phone away from my face so he couldn't hear the telltale sniffling, the beginnings of my breakdown. Struggling to regain control of my voice, I finally said, "Sorry, I've got to run. I have my own celebration to get to. Tell Julie and Henry congratulations and I'll talk to them later."

For a long time, I sat with my head in my hands, allowing

the tears to fall, wondering how I always managed to let him win. How had I gone from feeling ten feet tall, walking on air down 4th Avenue, to being a crumpled, defeated mess bent over in this chair? Even though I knew it was a competitive salary, Paul was probably right; I could have asked for more. And gotten it.

Even worse, I'd managed to distract the attention away from Julie. The night should have been all about her and Henry, but I'm sure Paul made my blunder the main topic of conversation. And I couldn't even call back to apologize or try to fix things, not without risking another encounter with Paul anyway.

Hours later, after I cooked myself dinner and made reservations for my celebration with Daniel, my phone rang again. "Hey, Maddie," Julie said softly. "I hear I should be congratulating you, too. That's really great. I'm so proud of you."

"Thanks," I said, pouring the last of the wine into my glass. "But first, I want to hear all about you and Henry. Tell me how he proposed." She told me Henry took her to dinner and had the restaurant hide the ring in her dessert. When he got down on one knee, all the other diners clapped and cheered. "Half of Graverton knew before our parents," she laughed.

After a while, I glanced at the clock. "Hey, isn't it pretty late there? Don't you have to rest up before you go start picking out china patterns or something?"

"Plenty of time for that. Believe me, between Mom and Mrs. Nowak, they'll make sure I devote every waking minute to wedding planning from now on. No, I called to hear all about your news. I'm sorry it got overshadowed. Tell me about the new job."

If I couldn't talk to my mother tonight, my sister was the next best thing. She asked the right questions and said the right things. She knew exactly what I needed. After another hour of laughing with Julie, I was happy again. "Hey, Jules, thanks so much for calling. I really appreciate it."

"You bet. You'd do the same."

28

"Madeline? It's Julie. I really need you to call me as soon as you get this, even if it's late. We have a big problem here, and I, I need to talk to you."

Hearing Julie's voice on my answering machine surprised me, and her message concerned me. A big problem? What kind of problem? Knowing my father, a pretty wide range of possibilities, each one more disastrous than the last, sprang to mind. But it was already ten o'clock here on the West Coast. That meant it was one o'clock back east. She did say to call even if it was late, but I didn't think she meant this late, especially not on a weeknight. But would I be able to sleep without knowing what the problem was? While I debated whether or not to call, the phone rang again.

"Oh, Maddie, thank God you're finally home," Julie sighed into the phone.

"Yeah, I was working late. Big project on a deadline. I just walked in the door. What's going on?"

She started crying. "I ... I just can't believe it. He's threatened to do this before, but we always thought he was bluffing. Just blowing off steam. No one ever thought he would go through with it."

"Slow down. What are you talking about?" I could guess who "he" was, but what was "this?" What had Paul done? My heart started to pound with apprehension. "Julie? What is it? What happened?"

"Dad sold Cutler Enterprises! No warning, no discussions, no nothing. Nobody saw it coming, not even the other executives. A bigger competitor made an unsolicited offer, and he decided to accept it and just walk away. No negotiation, no getting any advice, no talking to an accountant or a lawyer or anything. He didn't even tell Mom before he did it!"

Surely, there was some mistake. Paul would never sell the family business. It was Trip's legacy. It meant everything to Paul, to our family, even to the town. "Julie, are you sure? That's crazy. Why would he do such a thing?"

I listened as she tried to choke out the details through her tears. With a trembling voice, she told me how Paul claimed he had gone into debt, borrowing too much money over the years to put the three of us through school and to channel more capital into the business. He had a chief financial officer who usually kept a lid on company spending and borrowing, though Paul often scoffed at his advice. "What's the point of being the boss if I can't spend the money the way I want to?" he liked to say. On that basis, he ignored sound financial advice on more than one occasion; luckily, Cutler Enterprises had been able to bounce back thanks to periodic construction booms. This much I already knew because it was Paul's pattern even when I was still living at home. What changed?

I called my mother the next morning. "Mom, what's going on? Why would he do such a crazy thing?"

With a heavy sigh, she explained that business had been really slow recently. "Nobody is building anything new around here anymore. No new businesses opening, no new houses. A few people around town are fixing theirs up, but that's not nearly enough to keep a company of our size going. Your father has been cutting staff, taking out loans. In the end, it just wasn't enough."

"But just to take the first offer? Not even try to see if he could get a better one? After he gave me so much shit about not negotiating my salary?"

"Well, he didn't consult me about any of it, so I don't know." I could hear the trembling in her voice. Part sorrow, part anger, part confusion. "In fact, he's been refusing to talk to me any more than necessary lately."

As I tried to weigh what all this would mean, I dreaded asking the next question. "Mom, what's going to happen to you?"

"I'll be all right, honey. Don't you worry about me."

Too late. I was already plenty worried. The sale figure Julie quoted to me sounded like a nice chunk of money initially, but my parents were still relatively young. They would need income for many more years before they thought about retirement. There was the remaining college tuition for Trip to consider as well. And if Paul's debts were as massive as he claimed, paying them off would wipe out a pretty sizable portion of what he made on the sale. What was worse was that, as a condition of the sale, he had stepped down as chief executive officer. He didn't even have a job anymore. Typical of Paul, he just shrugged and said, "I made sure I kept my pension." What was he thinking?

During the days and weeks after Julie's phone call, I felt like I was watching a slow-motion train wreck through a telescope. Every time I looked, another car jumped the track and burst into flame. From Julie, I got copies of the local paper's reporting on the sale, which was full of quotes from angry, fearful employees. The sale hadn't included any assurances about maintaining staffing levels or keeping warehouses open, they said. People were worried for their jobs, and the whole town knew that if that many jobs were lost, the ripple effect would be massive. Other businesses would close. More people would move away. The whole town might just die.

Every article concluded with "Paul Cutler could not be reached for comment." According to Mom, all he would ever say was that he had carefully considered his decision and it was the best one for all involved.

After a while, I stopped calling home. Paul was there all the time now, and I didn't want to talk to him. I wanted to stay away from the chaos. I didn't think my presence in Graverton would help the situation, so I didn't visit either. I tried to give Mom and Julie some measure of comfort when we did talk on the phone. I offered to send Mom some money, but she declined, insisting she and Paul were fine. "I'm not going to let you go broke fixing this," she said.

I stopped checking in with Trip, too. His attitude was infuriating. It seemed that all of this interrupted his partying, got in the way of his good time, wrecked his whole college experience. He insisted that he wasn't worried about his own future at all. He had plenty of time to figure things out. Maybe go to work for the new owners. Maybe do something else entirely. It wouldn't be that hard to buy the company back at some point, right? Meanwhile, well, all that beer wasn't going to drink itself, was it?

In spite of all my worrying, the town and the company seemed to be fine. The buyers, who had been looking to expand into new regions, clearly intended to keep Cutler Enterprises going, just under a new name. They did bring in a few new executives, but those they replaced were given generous severance packages. The company stopped making headlines, and the gossip moved on to juicier topics.

About a year later, however, the company began to suffer again. The buyer, being too far away and too large and not "family owned and operated," didn't do a good job managing on the local level. Some said they had expanded too fast, and some said that they didn't understand the market in our area. Whatever the reason, people slowly began losing their jobs through layoffs and cutbacks. A lucky few relocated to more successful branches of the new parent company. The company still had a presence in town, but it was just not the same.

Julie told me that she and Henry couldn't go anywhere anymore without hearing someone discussing and debating whether it was Mr. Cutler's fault. "Half the town seems to think the business was reasonably successful when Dad sold it," she said. "If he had just kept it going. If he had negotiated a better deal. If he had given employees a chance to buy him out. Then there are the people who want to believe that the buyers messed everything up. They didn't understand the market. They couldn't work with the employees. Those people don't blame Dad at all.

"I really wish he had done a better job explaining things to people. As it is, all they have are their theories. Lots of grist for the rumor mill." Her voice sounded terribly weary.

"How is Mom holding up?" I asked.

"She doesn't go out anymore," Julie reported. "She gets up early so she can go to the store before it gets busy and doesn't have to run into anyone she knows. Nobody invites them to parties or anything. I don't even think she goes to bridge club."

When I tried to discuss these developments with my mother, she brushed off my concern. "I think most people are giving your dad the benefit of the doubt," she insisted. "It's a small town. We protect our own. People seem to see that the problems are the new owner's fault."

"But he still won't talk to you about it? Give you any clue as to why?"

"Oh, sweetie, I stopped asking," she said with a humorless laugh. "You know how he is."

When I did return to Graverton, each visit was more strained than the last. Mom did the best she could to make the holidays festive, just like always, but I could see the fraying edges and the cracks and the beginnings of collapse. None of us talked about the sale, but the topic lurked beneath the surface of every conversation, threatening to break through into a geyser of blame and frustration and tears. I would try to talk to Mom alone, but she wouldn't listen to any criticism of Paul. "Honey, your dad did what he thought he had to. I'm sure it broke his heart, so he wouldn't have sold if it wasn't absolutely necessary."

For his part, Paul kept himself detached from our discussions and interactions. I knew he listened to us speculate about the future with a permanent smirk on his face. I interpreted the way he was treating my mother—pretty much ignoring her—as his way of avoiding how much he had hurt her. I wished she had left him long ago, but that was impossible now. Once, I tried to appeal to his feelings for her.

"Have you noticed how this is affecting Mom?"

Paul narrowed his eyes a little as he stared at me a moment before responding. "She understands."

"Understands?" I argued. "How could she understand when you haven't told her anything? Meanwhile, she's embarrassed. She has to avoid her friends because they're all angry and upset about what you did. She hasn't bought herself anything new in more than a year. This has turned her whole life upside down! Did you even think about that?"

"Interesting that you see it that way," Paul said. "That I'm the one who didn't think about her. You're so sure she always thought about me."

"Of course she thought about you. You're her husband. Everything she ever did was about making you happy."

"Like I said, your mother thoroughly understands this situation. I don't owe you any explanation about how things work between us." With that, he snapped open the *Graverton News* in front of his face to signal that he didn't intend to talk about this anymore.

And then there was Trip, who continued to maintain that it was no big deal. We were at a tavern a few miles outside of Graverton, the place where many of my classmates had first used their fake IDs in high school. I wanted to get a better grasp on his baffling attitude, and he was eager enough to be treated to a drink.

"How did he explain it to you? The sale and everything after?"

Trip waved his hand and let out a little puff of air, as if my concerns were so lightweight he could easily blow them away. "Never said a word to me, actually. We really haven't talked much at all."

"Doesn't that seem weird? That he's not talking about it, even with you?"

"Why should it seem weird?" Trip laughed. "You know how Dad is. 'You understand me,' he says, and then he gives you the look. The one that says we're not talking about this anymore. Shit, I'm not going to push him if he doesn't want to tell me anything."

When we were growing up, "You understand me" (as a statement, not a question) was the phrase Paul had always used to indicate that he was finished talking and that we had better have learned whatever lesson he was trying to teach. And we had better be clear on what his expectations were. Because there would be no further explanations. No further discussion. No more questions or clarification. His patience and the conversation were at an end.

This was the most frustrating exchange I'd had in a while. "I can't believe you're just accepting 'the look' as his explanation. That you're not mad at him."

"Mad at him? Hell, no," Trip declared. Leaning a little closer, he added, "I'm glad he did it."

"You are?" I was shocked. "How could you be? He yanked your future away from you."

"No, no, it's not like that. Dad was smart to get out now. Fucking brilliant, in fact. Look what's happened. He would have lost so much money if he kept the company. Might have had to declare bankruptcy, for Christ's sake! Instead, he got himself a golden parachute, and now he's safe."

"He might be safe for now," I said. "But that money isn't

going to last forever. He and Mom still need an income of some kind."

"Did you forget about his pension? Again, fucking brilliant. They can live on that." He lifted his beer mug, toasting Paul, as if he were a hero. "And you know what? I have a pretty brilliant plan of my own." His eyes had that familiar gleam, the look that told me he was so confident in his own plans that nothing could persuade him it was a bad idea. "I'm going to graduate in a couple of years and get a job and start saving up my money, get some business experience, and then I'll buy our company back." Sitting back to take another big gulp of beer, he smiled smugly. "These new guys didn't know how to run things right, not like Dad did. It's tanking already. In a couple of years, they'll be dying to sell it back, and I can swoop in and get it for a song. You'll see."

I tried to get Trip to see the many flaws in his supposedly brilliant plan. That Cutler Enterprises had downsized to the point that it didn't really exist anymore. And even if the new owners put it back on the market as a subsidiary or something, it would take considerably more to buy it back than he seemed to realize, even if it was "tanking." It was a lot more likely that they would just shut down in this area. There wasn't going to be anything left to buy back. But it was no use. He could see no limit on his own earning power. Or his potential as a business genius. And he was determined to defend Paul's decision, firm in his conviction that "Dad is fucking brilliant."

Paul remained tight-lipped about the whole thing. Instead of explaining why he did it, he just kept saying how much he was enjoying his newfound freedom. "I really wish I had done this a long time ago, to be honest," he kept saying. He slept late, puttered around in the yard, read spy novels, and watched TV game shows all afternoon. It seemed to make him feel superior to know the answers long before the contestants.

You would never convince him that he wasn't smarter than everyone else.

When the entire business shut down for good, no one was surprised.

29

When I moved into my new neighborhood, the proximity to public transportation was a real selling point, and most days, I enjoyed the leisurely three-block stroll past coffee shops and restaurants, nodding to the local long-haired grunge musicians who were slouching down the street, and breathing in the fresh green smell that infiltrated the breeze after a good Seattle rain. I often stopped at the window of the shoe store to covet their merchandise. The short walk was a good time to review the high points of my day and just revel in my life as a young professional in Seattle.

But this week, the distance from the train station to my apartment building felt like the longest, most arduous part of my commute. I had been working extra-long hours, trying to complete the coding on a new project, with a staff that was grumpy about having to redo their work over and over again because of management's changing directions and expectations and my new boss's insistence that we get it absolutely, positively one hundred percent right. On this particular late spring day, in spite of the warm weather and a sunset made more colorful by the lingering rain clouds, three blocks felt like a trek over Mount Rainier. I motivated myself to walk a little faster by thinking about the bottle of wine chilling in my fridge and a long, hot bubble bath to ease my aching muscles.

On the other hand, I wasn't eager to be greeted by the glowing, not flashing, red light on my answering machine, meaning there were no messages from Daniel. It would be so comforting to talk to him after such a long, confidence-shattering day, maybe even invite him over for a late dinner.

He was so adept at taking my mind off work. Always knowing exactly the right music to put on. Steering clear of hot-button topics like families and the economy. Talking about his hopes and dreams with so much positive energy, never allowing for the possibility that he might somehow fail to achieve them. But those days were over now.

When we met, Daniel and I were both starting out on promising careers, both of us ambitious, both driven to succeed. We talked endlessly about how we loved the relaxed Seattle vibe, the way the city supported young people who were willing to work hard without condescending to those not competitive enough. It was refreshing to be with someone who truly understood when I had to change or cancel plans for work because he did it all the time, too.

Somewhere along the line, though, we started breaking plans more often than we made them. One day, I realized how long it had been since we had actually seen each other, been in the same place at the same time, much less spent a night together. So, I suggested a weekend away, a bed and breakfast on Puget Sound, just the two of us, to reconnect. Daniel loved the idea until we checked our calendars. It would be almost six months before we both had an entire weekend free at the same time. I wanted him to give up a bachelor party for a guy he hadn't seen since college; he said I didn't need to set aside so many Saturday hours to stay in my office. All of a sudden, we were arguing, each becoming increasingly angry about the other refusing to change plans so we could be together, each accusing the other of not making our relationship a priority. When the dust settled, we were broken up.

Lost in the confusion and regret of reliving that last conversation with Daniel, I failed to notice the car parked at the curb by my front door until I heard a familiar voice yell, "Surprise!"

Trip. Here. At my apartment. Unannounced.

Before I processed all this information, my brother covered the distance between us in a few bounds and wrapped me up in a huge hug. It became very real as he squeezed too hard, pinning my arms to my sides and lifting me a few inches off the sidewalk.

"Oh, Mad, it's so good to see you," Trip exclaimed as he set me down and took a step back. "I've been waiting for hours! Do you always get home this late?"

"Not always, just sometimes," I answered. "What are you doing here? Why didn't you tell me you were coming?"

"I wanted to surprise you," he said. "Weren't you listening?"

I was still bewildered, still trying to wrap my head around what I was seeing and hearing, still sorting through the dozens of questions that sprang to my mind in rapid succession. "How did you get here? Is that your car? Do our parents know you're here?"

Trip was laughing, but I could tell he was a bit annoyed that I wasn't as enthusiastic about seeing him as he had clearly expected me to be. To tease me, he spoke very deliberately and slowly, bowing slightly in rhythm with his words. "I drove here in this car. Yes, it's mine. I used the money Aunt Elaine gave me for graduation to buy it. Remember how I graduated from college? Just a few weeks ago? At age twenty-two? You know, when you're an adult and you don't have to check in with your mom and dad anymore?"

Wow. Additional confusing information. I should have thought about my questions and reactions more carefully, but I didn't. I foolishly said, "Aunt Elaine gave you enough money to buy that car?" It was starting to get dark, and I couldn't see clearly, but it looked brand new. And it was not an economy car. That wouldn't be Trip's style.

"Enough for a down payment," Trip said, waving his hand dismissively. "Getting financing is crazy easy right now." Then his enthusiasm at seeing me overwhelmed his impulse to give me details about the great deal he got. "Come on! Aren't you happy to see me? Don't I get a tour of your neighborhood? I'm starving. Let's go grab some dinner, and we can get caught up." He was taking my arm and trying to turn me around to head back the way I came. Trying to get a grip on the situation, I said, "At least give me a minute to take my stuff inside." I gestured at the briefcase I was carrying, as well as the jacket I had worn this morning when it was chilly.

"Good idea," Trip agreed. "Let me grab my suitcase. No point in tempting someone to smash and grab, right?"

Suitcase. A pretty big suitcase, in fact. Just how long did he plan to stay?

Walking to my favorite local restaurant—"They have a bar, right?" Trip clarified—he was full of stories about his cross-country drive. Getting kicked out of a campsite for sleeping in his car. "Well, I shouldn't have to pay if I'm not using any of the power or water, right?" Avoiding a speeding ticket by making the cop think some other car was the one going seventy miles an hour. "They always assume it's the car in the fast lane that's speeding. The radar gun can't tell the difference." Trying to pick up some girls in a roadside tavern somewhere in Iowa. "Yeah, that turned out not to be such a great idea after all." He didn't stop talking long enough for me to ask any questions. And I had plenty. Why hadn't he told me he was coming? What did our parents think of this trip? How was he making payments on this new car without a job?

Finally, when we were settled at a booth, Trip stopped talking long enough to take a long gulp of his beer. So, I jumped in.

"Okay, Trip, what are you doing here, really?" I began. "I'm glad to see you, of course, but I don't think you drove across the country just to visit me on a lark. What's going on?"

Initially, he looked offended, as if he couldn't believe I was questioning his motives. Then he chuckled, shook his head, and responded, "The thing is, Mad, I got to make payments on that car. I need a place to live. I want to have a nightlife. So, I need a job. Since I wasn't having any luck close to home, I figured you were my best chance to get one."

I took no satisfaction in being right about him having an ulterior motive. While I was shocked at what that motive actually was, I admired the self-confidence he needed to take that kind of risk. And a part of me kind of liked that he still depended on his big sister, the one who had her life together. He wouldn't be asking if he didn't think so.

However, that didn't change the facts, and I had to set him straight. "You thought I could get you a job? What would make you think that? I don't have hiring authority. Even if you were qualified to do coding, which I don't think you are, there are no positions open in my department. And hiring my own brother? Not a good look. Trip, I'm sorry, but you've really wasted your time."

"Come on, it's a big company! There have to be jobs open in some department somewhere. If you put in a good word, I would be a shoo-in. Can't you do that for me?"

"You know I work for a software company, right? And your degree is in, what, history? Have you ever even worked a part-time job in your life? What do you think you're qualified to do?" Even if I admired how bold he was, I was tired and cranky and hungry, and I didn't have the capacity to soften the blow. I really couldn't help him.

"Jesus, Maddie, it's like you haven't known me my whole life!" Trip's voice was rising as he tried to make his point. "I would be a genius at sales. You know I would. Nobody schmoozes better than me. Even a software company needs that, right?"

He had a point; he would be a good salesman. Trip had talked his way out of a lot of scrapes in his life, and he could be very charming when it suited him. But he had no real sales experience, no real job experience at all. Up until just a couple of years ago, he thought he had a guaranteed position at Cutler Enterprises, including on-the-job training, as soon as he was ready. Paul had always made sure Trip, and everyone else, understood that. Building up his resume had never been a priority. If I stuck my neck out and convinced someone to give him a chance, even with no experience, he might just figure out how to be a really great software salesman. Or he might just figure that he didn't need to work very hard because his sister would cover for him or he could just be his charming self and get away with doing as little as possible. I wasn't willing to stake my reputation in the company on which way he would go. I had worked too hard to get where I was.

Then again, here was my little brother staring at me across the table, asking for my help. I couldn't refuse him outright, but maybe there was a way to help him without risking my own credibility. "Look, I'm just not senior enough in the company for anybody to pay much attention to my recommendations." When he started to protest, I held up my hand. "But mine isn't the only employer in Seattle. Why don't you hang out for a little while and look around? You'll have to make a lot of cold calls and pound the pavement, but if you're going to be a good salesman, those are the skills you need. So, that's the deal. I give you my couch for a couple of weeks, and you prove you can sell yourself. If you don't find anything here, you need to move on. Deal?"

Trip broke into a big grin and thrust his hand toward me across the table. "Deal," he said. "You'll see. I'll land myself such a fucking cushy position, you'll be begging me to hire you!" He looked around for our waiter. "Hey, another round here! We're celebrating. Right, Maddie?" By the time I paid our tab, Trip had polished off four beers and an appetizer, entrée, and dessert.

The next morning, I left for work before Trip woke up. The note I put on the kitchen table detailed where he could find a spare key, how to log on to my home computer so he could draft a resume, and what he would find in my refrigerator for his lunch. Early in the afternoon, as I ate my own lunch at my desk, still struggling to complete a difficult facet of my current project, Trip called my office. "Hey, I can't find your remote," he said. "Where do you hide it?"

When I told him, he said, "Oh, yeah, there it is. Thanks!" And he hung up before I could ask why he was watching television instead of beginning his job hunt.

When I got home, he was still watching TV, looking as if he had been sitting there all day. Unshaved. Still wearing the T-shirt and shorts he had slept in. An empty beer bottle and a crumpled napkin on the table next to him.

"Maybe I wasn't clear," I said. "The deal was you look for a job while you stay with me. You aren't going to find one on television. Unless you want to drive a truck or something."

Trip grinned his most charming and disarming grin. "Yeah, I know. I'm sorry. The day just got away from me. I was still pretty tired from the long drive, and I felt like I needed a day to ramp up, you know? Tomorrow, I'll hit the ground running, I promise."

With a sigh, I headed to my kitchen to make some dinner. Trip followed me, apparently because he needed to apologize for the mess he made in there. Dirty dishes, food not put away, spills not wiped off the counter. He needed to apologize, but he didn't. Instead, he said, "Oh, are you going to cook? I thought we could go out again. Wouldn't that be faster?"

Two weeks later, Trip was no closer to finding gainful employment. Every evening, he had a fresh excuse:

"Everybody wants experienced salespeople."

"I had never heard of this company, but they were advertising that they had all these open positions. And then they expected me to know everything about them. I mean, how am I supposed to do all that research before I even answer an ad?"

"I'm starting to think these companies place want ads just to see how many people they can get to apply. It satisfies some sort of Equal Employment Opportunity bullshit, but they've already filled the positions."

"Hey, can you proofread that cover letter? I can't do anything about that job till you do."

"It was raining really hard today."

Worse, he was behaving like a hotel guest, expecting the housekeeping staff to clean up after him, do his laundry, and keep the kitchen stocked with his favorites. I had forgotten how hard it was to live with Trip and his cocky certainty that someone else would always take care of him and his stuff and his messes. We were headed for a massive blow-up, but I seemed to be the only one who knew it.

In fact, Trip was so blissfully unaware of how worn out his welcome was that he actually asked me for a loan. "Got a car payment coming up, you know? Just need a little advance till I have an income of my own. You can use the car any time you want, you know that, right?"

How could he not know he had lit the fuse? There I was in my own living room, clenched fists, red face, heart racing, blood boiling. "You're actually asking me for a loan?" I growled through clenched teeth. "You've got to be kidding! I've already 'lent' you plenty of money! You live here rent free, more than doubling my utility bills! Not once have you paid for a single bag of groceries or even a damn roll of toilet paper!" I saw a sly smile creep across his face when I swore because he liked knowing he had gotten to me. Just like Paul. But I kept up my rant. "You showed up here unannounced, expecting me to get you a job. I went above and beyond just giving you a place to stay for a couple of nights. Our deal was that you would get yourself a job and get out of here! But instead, you've just been abusing my hospitality ever since you got here. You sleep late, you watch television all day, you eat all my food, drink all my wine, and you have nothing to show for it! So the deal is off. You need to go!"

The charming grin was gone from his face, replaced by a kind of unexpected serenity, no particular expression, really, just calm. His head tilted to one side, arms crossed over his chest, he said, "You could've mentioned this before. I really had no idea it was such a huge problem. You're doing so well for yourself out here. The hotshot career girl in the booming industry. Raises and bonuses and stock options and all that shit. That's what Mom tells everybody when they ask why you don't visit. I wouldn't have thought it was such a big fucking deal for you to share the wealth a little. Is it really going to break you to feed your only brother for a couple of weeks? I have lots of good job leads, leads that'll get me the kind of job I really want. It's not going to take much longer. I don't think you're going to go broke by then."

Staring in disbelief at my brother, who was sitting there so completely at ease, so confident that he was in the right, that my attack was unprovoked and unwarranted, I suddenly realized just how much he had learned. Not in college, not in any classroom, but at his father's knee. He was Paul Cutler the Third. He didn't owe me or anyone else anything at all; the world owed everything to him. He was utterly convinced that he would do great things, and he had no notion that the rest of us wouldn't want to invest in him, in his remarkable future. We should all be grateful just to be touched by his magic. My anger actually came as a complete surprise to him. He honestly and truly thought I would make his car payment for him, no questions asked. How dare I say he wasn't looking hard enough? Of course, he needed to find not just a job but the right job, one that was worthy of him.

And he had quite skillfully tossed in major guilt, too, casually mentioning how our mother's friends ask why I never visit. I'm sure that comment was meant to catch me off guard and deflect my rage. Oh yeah, he was good.

Unfortunately for him, I had learned, too. Being on my

own, away from Graverton, away from Harding Street, away from Paul, had given me a new perspective on how things really work. Being well known in a small town means nothing in the big wide world. If Trip was planning to coast his way to success based solely on being Paul Cutler's son, way out here, two thousand miles away from anybody who gave a shit about our family or our business, he was in for a rude awakening. For a fleeting moment, I thought about letting him find that out on his own. Let him try to get by on his charm, on his sense of entitlement, on the certainty that being Trip Cutler was enough. It would be good for him to fall flat on his face and learn some humility. Maybe even go broke. The thing was, here in Seattle, I was his only safety net. If he fell, I would have to catch him. And that wasn't something I was ready or willing to do.

My anger dissolved into pity as we continued a wordless stare down, Trip's expression never changing, his confidence in his position never wavering. "New deal," I said finally. "If you're not gainfully employed by the first of the month, I'll make your car payment. And I'll even fill up the gas tank for you. And then I will wave goodbye to you as you head home." He didn't respond. "The first of the month. Are we clear?"

"Yeah, okay, we're clear." He didn't move or smile or take his eyes away from my face. Without another word, I retreated to my bedroom, unsure of whether to feel triumphant or not. Trip had received plenty of ultimatums in his life from our parents, from teachers, from girlfriends, and he was pretty adept at working his way around them. He was probably sure he could call my bluff, so I would have to be ready with a plan to make sure he observed my deadline.

Neither of us anticipated the wrecking ball that was about to crash through our lives.

30

Trip was still camping out on my couch when we got the news. Mom was sick. A lump in her breast. Stage three. Surgery and then chemotherapy, but only "catastrophic illness" insurance coverage to pay for it. Suddenly, Trip and his money problems, his job search and his ego, and my anger and my deadline were all so ridiculously unimportant. I paid for two airline tickets and said we would worry about the car later. I had something new, something much bigger, to be angry about now.

When Julie met us at the airport, she gathered Trip and me into a three-way sibling hug. I breathed in the comforting smell of her, the damp wool of her coat, the lingering shampoo fragrance in her hair, the Tic Tac mint on her breath. So much like Mom. Already, she seemed to be taking over as the matriarch, the one who would offer us all nurturing, compassion, and strength through this ordeal. It was the role she was born to play, but no one, least of all Julie herself, wanted it to be thrust on her like this.

"How is Dad doing?" Trip asked as Julie navigated her car out of the airport parking garage. It was a perfectly reasonable question. But before she had a chance to answer, I couldn't help snorting with derision, thinking that Paul's emotional state was the last thing we should be concerned about. "For once, can it not be about Paul?" I fumed from the back seat. "He'll do enough to be the center of attention all by himself. We don't have to help him with that."

In the rearview mirror, I could see Julie scowling at me. "Actually, Dad is having a pretty hard time with all this," she said. "I know you think he only cares about himself, but he's been going to the appointments with her, helping her make the decisions, trying to keep her comfortable at home. I think the word I would use is stoic. That's how Dad is."

My sense was that Paul's actions were all about keeping up appearances, as they always were. He knew what his friends would think, what the gossip mill would churn out, what people would whisper if he didn't act like a doting husband. That he was being so deceitful was just one more reason for me to be angry at him.

At the house, the aroma of all our favorite comfort foods greeted us at the front door. Fried chicken. Macaroni and cheese. Even chocolate chip cookies. We found Mom in the kitchen, acting as though Trip and me being home for a visit was cause for celebration. She was delighted to be cooking for us. As much as we tried to get her to sit down, rest, and let Julie and me help, she insisted that staying busy kept her mind off everything else.

"I'm just so happy you're all home," she said, smiling and touching my cheek, pausing in all her bustling around the kitchen. "You know I love spoiling you kids." Her smile faded as she added, "But as glad as I am that you're here, it's really not necessary. I'm going to be fine."

And even after she came home from the hospital after surgery, she kept repeating, "Really, this is all just so unnecessary." In spite of her brave words, she seemed broken to me, as if the surgeon's scalpel had created a crack through which everything strong and sensible and smart and spirited about her had fallen away. But still, she insisted, "I'm fine. Really. You don't have to stay. Julie will help me if I need it, but I just don't think I will. And, of course, your dad is right here. I don't have to have all of you fussing over me." Then she smiled and cradled my cheek in her palm in that motherly gesture I knew so well. Her hand was still so smooth and soft. I leaned my head toward it to make the warm contact and comfort last just a little longer. By the look in her eyes and the way she stayed locked on my face, I knew that my own sadness was showing. I wanted to be strong for her, and I was failing so badly. "Really, Maddie. It's okay."

Paul was always very quiet during these conversations, watching me closely as I reassured Mom that I wanted to be with her. I agreed that I knew she would be fine and said it wasn't a big deal for me to be away from work for a few days.

Privately, Paul was pessimistic about her condition. "Your mother puts on a brave face, but she's just not being realistic," Paul told the three of us one night after Mom had gone to bed. "This is cancer. Cancer. These goddamn doctors want to put her through all kinds of treatment, but it's not going to help. In the end, it'll just be expensive. And she'll spend the last year of her life tired and nauseous and bald. It'll be even harder on us than it is on her."

"Did the doctor tell you that Mom only has a year?" I asked. "What if the chemo buys her more time, more years?"

With a stony face, Paul locked his eyes on mine and leaned forward for emphasis. "My father had cancer," he reminded me. "And everybody kept telling me how strong he was, that he could 'fight' cancer, that radiation would extend his life. Bought him an extra few months, time he spent in bed being miserable. They were right, he was strong. And that just made it harder for me to watch him fade away. At the end, he was in so much pain he was just screaming. I don't want to watch that again."

"Daddy, I'm sorry you went through that," Julie said, touching Paul's arm gently. "But let's remember, that was what, thirty-five, forty years ago? Cancer treatment is a lot better now, more effective. Mom could beat this."

Shaking his head, Paul replied, "You sound like those doctors, trying to be so positive when they know the truth that the outlook is just not good."

This seemed like an extremely cold and heartless position to assume, even for Paul. This was his wife, his life partner, the mother of his children. How could he be so willing to just give up, to say it was the end, to admit defeat on her behalf? Finally, my own brave face broke open, and I could no longer hold back my rage.

"God, you are unbelievable!" I burst out, turning my back on him to pace away. "This is your wife we're talking about! Our mother! You don't get to decide for her how she lives her life, even in her last years. She gets to say whether she wants to go through this treatment, not you. You're always the one who's so concerned about appearances and what everyone else will think. How is it going to look if you decide to just let your wife die?"

When I was a teenager, such an outburst challenging my father's absolute authority in anything would have earned me a stinging slap across the face. But at this moment, I was met with complete silence. Julie and Trip, shocked at my words and nervous about their aftermath, stared at me with wide eyes. And I watched the color rise in Paul's cheeks, his face slowly turning red, as if his temper was burning him from the inside. When he finally spoke, through clenched teeth, with deliberate, measured words, his response was unexpected.

"You think you're the only one who's angry. The only one who has any reason to be angry. You think you know everything there is to know about me and your mother. But you don't. You don't know anything, Madeline, not a goddamn thing. I have my own reasons to be angry. Don't you dare presume to question me where your mother is concerned. She can do whatever she wants. Whether I support her or not is my business. I'm just trying to prepare you three for the inevitable. But I'm not going to take any shit from you. You understand me."

Even though I was nearing my thirtieth birthday, I reacted the exact same way I always had when I was a child: I fled the scene.

This time, though, fleeing meant I found myself not in the

room I shared with Julie, flung across my bed, pounding a pillow in frustration, but back in Seattle. I left Harding Street the next morning and flew home, where I was all alone with my hostility, my heartache, and my helplessness.

I sold Trip's car for him and sent him the money, along with some advice to not buy another vehicle until he could make the payments himself. I tried to call and talk to Mom every day, usually first thing in the morning, before my run. That way, I wouldn't have to worry all day about how she was doing. More importantly, Paul had taken to sleeping in very late, and he was usually not awake yet, so I didn't have to deal with talking to him.

In fact, I didn't speak to my father again until it became clear that his predictions proved correct. Mom didn't have much time left when I returned to Graverton to see her, and fail her, one last time.

PART SEVEN

1998

31

I wasn't prepared to take a second call from Henry, with him choking up and trying not to cry and me working hard to stay calm and figure out what happened. The first call, telling me about the accident initially, was gut-wrenching in so many ways, not the least of which was that Henry was usually so strong and stoic. To hear him, again, struggling to get the words out, to relate the latest emergency, was more than I could stand. I didn't have the details, and I didn't need them. I just knew I had to get to the hospital quickly because Julie and her baby were in danger.

All this time, the doctors had been monitoring Julie and the baby carefully. Keeping her in the medically induced coma was supposed to allow her body to focus on growing the baby and healing itself. But until she woke up, they wouldn't know the extent of her injuries. She might not wake up at all, or she could wake up and not be herself, and even if she woke up with no effects from the head injury, she could still be paralyzed. Whatever her condition, it could be temporary, or it could be permanent and life-changing. Surgery, even an exploratory procedure to determine the problem, was not advisable until after the birth. For weeks, I listened to all these explanations, grappling with the concept that the woman and baby the doctors discussed in such impersonal, clinical terms were my sister and my niece. And if the damage was both severe and permanent, well, nobody was even willing to talk about that possibility.

But now, one of the worst-case scenarios had reared its ugly head. All along, the doctors talked about how the impact of the accident had caused the placenta to become separated from the uterus. It was a concern, they said, but not an imminent danger. The remedy, even for a healthy mother, was bed rest, another reason to keep Julie in the hospital. If the separation started to grow, if more of the placenta detached itself somehow, there could be problems.

And that's exactly what happened.

Henry and I stood over Julie's bed as the doctor explained that a Cesarean section was the recommended course of action in this case. And sooner rather than later. "She's at thirty-one weeks," he said with a confidence that my pounding heart desperately wanted to believe in. "The baby will likely need some time in neonatal intensive care, but the survival rates are really good in these cases. Delivery now gives the baby the best chance. There are risks to the mother, of course, especially in her state. But once she's not pregnant anymore, then we can get serious about figuring out what's going on with her injuries. We'll take her out of the coma and go from there."

He stood up and concluded his remarks with, "You should talk about it and decide how you want to proceed. We can do the C-section as early as tomorrow morning if that's the way you want to go."

"Well, what is there to discuss, really?" I asked as soon as the doctor was out of the room. "If this is what the doctor thinks you should do …"

Henry looked utterly devastated and lost, even hopeless for the first time. "Yeah, I know, the doctor is optimistic," he sighed. "But it's not his wife and baby we're talking about, is it? No matter what I decide, there are risks. I could lose them both, I could lose one or the other, they might both survive but be …" His voice trailed off as he hid his face behind his hands.

"Or they could both be just fine," I said softly, touching his shoulder. "The chances of that are really good."

"I never imagined I would have to make a decision like

this without her," Henry whispered, looking at Julie. "She's the strong one, the smart one. Always knows what to do. What to say. How to figure things out. It would destroy everything if I lost her."

"We're not going to lose her. She's strong, just like you said. There's no way she would go out like this, that she would let your life together be destroyed. Let's meet your daughter, and then we can get your wife back."

Henry nodded for a second, and then his expression changed. "Wait, daughter? How do you know that?"

"I'm so sorry. Dr. Faulkner let it slip a while ago. I didn't know if you wanted to know, so I didn't say anything."

He managed a small smile. "A girl, huh? Yeah, okay." Then he looked at me carefully. "I didn't know you were so good at keeping secrets."

32

I don't know anyone who likes hospitals, even under the best of circumstances. The smells, the mysterious sounds, the sterility that takes away any pretense of comfort, the unseen lives ending and hearts breaking behind the closed doors you pass. So many of the worst moments in anyone's life might be happening just a few feet away at any given moment. So much to bear. And I had spent too much time in this particular hospital watching over my broken family members, trying to wish them back to health.

And now it was almost midnight, and I was sitting in the Neonatal Intensive Care Unit, touching a tiny premature newborn in her incubator, stroking her smooth skin with its purplish undertones, and whispering reassurances that were really not mine to offer. Henry was in Julie's room, where my sister faded in and out of consciousness, wavering between despair and bravery, trying to absorb all the information and realities that had come crashing down on her, and all the rest of us, in the last few hours.

After delivering Julie's baby girl, the surgeon had finally been able to explore the extent of Julie's injuries. The news, while not our worst fears, was still not good. She opened her eyes but didn't talk. So, there was still no way to know whether she'd ever be herself again. To make matters worse, the damage to her legs and spine was more extensive than they thought and probably couldn't be surgically repaired. Although some of the injuries might still heal on their own, it seemed unlikely she would walk unassisted ever again.

The doctors delivered all this news as Henry held Julie's

hand, kissed her forehead, and never left her side.

I, on the other hand, did what I do best: I fled. I backed quietly out of Julie's hospital room, waiting till I was past the nurses' station to break into a run. Down the stairs, across the hushed lobby where the lights were dimmed for the evening, and out into the night. Stopping on the sidewalk, I bent over, hands on my thighs, taking deep breaths. I knew I should focus on my sister and her family and what they needed from me, but somehow, the rubble of my own life blocked my way. I was still desperate to shrug off any responsibility to this family, still wanting to say, "Not my problem." I was still unwilling to acknowledge how much damage and despair I had heaped on my mother by being so focused on my father. Still struggling to recognize the dangerous self-centeredness Paul had passed on to me, still not willing to admit that Julie was right: I was just like him. All I wanted to do was run away, leave Graverton, and never look back.

I paced under the streetlight by the hospital entrance, steeling myself for the conversation I would need to have with Julie and Henry eventually. I just can't stay here any longer. Then I heard a comforting voice and felt a reassuring hand on my shoulder.

"Madeline?"

How Derek knew where to find me, I could only guess. In a small town, big drama in the hospital gets around pretty fast. His presence had become so familiar that I didn't even need to look into his face. He wrapped his arms around me and pulled me close, trying to stop my shaking sobs. "It's going to be okay," he kept repeating. I breathed in his warm, spicy fragrance, felt the soft weave of his sweater on my cheek, and let his fingers stroke my hair. It felt so right at this moment, but it felt wrong to accept his comfort when I was planning to abandon him along with my family.

After a minute, I stepped back, keeping my eyes down, avoiding his gaze and shaking my head. "It's not ..." I whispered. "It's not going to be okay. What if she doesn't recover?

What if she can't walk? I can't handle that. I, I can't be what Julie needs right now. They all need so much more than I can give."

Derek put his forefinger gently under my chin and lifted my face. "How do you know that? Maybe all she needs is to know you care. That you love her. For now, that just might be enough. No matter what happens to your sister, you can do that for her. For once, Cutler, trust yourself to be enough."

"I grew up believing I wasn't enough and I was never going to be," I admitted. "I spent so much time trying to be good enough for my father. Trying to meet his impossible expectations. Trying to show him I really was good enough. Now I'm terrified he was right all along."

"So, prove him wrong. Go back in there and be a good sister. Let her lean on you. If I've learned anything getting to know you, it's that you're plenty strong enough to handle that. I know it. And you know it, too."

Now I sat next to baby Olivia, all three-point-eight pounds of her, telling her how much her parents loved her and how happy they were that she was here. I tried to explain to her why her aunt was with her and not her mommy or her daddy. I told her how brave and strong they both were and what great parents she had been born to. How excited her brother was to meet her. How her grandparents would have been so proud of her. How I was going to stay with her all night and keep her company.

All of that was true. All of that poured out easily, along with my tears. What was much harder to say out loud, even to a baby who didn't understand the words, were the other awful truths looming in all of our futures. Olivia, we don't know if your mom is ever going to walk again. Your Aunt Maddie still wants to run away, to return to the life she built to spite her father, the life that was supposed to prove once and for all that she'd been good enough all along. Even now, I had one foot out the door, but the other was still firmly planted here in the place that made me who I am.

Looking ahead, I could see that Henry and Julie would fight a fierce uphill battle, trying to get by on Henry's salary while also trying to pay for Julie's recovery and childcare and physical therapy and wheelchairs and walkers and medical equipment over and above all their current living expenses. And who knows what health issues a premature baby might present? There was also a little boy, asleep at a friend's house, whose mommy might never run and play with him again. So much pain. So many pieces to pick up and put back together. Was a broken person the right one to do it?

Staring at this tiny baby, this precious new life, this promise of my family's future, this newborn who was not my child but was somehow mine all the same, I began to realize what I had to do in spite of how much I didn't want to do it. I had to break the cycle. I searched my heart and my mind for any other logical, workable option, but there wasn't one. I couldn't fix everything that selfishness had broken. Some of it was beyond repair. But I could become my mother's daughter instead of my father's, stop being selfish, and begin to rebuild my life, my family, our hope.

Confessing all of this to Olivia, I let my tears flow, mourning all that was lost. I cried for Julie and Henry and Michael, whose lives were changed forever. For my mother and J, whoever he was, and what could have been. For Trip, who would never even know all he lost.

I even shed tears for my father. For the first time since his death, I wasn't crying because of him, but because I was beginning to understand how much he missed out on, and that was so sad. I cried for the life I had so carefully constructed for myself, thinking it was exactly what I wanted, but now seeing just how empty and lonely it really was. I cried for what was ahead for me and my family. But those tears were also washing away my doubts and my anger, cleansing all my wounds so that I could finally heal.

I would tell Julie and Henry in the morning. I was going to move back to Graverton to help them.

33

The moving van rumbled down Harding Street, announcing itself with noise long before it reached the driveway. Julie and Henry's new minivan followed close behind, and as soon as I saw them pull up, I ran outside to help. By now, Julie was pretty adept at maneuvering herself from the van to her wheelchair, but she still needed someone to get the chair into position. Henry could handle that, which left me to corral an excited little boy and an almost one-year-old girl, both of them still confined to car seats.

"Wow, they did a great job on the ramp," Henry commented, looking at the revisions to the front porch that allowed the wheelchair easy access to the front door. It had taken several months to get all the work done on the Harding Street house, but now we had not only a ramp but also a new bedroom and full bath on the first floor. With the settlement money that Anthony Marossi helped Julie and Henry get from the other driver, we had done all the repairs Paul never got around to, and we had cleared away all the faded furniture full of memories, good and bad, that didn't fit with the house's new life. It was ready for all five of us to take up residence here and make it a happy home.

As Michael tore up the stairs, eager to make sure that Trip's old bedroom had been transformed according to his exact specifications, I unstrapped Olivia from her car seat and carried her into the front hall. With a pacifier still stuck in her mouth, her soft gray eyes took in the newness and the changes. She had no memories of the house as it had been for so many years; her reference points began during the mad rush of construction in the last year or so. Her eyes were wide open, trying to understand how these rooms could look like they did now, based on how ripped up they had been just a few short weeks ago. Someday, her mother and I would show her photos from our childhood and tell her how her room, Michael's room, the living room, and the kitchen used to be and how hard we worked to rebuild it all.

"What do you think?" I asked her, nuzzling her soft cheek and hoping for a smile or some noise of approval. Instead, she pointed over my shoulder toward the stairs to tell me she wanted to see more. From a perch on my hip, she got a guided tour—her new room; Michael's room, which would probably be off-limits to her most of the time; and my room, the one Julie and I used to share.

"See, Olivia?" I said. "Aunt Maddie will sleep over here and work over here." My desk, computer, printer, and fax machine occupied what was once my side of the room. After much negotiation, I arranged with my employer in Seattle to allow me to work remotely as a contractor for at least a year. That would come to an end soon, but I was quickly learning that lots of people and businesses in Graverton could use expert tech support and advice. So, I was building a consulting practice. "Your mommy is going to help me make sure I manage my business the right way. She's so good at that!" Grinning, I gave Olivia a little squeeze. "Someday, I'll teach you how to use a computer," I promised her.

Coming down the stairs, I heard Michael yelling, "Derek's here!" I smiled to myself. Of course he's here. A year ago, when I told him I planned to stay in town, I expected him to freak out. After all, I began our relationship by emphasizing how much I liked my life in Seattle compared to how much I didn't like it here, so he had every right to expect that ours was a no-strings-attached kind of fling that would end when I left town. And here I was, suddenly changing the ground rules. To my surprise, he smiled and gave me a bear hug. "That's great news," he laughed. "After my mom, you were going to be my only guaranteed repeat customer. Now, I know my restaurant is going to be a success!"

From the doorway, I watched Derek walk up the ramp with an arrangement of bright pink stargazer lilies in his hand. "A little housewarming gift," he said, tousling Olivia's hair before giving me a quick kiss. "How can I help?"

I set Olivia on the living room floor, put the vase on the mantel, and said, "Come on, let's grab the suitcases out of the car before the movers start bringing in the furniture." On my second trip out the front door, I saw Michael turn away from the car with an armload of toys and stop dead, his jaw dropping.

"Daddy! Aunt Maddie! Olivia!" he cried, pointing behind me.

When I looked, there was Olivia wobbling through the doorway, taking unsteady but determined steps towards us.

"Oh my God, she's walking!" Henry gasped. "Julie! Julie! Where are you? Olivia is taking her first steps!" He ran to his little girl, who was holding her arms up, ready for Daddy to sweep her proudly into his grasp and hug her with all his might. He set her down again a few feet from where Julie was waiting. "Show Mommy, Olivia," Henry coaxed. "Show Mommy what you just did."

Smiling, confident in her new skill, Olivia lurched and swayed and waved her arms for balance and slowly made her way across the floor to her mommy. Laughing with delight, Julie lifted Olivia into her lap and kissed her noisily on the cheek. "Oh, sweetie, I'm so proud of you," Julie said. "I thought you and I would learn how to walk together, but you're way ahead of Mommy. Maybe you can help me when I'm ready to walk again."

Over the last year, Julie had refused to give up on her physical therapy, insisting that she was getting stronger every day, that she was sure the feeling was returning to her legs. Nobody seemed willing to tell her any differently, and just a few weeks ago, she had been able to stand up with the walker. The doctors just kept saying this kind of injury is unpredictable; there are no absolutes. But Henry and I had an unspoken agreement that we wouldn't argue with her, that we would support whatever decision she made, that we would never stand in the way of her determination.

Watching her now, overflowing with maternal pride and making room for Michael in her lap, too, Julie reminded me so much of our mother. Everything she knew about being a good mom she had learned here in this house at our mother's knee. Somehow, in spite of Paul, Julie figured out how to build a happy family. She was giving me a chance to finally be part of it.

EPILOGUE

FIVE YEARS LATER

34

The last day of school. When I was young, I started looking forward to it as soon as school began. The promise of summer, of sleeping in, of freedom from homework, of lazy days with no schedules and no expectations. Lucky for Michael and Olivia, Henry was a teacher, and he completely understood the lure of lazy summer days, the importance of ice cream for no reason other than how hot it is in the evening, the sweet chlorine-scented exhaustion at the end of a day at the pool. After today, Henry would take over the day-to-day childcare until school started again.

Today, I was still on parent duty, so I waited in front of the elementary school that hadn't changed since Julie and I walked here from our house. Solid and square, its red brick walls were interrupted only by a few concrete decorations and metal-framed institutional windows. Even all the way out here on the sidewalk, I could almost smell the chalk dust lingering in the long, narrow hallways.

While I stood waiting, I wondered if Michael would die of embarrassment to find me here. This was not just the last day of the school year for Michael; it was the last day he would spend at this particular school. In the fall, he would be in seventh grade at the junior high. We all knew he was a little apprehensive at the prospect of a new school, but he would never, ever let on.

Olivia, however, was going to be thrilled to see me. She was finishing first grade, but the girl seemed to rule the school. She had a lot more self-confidence than the average six-going-on-seven-year-old. Just a few weeks ago, she had begun insisting that we express her age that way. I was pretty sure her teacher had her hands full all year, reining in Olivia's enthusiasm, and second grade was probably bracing for her already. I watched the front door, anticipating the explosion of happy kids.

"Excuse me, are you Madeline Cutler?"

I turned to face a handsome older gentleman. Dressed casually in a dark polo shirt and khakis, he was tall and trim, standing very straight with his shoulders back in the stance of a younger man. But his hair, though it was thick and wavy, was completely white, and even though his eyes twinkled with a youthful sparkle, there were crinkles around those eyes that belied his posture and gave away his years. He smelled of a spicy after-shave that reminded me of my father. I didn't recognize him right away, but there was something familiar about him. And he clearly knew me.

"Well, it's Bridges now, but yes, I'm Madeline," I said. Looking at him more carefully, I added, "I'm sorry, I don't think I know you."

He smiled at me for another second. "I knew your parents way back when. My name is Jerry Baines."

It took a moment before I trusted myself to speak. Jerry. With a J.

"Um, sorry," I stammered. "Your name isn't familiar, but I do seem to remember a Jodi Baines, I think, maybe in the class ahead of mine?"

"Yes, Jodi is my daughter. She moved to Brockport when she was in high school because her mother remarried. I left Graverton even before that, after we got a divorce. Now, Jodi and her husband are back here, and I've come for a visit. They dispatched me to pick up their son. Jason's in second grade."

With this simple explanation of what he was doing here, Jerry might have filled in all kinds of holes in a story I carefully buried in my memory. If he was the elusive and mysterious J from my mother's box of letters, it seemed that her help and advice and counsel had not kept him and his wife together after all. If he left town, that would explain why the correspondence stopped, maybe why my parents had stayed married, why I had never known anything about J. The only evidence was that shoebox full of letters, which I had destroyed years ago. At the time, I resolved not to think about those letters anymore, not to tell Julie or Trip or Henry or Aunt Elaine about them, and to steadfastly pretend I had never even seen them.

Now, here was this guy who could very well have all the answers I sought.

"When I knew your parents, they were both very proud of you and your sister," Jerry was saying. "Your mother especially. She talked about you a lot."

"Yeah, that sounds like Mom," I said.

"And your brother? How is he doing?"

"He lives in New York City now. Well, in New Jersey, actually. He works as a salesman in a men's clothing store in Manhattan. He talks about opening his own store someday. We'll see." As I spoke, I kept staring at Jerry's face, searching for any clue, any answer, any indication of what the truth might be.

Then Jerry flashed a charming grin that sent a chill right through me. I could see Trip in his face, I was sure. Just as quickly as it appeared, his smile faded when he said, "I was sorry to hear that both of your parents are gone. I didn't really keep in touch with many of my friends here, and I didn't know your mother had died until a few years after the fact. And your father. So sudden. And then everything that happened right after." He reached out to touch my arm, looking into my eyes with true sympathy.

"Thank you," I managed to say. "But it's all okay now. Julie's using a walker, but she can get around pretty well. And her daughter is thriving. You'd never know she was a preemie."

He looked ready to say more, but just then, the school bell rang, and the sound had barely finished echoing when a flood of children broke through the front doors. For a moment, I turned my attention from Jerry to looking for Michael and Olivia. Olivia appeared first, running exuberantly toward me. Plopping down on the grass at my feet to open her bright pink backpack then and there, she began showing off all the artwork she was so proud of.

Over her head, I scanned the crowd for Michael. As I predicted, he was striding along with a bounce in his step, laughing with his friends, until he saw me. Immediately, his face clouded over, and he looked intently away. I heard him say, "You guys go ahead. I'll be right there." He stood and watched his friends amble away, making sure they weren't looking before he approached me and Olivia.

"I'm going to Aidan's house," he announced, staring defiantly into my eyes. "And I may stay there for dinner." I noticed that it wasn't a request for permission but a declaration of intent. He had recently begun to complain about having an extra parent cramping his style, enforcing unfair rules, watching him with an eagle eye. "I never get away with anything!" he declared. Even though I didn't live with them anymore and I helped out as a caretaker only as much as my consulting business and Derek's restaurant allowed, he was probably right. So, I made an effort to defer to parental authority, to remember my role as aunt and not mother.

"All right, honey," I said patiently. Even though I wanted to, I didn't point out that maybe it would be better to ask if it was okay. "We'll see you later."

As I took Olivia's hand, I suddenly tuned in to Jerry's conversation with his grandson. The little boy wasn't smiling and happy the way the other kids were. "But I really liked my teacher, and all my friends were in my class," he complained to Jerry, who was crouching next to him, nodding patiently. "What if third grade isn't fun anymore? What if my friends have a different teacher?"

"Well, the end of every school year is an important milestone, and it's okay to be both happy and sad," Jerry said. "See, the thing about milestones? They don't just show your progress toward a new place. They also mark the path away from where you've been. You might have liked that place a lot so you're sad you're leaving it. But you're going to have such a fun summer! You can worry about third grade later."

Jerry became aware that I was staring at him and his grandson. "That's something my mother used to say. That thing about milestones," I explained, hoping he wasn't offended at my eavesdropping.

"She was a wise woman," he replied, rising to his full height again.

Taking a deep breath, I ventured, "We should, maybe, meet for coffee sometime, you know, while you're here. I think, um, I would enjoy talking to you about how you, you know, remember my mom."

With the fleeting but knowing look that Jerry and I exchanged at that moment, so much doubt and sadness fell away from my heart. Yes, my mother was wise and wonderful, giving and generous, beautiful inside and out. Maybe I hadn't been aware of it at the time, and I could never get back all those years I ignored her, shoved her into my father's shadow, broke her heart, and tried to make out like I was the victim. But now that I knew the truth, I could make sure I remembered her for her beauty, her wisdom, and her loving heart. And I could become more like her.

Acknowledgments

So many kind and generous people helped me take this story on its long journey to becoming a published novel. Thank you all for the support, encouragement, patience, constructive criticism, and friendship you provided.

My family, especially Charlie, Alex, Carol, Stephen, Liza, Karen, and Rick.

The staff at Atmosphere Press, especially Colleen Alles.

The wonderful women in my book group, especially Barbara Moulton.

Vicki DeArmon

Mary Widdifield

Danielle Hougard

Greg Epstein

Vivian Volz

Susie Becker

Wendy Swenson

Scott Fay

Mindy Uhrlaub

About Atmosphere Press

Founded in 2015, Atmosphere Press was built on the principles of Honesty, Transparency, Professionalism, Kindness, and Making Your Book Awesome. As an ethical and author-friendly hybrid press, we stay true to that founding mission today.

If you're a reader, enter our giveaway for a free book here:

SCAN TO ENTER
BOOK GIVEAWAY

If you're a writer, submit your manuscript for consideration here:

SCAN TO SUBMIT
MANUSCRIPT

And always feel free to visit Atmosphere Press and our authors online at atmospherepress.com. See you there soon!

About the Author

In 2008, **SUSAN PICK** left her corporate communications career to become a full-time mom and writer. In 2024, she celebrated her son's college graduation and the publication of her first novel. She lives in northern California with her husband, Charlie.

Milton Keynes UK
Ingram Content Group UK Ltd.
UKHW031143121124
451094UK00006B/518